The Family

BUCHI EMECHETA

The Family

GEORGE BRAZILLER
New York

Some of the place names in this novel are imaginary,
others are real

First published in the United States in 1990
By George Braziller, Inc.

Originally published in the Great Britain
by Williams Collins Sons & Co. Ltd.
(Published in Great Britain as *Gwendolen*)

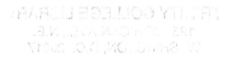

LIBRARY OF CONGRESS CATALOGING-IN-PUBLICATION DATA

Emecheta, Buchi.
The family
I. Title

PR9387.9E36F36 1989   823   89–70783
ISBN 0–8076–1245–6
ISBN 0–8076–1250–2 (pbk.)

Printed in the United States of America
First Edition

To that woman in the Diaspora who refused
to sever her umbilical cord with Africa

CONTENTS

1

Parents

She was christened Gwendolen. But her Mammy could not pronounce it, neither could her Daddy or his people.

She could remember, though not too clearly, what Daddy Winston looked like. She saw him in her mind's eye the day he left for overseas. She could not recall much before that day. In her memory, that was the day she was born, that was the day of the very beginning, the day the world began. Before then, there had been nothingness and void.

After endless shouting and arguments from Granny, her Mammy and Daddy had to go to the office to get married.

Gwendolen's dress was made from organza. The skirt, shaped like Granny's 'coolies' umbrella', was a full one. Her Mammy threaded a few yards of blue ribbon around the waist instead of a belt. Her hair, after it had been pressed, was parted in the middle and tied on each side with more blue ribbons. Granny Naomi gave her a small, black, plastic purse with a string, which she slung across her shoulder. She had a pair of black patent shoes and white cotton ankle socks.

Everybody looked at her, smiled, nodded and then agreed that she did look smart and pretty. They said that she was a lucky girl. Some said, 'You'll go to England and join your Daddy soon, gal.' And then they'd touch her cheeks, or gently pull her hair. But Johnny always touched her thighs. Gwendolen had smiled happily, her brown and white eyes dilating translucently in childish pleasure.

She had no idea where or what England was. But she sensed that her Daddy's people who lived down in Kingston and who were so incredibly sophisticated – because they all wore white gloves – thought it a good place. All she knew was that England was responsible for her Mammy marrying her Daddy in the office that very morning and making her Mammy cry all through the arguments and laughter.

It was all terribly confusing then, because one minute they said it was a good place to go and it was good that her Daddy was going, and that since her Daddy was going he had to go to the office and marry her Mammy because it was not nice for her Mammy and Daddy just to be 'stuck up', next minute her Granny Naomi was shouting and her Mammy crying.

She was then only five and still wet her bed. Granny frequently shouted at her and told her that she wet her bed because she drank too much water and ate too much dumpling. But on that fine, sunny day when her Daddy was leaving for England all that was forgiven.

Her Mammy's dress was similar to hers, only Mammy's was pink. Granny wore a flowered shift and a straw hat with little flowers on the brim. Mammy bought Granny the hat specially for the wharf. Uncle Johnny came with them too. There were so many relatives and friends. After the wedding at the office, they all took a bus down to Kingston where her Daddy lived.

Gwendolen had not known or seen her Daddy all that much, because mostly he worked on the ships way down Kingston. But whenever he came to visit her Mammy and herself on the hill in Granville, he would let her sit on his knee and give her boiled sweets.

She was always impatient to run outside and tell her friends, Shivorn and Cocoa, that Daddy had brought her sweets all the way from Kingston. She would show the sweets, allowing them to have a lick while she held the greater part. She never trusted Shivorn, not since the day Shivorn swallowed one right out of her fingers. So, she would hold the best part of the sweet and stand on tiptoe, whilst at the same time reminding her friends to make sure they did not again swallow it by mistake. It never occurred to her to lick all the sweets by herself. She knew she just had to share, because that was the way things were in Granville.

Now her Daddy was going away to a far, far place called the 'Moder Kontry'.

There were too many people and it was too hot. Uncle Johnny, who came in his smart church clothes with stripes, held her by the hand. Mammy was busy crying and Granny busy telling her Daddy off. All the others seemed to be talking and laughing. They all had so much to say in excited voices. At the wharf, there were different-coloured dresses, suits and hats, and more people than Gwendolen had ever seen in their church in Granville. Once in a while Uncle Johnny would ask her, 'You all right, gal?' And she would nod that she was OK. He would smile at her, displaying his golden tooth. Sometimes Uncle Johnny would smile at Granny Naomi too. Once she had caught them winking at each other. At other times, he grinned hugely at Gwendolen and called her 'Smart Juney-Juney'.

Soon it was time for Daddy to go. There was a great deal of rushing and pushing. Then her Daddy remembered her, lifted her up for a goodbye kiss. Gwendolen touched his face. He had a lot of flesh and his head was soft. Her Daddy was a big healthy 'African' as her Mammy used to say. He was really black. He had eyes sunken right into his head. He was tall, with very broad shoulders. He was a silent man who stammered whenever he tried to talk rapidly like his friends, so not infrequently he grunted instead. Gwendolen felt safe, that split second he held her up to say goodbye. But unfortunately, in so doing, he was exposing her legs and knickers, because her full skirt was stiff. Mammy saw it, looked horrified and pulled her down very quickly. Years later, Gwendolen was unbelievably sorry for her mother's haste. She would have liked to have spent a longer time in saying goodbye to her Daddy, because even then she knew that

11

Daddies could go away for an awfully long time. Shivorn's Daddy had been away to become a famous boxer. Cocoa's Daddy was working in the hotels down the coast, but unlike Gwendolen's Daddy Winston, Cocoa's Daddy very seldom came to Granville. Cocoa's Mammy had to go down there to get money from him for Christmas. Sometimes Cocoa's Mammy came back with no money.

Anyhow, on this day, Daddy Winston went into the boat and it soon hooted away. Everybody waved and waved until the boat disappeared on its way to the big ship that was waiting in the middle of the ocean. Her Mammy Sonia lifted her and showed her the ship that stood so far away from land.

Mammy Sonia did not cry much after Daddy left. She took Gwendolen's hand and did not allow Uncle Johnny to hold her again. Gwendolen felt she now had all her Mammy's attention. Mammy had been fussing around her Daddy all day. Now the boat had taken him away to the big ship. None the less, Uncle Johnny winked at her behind Mammy's back, and she winked at him too, just as if they were playing hide-and-seek. There seemed to be an understanding between her and Uncle Johnny. He was a fine funny man, Uncle Johnny, a good friend of her family and a neighbour. He looked jaunty and funnier still that day in his striped suit.

Another bus took them near home. It was a dull, long, uphill walk back. Mammy carried her most of the way, for by the time they reached home in Granville she was asleep. She dreamed of her Daddy with his soft shaved head, smart black suit and bow tie that smelt of camphor, on his way to England, the 'Moder Kontry', where they said her Mammy would soon go. Was England as big as the White Road down Kingston way? she wondered.

Gwendolen remembered each time Daddy Winston wrote from England. The sun always shone, but it seemed to have a special balm when England letters came. Mammy would put the letter on the table by the window and sit there looking at it for a while. She would then send her to tell Uncle Johnny to step this way in the evening because Daddy Winston had sent a letter from England. Uncle Johnny would say, 'Right-o, Ah sure to be there. And how's my Juney-Juney?'

'Me OK, Uncle Johnny, thank you.'

Gwendolen would skip happily back to her Mammy quite well aware that the letter brought exciting news.

Uncle Johnny came every evening anyhow. His lean-to shack was only down the road. All their friends lived on this side of Messina Road. Those on the other side lived in trailers. Her Mammy said they'd been there since the big hurricane and they'd never left. Gwendolen had asked Shivorn when she thought those people living in the trailers would go. And Shivorn had said that they would go when another hurricane struck. Maybe that was why they lived in houses on wheels, Gwendolen thought.

However, on days Daddy Winston's letters arrived from England, she did not let such thoughts bother her too long.

Uncle Johnny would be given a chair by the window to catch the light. But sometimes, when he came too late, he would read with their hurricane lamp. Granny would sit on her bed, which was on one side of the room. Her Mammy would sit on her sewing chair and Gwendolen would sit on the grass mat on the floor. Their eyes were fixed on Uncle Johnny's face as he spelled and mouthed the words first to himself and then aloud to them all. Mammy always asked Uncle Johnny to read it all over again. Uncle Johnny would say, 'Right-o, sure do.' This often made Granny Naomi laugh and say, 'You good to us, Johnny.'

As for Gwendolen's Mammy, she would smile and nod and say, 'Me know, dat's a'right. Dat's a'right.'

But it was not always all right, because Mammy would take the letter to the Indian teacher down Victoria Avenue to read it again. Then Mammy would be happy and sing joyful church songs. And Gwendolen noticed that most of the letters contained paper money. Mammy would then take her to the big post office in Kingston to collect the money Daddy Winston sent. As soon as Mammy had collected the money, Gwendolen would ask, 'Mammy, Daddy send money today?'

'Yeah, June-June, your Daddy send money today.'

'It's a happy day, and we have nice Daddy, not so, Mammy?'

Her mother would nod in agreement and smile at her while her bottom cheeks dimpled outside her mouth. Mammy did not always open her mouth when she smiled because her teeth were bad. Granny Naomi said it was because she had a sweet tooth as a child.

'Cocoa and Shivorn's Daddy don't send no money, don they, Mammy?'

'Come on, you little Marm, you love your Daddy so, eh? No, Shivorn's Daddy can sen' no money because 'im be big, big boxer one day.'

They would then shop and buy material to make dresses for church. They would buy meat for food and plenty of biscuits for friends and neighbours. They would buy a bottle of rum for Granny Naomi and another for Uncle Johnny. Then they would pass Victoria Avenue to pay the Indian letter-reader. Mammy would then sit and dictate a letter to her Daddy, telling him at the end of it that his daughter 'June-June is a big 'oman nuh, and sends she love'.

Mammy would pay the man for writing the letter. On the way back with all their shopping they would pass by the little post-box and Mammy would let her drop Daddy's letter into it.

On Sundays, they would wear the nice dresses Mammy had made and go to church where they would sing and clap and praise the Lord. Granny Naomi always danced in the church, but Mammy never did. Gwendolen was too shy to dance, even when her friends invited her. But she knew all the words of the songs by heart, and she could really sing.

14

She really liked going to their Pentecostal church on Sundays in Granville.

Soon, another letter arrived to say that her Mammy was to go and join her Daddy Winston. Gwendolen was quite restless when Uncle Johnny mouthed the words. Why should her Mammy go and leave her with Granny Naomi? Why could she not take her along? They said her Mammy would send for her. This time was different; she was not so calm about her other parent going. She was even afraid. She did not miss her Daddy that much because he had not been living with them anyway. But she was going to miss her small Mammy Sonia. Sonia was a small woman with bow legs. She was very dark too. She had a small head and this smallness was emphasized by her lack of hair. Her hair was so short that one could see patches of her skull. Half her teeth were broken. They said it was because she ate too much honey and too many sweets. But how could she have resisted eating honey and sweets since her parents collected honey for their living?

Mammy told her that Grandaddy Richard used to look very strange in his work gear. He wore a huge straw hat with nets at the brim covering his face, before going to the bee hill on the farm. As soon as her Mammy was old enough, she too had helped in collecting honey. Mammy Sonia taught Gwendolen how to remove the wings and bodies of dead bees from the honey, ready for Granny Naomi to process. There was nothing her Mammy loved like munching the half-processed honey. She would chew the dry pieces for hours on end. Sometimes she would be so full that she went without her dinner saying, 'Me belly full of honey, me no wan' dinner.' Granny would raise her gritty voice and tell her that too much honey was bad for her teeth. Mammy would not listen. Also, she favoured boiled sweets sold by the coolie women down the foot of the hill. She invariably gave Gwendolen some.

Now that her Mammy Sonia was going, and Grandaddy

15

Richard had died, she was going to be the only one left to help Granny Naomi on the bee farm. She did not like the bees, because she knew they could sting.

She tried once to stop her Mammy from going to England. She pointed out that there were no bees there, so where would she find enough honey to chew as she was used to in Granville? Her attempt failed to have her intended effect, and they laughed at her. Mammy laughed the loudest, displaying proudly her new set of teeth, teeth which were too white and too many for her face, giving her the look of the grinning skeletons which Gwendolen had seen in a book Shivorn's sister brought from America. 'So many tings to eat for England, me forget honey self,' her Mammy said in reply.

This made Gwendolen shut her mouth and pray that it would not be too long for her parents to send for her.

A few days before Mammy left, she busied herself in making her house-dresses and church clothes. Gwendolen sat in the corner by their bed, sulking and watching her happy Mammy singing as she sewed. Mammy stopped singing, turned her little head and asked suddenly, 'June-June, you like school?'

Now what brought that on? Gwendolen thought. First she was going away in a few days, now she was asking her if she liked school. She'd seen older children go down to school in groups. The schoolhouse was far beyond the church, an open building with lots of open windows, standing in open grass fields. And you went to school without your Mammy. 'Me no like school,' she declared defiantly.

'You learn education for school, June-June. When your Daddy send money to Granny next time, you start nice school. Tomorrow Ah buy your uniform for Marcus Garvey School. Nice school. Shivorn soon start too when her Daddy send money.'

'Shivorn's Daddy no have no money for send she. Him going to be a big, big boxer, one day.'

Sonia laughed, displaying those horrible new teeth again.

Gwendolen was more used to her Mammy's old teeth. These ones made her look as if she was slipping away from her bit by bit. She was becoming a new Mammy. First she was singing and laughing more than usual, and now these new, too white, too many teeth.

'You're big clever 'oman nuh. You make plenty, plenty friends at school.'

Granny Naomi came in and asked what they were talking about. Granny was sweating. She'd been working in the yard among the chickens and the sweat poured from under her hair to her face. She removed the scarf on her head, wiped her face with it sighing all the time. She looked tired but happy. She too was looking forward to her Mammy going to the 'Moder Kontry'. Everybody wanted her Mammy to go away.

'Your grandaater no like school,' Mammy explained.

'Ho, ho, ho, ho, you no know how lucky you is. Good schools like Marcus Garvey's cost plenty money, you know. Education is the thing nuh, gal. Soon get used to it. After school, then you help ol' Granny on the farm and the yard, huh?'

'See you'd so busy, you won't miss me, eh, June-June?'

Gwendolen knew that with Granny she could not win. That the shack was built by herself and Grandad Richard was a fact she never allowed them to forget. Many a time she would shower Gwendolen with love and gifts. But when Granny Naomi got angry, she shouted and her coarse voice became unrestrained and would melt all her good deeds away. Gwendolen had learned never to answer Granny Naomi back, because her Mammy got upset. Granny Naomi was tougher than her Mammy though, because her Mammy's voice was not so loud. Granny always won. Anyhow, she had learned to share her love, to include all of them, her Mammy, her Daddy Winston, her Granny Naomi, Uncle Johnny down the road and all the rest of them, because that was the way things were done in Granville.

They trailed again to the wharf. This time Mammy did not cry. She laughed all the time looking stranger still with her new hair-do and the new teeth. The heels of her new shoes were too high so she wobbled in them. Gwendolen had never seen her so happy. But Gwendolen felt so lost that she cried. Not only did she cry because her Mammy was going, but also it looked as if her Mammy was happy to leave her behind, giving the impression that she was not really wanted. If that was not the case, why then was her Mammy so happy to go away and she so sad to see her go? Gwendolen felt cheated because everybody kept telling her that she was a big 'gal nuh' and should be able to look after her Granny Naomi. Her sadness made her nervous, so she kept tripping and falling on their way to the minibus. Nobody understood how she felt and she could not talk to anybody about it, because she knew she would look stupid. Even her friend Shivorn had said only last night, when she saw her crying in the yard, that she was a cry-baby. Her Granny would shout and remind her that she had her and all their friends and neighbours in Granville, did she not? That might be so, but Mammy going was the final act of rejection life had imposed on her. She wanted her Mammy not to go. Would she ever be wanted by anyone, she wondered, as they walked back to Granville after wishing her Mammy a hurried goodbye, for unlike her Daddy Winston who came on time to the wharf, her Mammy was late. It took her too long to fix in the hairpiece under her pink hat and to pick up this and that thing she was going to need in England.

Last night, amidst all the packing, Mammy told her that her Daddy's people who lived in Kingston White Road at number 33 would come and visit her from time to time. 'Me sure, they'll come visit you in Granville. Anyway, you soon come an' join me an' your Daddy in England.' She had smiled, tripping over her packing cases like a young girl playing with her dolls.

'Why we no go together? Me wan' go with you, Mammy.'

'Me soon send for you, June-June, never fear.'

All that was only last night. It looked today as if it was ages ago. That little sunshine hope she had last night seemed to be covered with rainclouds today because her Mammy looked and felt so far away already. But she remembered the address of her people in Kingston.

By the time they turned into Messina Road, the untarred dusty road in which her Granny lived, in which Mammy was born, and in which she was now being raised, the world had become black and grey. The shadows were indistinct. The lights from the hurricane lamps escaped from doors and windows of the lean-to shacks like their own.

'Home sweet home,' Uncle Johnny's voice announced heartily from the back as he and Granny Naomi were slowly bringing up the rear. Gwendolen felt that Uncle Johnny's jocularity was meant to cheer everybody up. But with her, he failed dismally.

After putting away her clothes in the laundry basket for her and Granny to wash the following day, Gwendolen crawled into her corner. She missed Mammy more now, because as far as she could remember they had always shared this corner of Granny's shack. Now the bamboo bed did not only feel empty, it was large. She felt the type of loss she could not give name. The loss was deeper because something inside her kept telling her that when she saw her Mammy Sonia again, things would never be the same as before. Here in their little village in Granville by the hill she had had her mother's whole attention.

Granny was kind too, but she became tired easily and tended to complain a great deal. She was getting old, nearly fifty; she'd said so so many times, 'Me's near fifty now, you know.' Granny sometimes made the age of fifty appear like a badge you wore in front of your dress.

Gwendolen started to sniff in an attempt to hide her tears. But Granny who sat on Mammy's now empty sewing chair

19

heard her and asked in a low voice, 'Lawd God Almighty, what dat sniff, sniff mean? You big 'oman nuh, June-June. So why you cry like small pikney for your Mammy? Nuh, you have a big, big bed to yourself. Your Mammy soon write from England . . .'

There was a knock on the door. Granny said, in the same low voice, 'Henta.' Even before he came in, Gwendolen knew it could only be Uncle Johnny. All their other close friends, Mrs Roza Blackson, Shivorn's Mammy, Shivorn, Cocoa and all the other male cousins who came to see Mammy off would be too tired to come for a late chat. Most of them were there last night anyhow, reminding her Mammy of this and that and her Mammy busy showing off to Roza and Cocoa's mum. The men just watched and laughed. But tonight, Uncle Johnny was the only one close enough to pay another visit and to ask how they were getting on without Mammy. He knew they both trusted him implicitly.

'She only gone five minutes, Johnny, but henta anyhow. You was always a God-bless soul church broder. Me miss Sonia, you know.'

Granny lowered her voice. Gwendolen knew that this was out of consideration for her. But she was learning to swallow her sorrow.

That night, when it was dark and the stars twinkled, she kept imagining where her Mammy would be and what she would be feeling. She heard Uncle Johnny and Granny celebrating. From the sounds of their voices, she could tell they were incredibly happy her Mammy had gone to England. She lay very still. She heard every sound made by Granny Naomi and Uncle Johnny. They thought she was now asleep, because she was usually asleep by this hour, but for her that night there was little sleep.

For to Gwendolen, it seemed, the end of the world had come.

2

Uncle Johnny

Gwendolen soon learned that you had to accept things you could hardly change. The hurt of mother's departure lay heavy and tangible on one side of her chest for years after. Pangs of jealousy razed through her mind whenever she saw Cocoa or Shivorn running to welcome their Mammies from the farm, or when she saw them going to church together. Yes, she had Granny Naomi, yes, Uncle Johnny paid them regular visits, and he and Granny always celebrated till very late, making their little lean-to shack warm with their merriment. But Uncle Johnny was not her Daddy and Granny Naomi was not her Mammy. They both tried very much to be kind though.

By the time two years had passed, she learnt to disregard their noise, and oftentimes slept through it. Their conversation did not mean much to her anyhow.

One such night, she dozed off however, but was woken by Uncle Johnny. He was kneeling on the bamboo bed. He was now touching her face and mouth, telling her not to cry, that he was here to take care of her. She struggled to get up, but he shushed her, telling her not to wake Granny who was very tired and now sleeping. Gwendolen could hear the rise and fall of Granny's snores. The hand Uncle Johnny kept on her mouth was firm, but his other hand touched all her body, as if Uncle Johnny had four hands instead of two. His breath smelt of rum, he had been celebrating with Granny Naomi. They must have had a lot of drink. He put his hand under the bedclothes and tickled her with his fingers. He wanted her to laugh and enjoy his playing with her, but instead fear and shock froze all her emotions. Was this man with the iron grip over her mouth the same Uncle Johnny who used to bring her and Shivorn sweets and lemonade drinks at Christmas, who used to bring her ripe mangoes from the tree during mango season? Was this Uncle Johnny who used to rub oil on her grazed knee? Was this Uncle Johnny who used to call her Juney-Juney and wink at her and she would wink back? Was this Uncle Johnny who Mammy had said cried all night when Grandaddy Richard died because they were friends? What was the matter with Uncle Johnny tonight? She wanted very much to ask him what he was doing, but she could not; his hand was firmly over her mouth and she could not struggle because her body was frozen. Only her eyes roamed and it was dark. He was on top of her. She almost suffocated, but he soon rolled to one side.

'Your Mammy gone na England to join your Daddy. Dem no want you dere, but me look after you, right? Me help your Granny on de farm and buy you tings, right? We one family nuh. This our secret, right? Don't tell nobody, because they'll say you're a bad gal. You'll do anything for your Uncle Johnny, not so, Juney-Juney? And if you wan' anything, anything at all, just tell me. We good friends now, good, good friends.' His voice was hoarse, his breath came and went and the sickly smell of rum escaped every time he opened his mouth.

Gwendolen could listen no more. She struggled out of his hands and rushed into the dark backyard. Her inside burned and she felt sore. She was going back inside to tell Granny of Uncle Johnny. She could not stand there for long because the night air, in contrast to the suffocating air in their shack, was chilly. 'Mammy, why you no take me with you?'

When she returned, she stood by the side of Granny's bed and peered into her corner of the shack. Uncle Johnny had gone, but still she snored and was deep in sleep. Gwendolen decided to go back to her corner. It was too late to wake Granny now. Granny would only start complaining and maybe blame her. She would tell her in the morning. She placed her mother's sewing chair behind the door to prevent Uncle Johnny from coming back. It took her a long time before she was finally able to fall asleep.

The crow of the cocks and cackling of mother hens in concert with the early birds did not wake Gwendolen. She was still tired and sleepy when Granny woke her. Granny reminded her that now her daughter Sonia had gone, they had to work hard and that meant waking up on time. There were the hens to feed, the room to clean, breakfast to get before they could go further up the mountain to the bee farm. Sonia was a good hard-working girl, and that was why she'd got herself a nice, nice husband. 'Sonia in England nuh,' she reminded her granddaughter proudly.

'Me know,' Gwendolen replied slowly as she cleared the night clothes from the bamboo bed so that it could serve as a seating place during the day.

Granny was right. They rushed through the morning work and were soon on their way up the hill, even before the rising of the sun.

Gwendolen could find no time to tell Granny what happened in the night. So she pushed it from her mind, hoping to do so when they were settled on the farm. However, as they climbed the hill, other bee-keepers joined them and the talk was of her Mammy. They were all saying how lucky her Mammy was.

'Some people sell them houses and land, you know, just to buy the tickets for England, but Sonia's man just sent for her,' Shivorn's mother said.

'Sonia make you jealous?' came the happy voice of Uncle Johnny. He appeared suddenly from the side of the track in his work-clothes.

'Where you going so early dis marning?' Roza asked.

'Naomi would need another pair of hands, Ah guess.'

Granny Naomi was very happy to see Uncle Johnny, but she too showed some surprise at seeing him so early. He used to come and help whenever he could spare the time but never this early. Naomi thought this gesture was to show her the depth of their friendship. They soon fell into conversation and the other bee-keepers took their various tracks to their various hives. Gwendolen followed them in a confused state. If what Uncle Johnny had done to her last night was wrong, how come he behaved so normally this morning? Telling her Granny now was out of the question, because she was so happy with Uncle Johnny's help.

Granny Naomi might not believe her anyhow. But there were two things she was sure of, she did not like Uncle Johnny troubling her at night, and she did not like to see Granny Naomi unhappy. She listened to their conversation without taking it in. Their talk was inconsequential banter, to her anyway. They were always telling each other how lucky they were to live this long and oftentimes praising the Lord for giving them enough to eat.

In the evening, Uncle Johnny brought Gwendolen the bottle of lemonade he had promised.

'Oh, Johnny, you spending so much money and time on us?'

'Me think the chile still missing she Mammy. This to stop her from crying.'

'Oh Johnny, you so kind. Looking after your friend's family like your own.'

'Yeah, those of us left must stick together, eh, Granny?'

'You sure right, Johnny, thank you. Gwendolen, whey your manners? Uncle Johnny bring you lemo – '

'Thank you, Uncle Johnny,' Gwendolen said quickly before Granny's voice became raised. She thought Granny looked silly putting on that childish voice just because of Uncle Johnny.

Looking back at that time as an adult, Gwendolen could not really pinpoint on which day and at what hour Uncle Johnny had started to make her feel guilty. All she knew was that as she grew older, she began to entertain the irrational fear that everybody would blame her if they knew her secret. She was beginning to learn by daily indoctrination that there was little a man like Uncle Johnny could do wrong. He was usually right, listened to and regarded as a very kind person. Who would believe her word against such a respectable man as Granny's friend Uncle Johnny? True he was not married to Granny Naomi, but theirs was a respectable relationship. Two middle-aged people, God-fearing and church-going. Yes, Uncle Johnny must be right. He had told her that they were not hurting anybody and that it was her way of showing him she loved him. It seemed at that time a sin not to love Uncle Johnny. He so good to them.

Mammy sent them a letter the Christmas after she left. She told them she had had a baby boy and she sent them some money. The money was good because Gwendolen could feel how hard things were becoming for Granny. In Granville people did not go hungry during the mango season, but Granny was counting and rationing the ones she picked. Uncle Johnny still picked them some and helped on the farm, but things were becoming hard.

The letter pleased Granny because of the baby but it saddened her for a while because Mammy wanted Granny to use part of the money to send Gwendolen to Garvey's academy. 'But, June-June, you such a help on the farm,' Granny cried. 'Me wan' you to learn education. Education is a good thing, but we produce little honey these days, not enough to buy bread and beans.'

'Dem no go school on Saturdays,' Uncle Johnny said. 'Dem have so many holidays in those schools, me tell you. Teachers nowadays don' like much work, not like our days. She helps on her free days, Naomi. Let she go.'

Granny's smile was slow and uncertain. 'June-June, you're a lucky gal, you know that.'

'Every child suppose to go to school on these islands, you know, Naomi, but many parents on the hills pay no mind to the law.'

'School cost money, Johnny. Dem school uniforms, books, and the parents losing all the help the child give at home and on the farm.'

'You start school nuh?' Shivorn shrieked when Gwendolen told her. 'Dem put you in baby class, you know, since you don' start school in time.'

'Me mammy wan' me to learn education,' Gwendolen put in weakly.

'Ah know. But, June-June, you too late to go nuh, private lesson better. You no sit next to a runny-nose pickney. When my Aunty send money from America, dat's where me go. Cheaper too. The teacher, she the Sunday school teacher, Miss Peters, she nice. You know she, June-June, she Yellow Nigger, Jamaica Brown, but she nice.'

Granny Naomi did not need much persuasion in sending Gwendolen to Miss Peters's private lesson. Miss Peters did not need to be a wizard to know that Gwendolen might be a shy and sensitive child, who was not interested in the intricacies of multiplication tables and the ABC. She did her best, though. She taught Gwendolen the catechism and some church hymns and Gwendolen began to recognize some words in the songs. For months on end, she practised how to write 'Jesus Christ Our Lord'.

This arrangement suited everybody. Gwendolen could work on the farm during the day and went to Miss Peters whenever she was not too tired and when there was not too much work to do in the house. They did not have to worry anyhow. Because Sonia did not send money for the next fees. So Gwendolen soon stopped going to Miss Peters, but Uncle Johnny did not stop coming to her on some nights.

26

Granny thought that by now Gwendolen would stop her bed-wetting. At first she used to tell her off mildly, but now she was beginning to lose patience. Once, she was so angry that she made Gwendolen carry her soiled beddings around their yard to shame Gwendolen into stopping. This worked for two days only. As soon as Uncle Johnny sneaked up to her again, she would wet her bed that same night. Granny made her eat her supper at five o'clock in the evening so that hunger would keep her awake. Hunger did keep Gwendolen awake, but the few hours of fretful sleep she did have, released her bladder again.

Gwendolen knew that Granny Naomi was at her wits' end. She'd heard her talk about it to Shivorn's Mammy several times. But one evening, her heart missed a beat when she heard Cocoa's Mammy suggesting Granny took her to a doctor.

'Me have no money, man. Sonia forget 'bout us nuh.'

'No, Granny, not dem white doctors, but the damn good black 'oman by the market. She good. She tell you why she bed wet so late. Some children take long to stop though.'

'June-June too long. Sonia not like that.'

Fear gripped Gwendolen so much that that night her bed-wetting was heavier than ever. What would the woman doctor do to her? Who should she ask, Shivorn or Cocoa? The two made fun of her for wetting her bed like a child. Cocoa always called her baby anyway. Should she ask Uncle Johnny? She knew the woman they were talking about. Some called her the magic or obeah woman. What would she do to her? And her going there would mean Granny telling everybody about her bed-wetting. Granny did not know that she was more ashamed of it than herself. Granny worried about the stink in their room, but for Gwendolen the shame sat on her like a perpetual load. She tried very much not to annoy her friends so that they would not call her a bed-wetter. But if Granny was going to tell everybody, because that was what going to the obeah woman meant, she would do something about it.

Her Daddy's people lived in the capital by the harbour. She saw them last when she and her Mammy went to see them the Christmas after Daddy left. But her Mammy never stopped talking about them. Gwendolen knew their address by heart, but the trouble was that she could not remember how to get there. She would chance it, White Road in Kingston and number 33.

Should she ask Uncle Johnny? Maybe he would give her some money. After all, he promised to help her, but suppose he told Granny Naomi? And suppose he told her not to go? He seemed to be right all the time. Her Mammy had been gone now over two years, but she had written only four letters. The first one arrived the Christmas after she had left. That letter came with some money. The second letter was in a parcel containing a new dress and shoes for her, a headscarf and some medicines for Granny. The next letter announced the birth of another brother and the fourth brought nothing but to say how difficult life was becoming with two baby boys to look after. Mammy even said she was lucky to have a mother like Granny Naomi who had agreed to take care of her daughter. Each time Uncle Johnny read such letters, he would lift his red-rimmed eyes and look knowingly in her direction as if to say, 'Did I not tell you that they will go there and breed and forget all about you?' So Gwendolen's hope of being sent for was still very alive, yet everybody around her told her that with the birth of other children her parents would not be able to send for her because things were expensive over there. That hope was very much at the centre of her dreams. And if only her parents could send more money to Granny Naomi, and more frequently, the bitterness in Granny Naomi's life would not be so severe.

But she was leaving. She was going to her father's people to avoid the shame of exposure. A big girl like her wetting

28

her bed. But sometimes she asked herself why it was that her friends, Cocoa and Shivorn, did not have the same problem. Many a time Granny said that it was because she ate too much, at other times she said it was because she drank too much water, but even though she reduced her water intake and altered her mealtimes, still that did not help. But she noticed it became worse after Uncle Johnny had left her bamboo bed. Telling Granny about that now would not help. People would ask, 'But why she kept quiet for so long?' And she was not even sure that that was the reason she wet her bed. She wished Uncle Johnny would stop though, because she came to dread it, especially these last months when Uncle Johnny kept asking jokingly, 'You no wan' make people know our tiny-tiny secret, do you, Juney-Juney?' Her mouth went dry each time he made a joke like that. The only thing to do was to leave Granville.

She was sorry she had to take some money from under Granny Naomi's pillow to pay for the bus ride. She promised herself that she would pay Granny back someday. If only Granny Naomi did not have to depend so much on Uncle Johnny. He made it his duty to take the finished honey down to the harbour and hire boats on which to sell the honey to the businessmen who owned the big hotels down the coast. Granny had lost the knack of doing this. Gwendolen knew that Grandaddy Richard used to do this until his death. Her Mammy Sonia had taken it over, but when she left for England she had assured them that Granny would not have to depend on honey for her livelihood. Granny now depended on it for their daily bread. Gwendolen knew that her own help was becoming invaluable too. Granny said that she was so good with handling eggs from the hens. When they had many eggs she sold them in the market-place and bought yams with the money. But Uncle Johnny brought enough money to buy fish, kerosene, rice and beans. What would happen to Granny Naomi if she left Granville and went to Kingston? She guessed they'd be able to look after one another.

The journey took most of the day and she arrived safely at the gate leading to the yard where Granny Elinor lived with her family. It took Gwendolen a long time to explain that she came because she wanted to see them and know her Daddy's people better. She found herself repeating this rehearsed statement over and over again to Granny Elinor's close and piercing questions. Granny Elinor was happy to see her, but, as she said, Gwendolen was better on the hill with her Granny Naomi because she could see 'how overcrowded we be, no room for breath here, lovey,' she explained grandly to Gwendolen.

Granny Elinor was young-looking and very pale almost like white people. All her children were like that. So how come her Daddy Winston was black? She had noticed this before, when she and her Mammy came to visit them the Christmas after Daddy Winston had gone. But now she was older and she became more curious about it. She looked so different, so much so that many of Granny Elinor's acquaintances were commenting on how black she looked, just like Winston. And she noticed that Granny Elinor did not particularly like the comment. Unable to keep it to herself any more, Gwendolen asked, 'How come my Daddy so black, Granny Elinor?'

'Your Grandaddy different from my last husband.'

'You mean my Grandaddy black and your husband Yellow Nigger?'

Everybody laughed, except Granny Elinor. For no reason at all, Gwendolen felt she could speak her mind here among these people. These might be her relatives but she did not and would never feel at home with them. She had nothing to lose by telling them what she thought of them. Most people in Granville were like her, except her tutor Miss Peters. Gwendolen had heard Granny Naomi refer to her as Jamaican

Brown or Yellow Nigger whenever she made any fuss about the delayed tutorial payment. 'All dem Yellow Niggers with these airs.' So Gwendolen had associated people with pale skin as people with 'airs'. She had seen many half-castes in Kingston before, but had never given their paleness any thought until Granny Naomi started calling Miss Peters 'Yellow Nigger'. She felt now that Granny Elinor did not wish to be reminded of her Grandaddy's blackness.

'Why Daddy go 'ngland, because him black, 'im different?'

'No, chile, nat so, nat so at all. 'Ngland, nice place to go. Him come back a rich big man,' Granny Elinor said in her nicest voice, but Gwendolen was not deceived. She was beginning to feel that if her skin had been paler like those of Elinor's other grandchildren, she would have allowed her to stay. Why was it that people with paler skin colour have airs, she wondered. Suddenly she realized that the only people she could ask were in Granville, not here among her relatives in Kingston.

A few patronizing jokes about her cute brown eyes and tight natural curls and how she laughed like Winston decided her. She would go back to Granny Naomi. She would tell her everything. At least she would be among real people, not these city ones. Their house was not that good either. It was not a shack like the ones they had on the mountains, but there were too many people. Granny Elinor seemed to have so many grandchildren. Gwendolen did not like the yard here; everybody's apartment door opened on to it. At least Granny Naomi had her own backyard. True they kept chickens there, but those were just hens and cocks and not people. She began to feel homesick.

When Granny Elinor told her that she must go back home, because Granny Naomi must be sick with worries about her disappearance, Gwendolen did not refuse. Granny Elinor bought her a red beret and a packet of biscuits and saw her to the bus station. She left her with strict instructions to go back home and that she would check from her Granny whether she had arrived or not. She did not tell Gwendolen how she was going to do it, but Gwendolen believed her. However, she did not need that threat; she had nowhere else to go. She must go back. Maybe one day, just one day, her parents would send for her. After all, the preacher at the church had said that 'In the name of Jesus, everything is possible.' Please Jesus help her now.

Granny Naomi caned her so much that she almost collapsed. She had caused Granny so much anguish. Everybody had been looking for her. They were going the very next day to report her loss at the police station in Victoria Road. Why did she have to go to those people who had never asked of her since her Daddy left? Was she that stupid, not to know that Elinor and her children thought themselves superior? Why did she have to go to them? Since her husband Richard died and her daughter Sonia gone to England, had Gwendolen ever seen her go to them in Kingston with plate in hand to beg for food? Why did she have to go to those snooty-nose people of all places? Why did she come back, anyhow, why?

'Because me love you, Granny,' Gwendolen whimpered. 'Me no have no one else, see, please, Granny.'

'Naomi, stop now, hear what the lill gal say. Make you stop now. She understands nuh,' Roza Blackson, Shivorn's Mammy, said. 'Don't you ever do no such thing again, June-June. Bad men could have tief you away, you know dat. All the way down the harbour on your own. Never do it again, you hear.'

Gwendolen nodded like a robot.

Granny looked straight at Gwendolen in the eye, just as one would at a real person. She usually looked above and beyond her, never at her straight. Why was the child running away from home? she wondered. A sense of guilt was enveloping her. After raising Sonia, and knowing that she could not have any more children, she had reconciled herself to her lot. She really did not wish to go through worrying after a young girl again, not since Sonia had dragged Winston from the coast to tell her bewildered parents that she was pregnant and that he was the father of her child. Naomi had thought that her only child would be a little school marm like Miss Peters, but instead she got herself 'stuck up' with an illiterate like Winston. She had given up trying to raise anybody proper. She was not good at it. She had even told Richard several times to sell his honey from a wooden shed, but he preferred boats tied to the coast because they were cheaper. When the heavy rain came that year he was drowned in the boat. Now Sonia had taken her Winston to England and left her with this child without sending enough money. She was not supposed not to love her only grandchild, because that was bad. But she wished Gwendolen were with her mother so she could worry about her own belly and her church-going. Was Gwendolen able to see all that? Was that why she ran to Winston's people in Kingston?

Gwendolen looked up and saw a new kind of sympathy and understanding in Granny's eyes. The look was new to her and she could not give it name.

That night, Gwendolen called her Granny and told her what Uncle Johnny had been doing to her and that that was the reason for attempting to run away in search of her relations in Kingston.

Surprisingly, Granny Naomi believed her. She called all their neighbours and they marched to Johnny and really started a fight. Everybody came and shouted at him, calling him all kind of names under the sun. Her Mammy's friend, Roza, suggested Uncle Johnny should be reported and sent to prison. 'You silly ol' man, troubling lill babies. Never seen such a ting. God damn you, you know.'

'Me just can't take it. He a Christian too.' Granny Naomi shook her head. 'What me tell Sonia, huh? Say me no fit raise she daater? Lawd ha' mussy.'

Most of their male neighbours were shocked at first, but they recovered very quickly and began to look rather amused. And Uncle Johnny could sense it. He did not deny the accusation, he just looked detached as if all the noises people were making had little to do with him.

One man, Jeffrey, who lived in a trailer across the road and who normally had little to do with those who lived in houses, even though the houses were wooden shacks, came up and thumped Uncle Johnny on the chest and asked, 'Dis true, Mr Johnny? You trouble the lill pikney?'

'Don't fex me, man. How Ah fit do such a ting, when Naomi dey dere? Me and Naomi friends long, long time, you know. Ah work my ass out on she bee farm, so this is thank you. Why June-June no shout, huh? Why she keep quiet?'

'Now, June-June, when did Uncle Johnny trouble you? Last night? Last Sunday?'

Gwendolen shook her head. She knew she would be ridiculed, she knew they would not believe her, but she prayed that at least after this night Uncle Johnny would stop worrying her. In a small voice which sounded unreal even to herself she replied, 'Long, long time.'

Uncle Johnny's hysterical laughter jolted everybody. 'See, see wharr Ah mean. Whey Naomi when Ah trouble you? In the same room? With your Granny watching? Lawd ha' mussy. E late, man. Long day tomorrow.'

Jeffrey shifted his cloth cap to his nose, hunched his shoulders and said as he swaggered across the road to his trailer, 'Maybe the lill marm love the job.'

There was an uneasy laughter among the men as people started to drift away.

The women still defended her, though their voices of protestation were taking a lower key. But Granny Naomi was incensed with anger. Gwendolen had never seen her so worked up. It needed the energy of hefty women like Shivorn's Mammy to pull her away.

Granny Naomi was not only bitter that Johnny had done this to her grandchild, but she was sorry and humiliated that it was done by the only man she trusted as a friend. Naomi banged at Uncle Johnny's windows, she threatened to burn his shack down. She cursed the fickleness of men. How could he? He was here when Gwendolen was born in that very shack. He had helped in watching over the child through cold and measles just like his own grandchild, and how could he? After a time, Granny almost choked and she actually threw up, but the women led her back into her shack, and started to talk sense into her.

She must remember that it was Gwendolen's word against that of Johnny. Granny must not forget Johnny's status in the society. All Naomi had to do now was to try to forget it and keep her eyes wide open that a thing like that would never happen again. Very few people would believe Gwendolen, she must never forget that.

Gwendolen felt like screaming every time people said that it was her word against that of Uncle Johnny. But she controlled herself. She had caused enough trouble for one night. And Granny Naomi seemed to have suddenly aged. She had spent the last couple of days looking for her, and now this. Some people were even giving her black looks. So she kept away in her corner on her bamboo bed.

Uncle Johnny stopped molesting her. But Gwendolen had lost her innocence. So adults could tell lies and wriggle out of tricky situations, simply because they were respected members of their community. People in Granville started looking at her differently.

Shivorn was at first very funny. She started waving at her over the yard and would not stop to talk to her as they used to on their way to sell mangoes. But Cocoa was curious.

'Why you don't shout when Uncle Johnny trouble you?' Cocoa asked two evenings later, after making sure there was no one near. Gwendolen did not know why Cocoa had to look this way and that before talking to her in this low breathless way. But Gwendolen needed her friendship. She could not bear it when people started avoiding her and looking at her with the corner of their eyes.

' 'E cover my mouth so.' Gwendolen went on to demonstrate.

'If na me, I bite so.'

Now why did she not bite Uncle Johnny? There was no time to think of that the first time because she was scared. And she told her friend so. She simply said, 'Me scared, Cocoa.'

'Cocoa! Co . . . coa! Curiosity kills the cat, you know. Let June-June be. Stop troubling 'er with questions,' Roza, Shivorn's mother, called from her yard. Cocoa quickly skipped away. Gwendolen would have liked to talk to her friends more about her ordeal. The yard suddenly looked larger and empty. The noises of the chicken grew louder and she felt so alone.

Days slipped by and people started to forget, but Granny Naomi's fierce defence was no longer so strong. Since Uncle Johnny had stopped helping them, and since her parents did not send money, Granny Naomi started to complain about so many things. She complained about the way Gwendolen walked, why she always rolled her backside when she moved about. Gwendolen was not aware she was doing that. Granny Naomi tried to straighten her up, by telling her to tuck her backside in, otherwise men would think she was a bad girl, inviting trouble. She would try to walk straight, she promised.

Soon Granny Naomi herself started calling her a bad girl. How come Uncle Johnny did not trouble the other girls? How come she was the only one? Because of her behaviour, they now had less honey to sell and less food to eat. Gwendolen started to pick mangoes and add to the eggs to sell by the street corner. But the trouble was that during mango season, everybody had mangoes. So, she ate many herself. At least her belly was full at this time of year.

By the time Gwendolen was eleven, life with Granny Naomi was becoming almost impossible. She'd stopped beating her, because Gwendolen had learned to run away whenever Granny's voice started to rise. Granny would then resort to taunt at the way she walked. That did hurt Gwendolen, because she knew Mammy Sonia walked that way. Now Granny was making it sound as if her walking attracted old men like Uncle Johnny, although Granny had believed her and was really angry at Uncle Johnny. Shivorn had told her though that Granny talked that way because she was getting old and afraid of where their next dinner would come from. After all, did not her Mammy walk that way, bending to one side? 'Pay her no mind. She ol' and poor. And maybe she miss she sweetheart Uncle Johnny. Whey he, anyhow? Ah don' see him long time now. He shame, you know. Silly ol' fool.'

That was the first time Gwendolen knew that her friend Shivorn was on her side. But the whole episode had succeeded in making her into a quieter girl. 'How come your Mammy stopped sending money anyhow?' Shivron asked as an afterthought. Gwendolen shrugged her shoulders to this question, because she did not know the answer.

A few evenings later, Uncle Johnny suddenly showed up. Gwendolen and Shivorn were as usual in the backyard, putting the chickens back into their baskets. Shivorn was at the same time busy telling her friend how she was going to look when she eventually joined her Aunt Monica in the USA. They had both talked of these dreams so many times that Gwendolen had learned not to ask, 'But when will Aunty Monica send for you, Shivorn?' She did ask once and her friend had burst out crying, cursing and even shouting at her, and said, 'And you, June-June, why your Daddy don't send for you?' Since then Gwendolen had learned her lesson. Now she just laughed and agreed to everything Shivorn said. She knew that her Mammy might never send for her. As for her Daddy, she believed he had long forgotten her.

Then suddenly, Shivorn who was facing the gap between the shacks that led to the front stopped. She started to rub her eyes dramatically. 'A ghost, June-June, a ghost. Ah sure see a ghost.'

Gwendolen, who had finished settling the hens for the night and was now breaking some firewood, dropped what she was doing and ran up to where Shivorn was standing. The sight that met her eyes was quite unexpected. They saw Uncle Johnny in a yellow shirt, with a kind of yellow handkerchief tied round his neck. He wore a pair of checked trousers and a cap of the same material. He looked really smart, and this smartness was emphasized by the jaunty way he walked.

The two girls opened their mouths wide and stared at each other. Instinctively they drew nearer the door as he knocked and Granny Naomi said in her worst voice, 'Henta.'

Then Granny Naomi shouted, 'Wharr you wan' 'ere you man with no shame . . .' The girls burst out laughing. Their laughter was so loud that the two adults inside the shack heard them. That probably made them lower their voices. Soon the girls thought they could hear Granny Naomi crying, but they were not quite sure. In no time at all Uncle Johnny walked out with the same jaunty air as he entered. Shivorn put her hand in her house shift and started to imitate the jauntiness. Gwendolen laughed and laughed.

When they had laughed their fill, and Gwendolen had finished breaking the wood for the fire and the sun was going down and they knew they would soon go to their different cooking places to start preparing food for the evening, Shivorn put into words what Gwendolen had wanted to say for the past half hour. Now Shivorn was speaking for the two of them. 'But what 'e wan' here nuh?'

'Me no know,' replied Gwendolen.

'Maybe him come for marry you, June-June.'

Gwendolen was not the cleverest of people. She could be slow, but she was not thick-skinned. She could not fight Shivorn, because she was slight like her Mammy Sonia. She hadn't the confidence for a verbal attack on her friend, not after her years of bed-wetting and the Uncle Johnny episode, which she knew people could throw back at her to hurt. But she could sulk and pout. She did that now, pulling her thin lips together and sucking her breath like a snake. Her friend knew she had offended her. There was no time to apologize because Roza's voice could be heard.

'Sheeeeeeeeeevorn, Sheeevorn, whey dat gal!'

Shivorn ran into her own yard, it was time to help in the kitchen.

That evening, after they had all eaten, Granny Naomi told Gwendolen that her relatives in Kingston had sent word that Mammy had had a fourth child and that they would soon send money for her to come to England to help her Mammy look after the family.

Gwendolen was too shocked to speak. She impulsively opened her mouth like a fish gasping for air and quickly closed it again. She felt that if she said anything Granny might prevent her from going to England. To England, where she could be herself – happy, trusting, Gwendolen again. To England where she would be able to answer friends like Shivorn back because they would not know about her bed-wetting past nor what Uncle Johnny had done. She would not risk this freedom by asking Granny any questions. But oh, she was burning to know how Uncle Johnny managed to get the information. She wanted to know where he had been all these months and how come he'd turned out so smartly dressed. She wanted to know when the money would be coming . . . she wanted to know many things, but since it was now beginning to look as if Granny was blaming her for what Uncle Johnny did, the little innocent openness that existed between her and the adults in her world had gone. She had to be really sure before opening herself to an adult again.

Why was Granny Naomi crying? Was she crying because she was going to miss her? The adult world was so complicated, one minute they made you feel unwanted, the next they said they were missing you.

3

Moder Kontry

'June-June,' Granny Naomi called weakly, as she watched Gwendolen folding and patting her tropical cotton dresses into shape, ready to put them into the tin portmanteau she was going to take with her to England. Granny Naomi knew from stories people had told her about England that most of those cheap dresses would be thrown away. Most of them were bought from cheap open stalls in Coronation Market in Kingston. Granny knew that Sonia and her husband must be doing very well, because not everybody who went to England could afford to send for the child they left behind. And they would not allow their daughter June-June to wear such dresses and carry a portmanteau with so many dents for long. But she was not going to tell Gwendolen all that. The child was happily preoccupied with her packing.

'June-June,' she called again with a kind of apologetic and uncertain smile. 'Ah may never see you again, you know, gal.'

The statement was so unexpected that Gwendolen stopped her packing. She did not know whether she was expected to give an answer, and, if she were to give one, what she was going to say. Granny Naomi did not wait for her reply. She had not finished talking.

'Well, England is a long, long way. And when you get there, you won't remember me no more. You busy making new life, new friends and won't remember these ol' bones no more.'

Gwendolen recalled the harsh, hand-to-mouth life she had been through with her Granny. For sheer existence, it was sometimes necessary for them to wake up as early as four o'clock in the morning as soon as the cocks start crowing. The work and the bitterness over Uncle Johnny and Mammy not sending enough money had all distanced Granny from her. The relation between her and her Mammy was like that of two women growing together. She could tell Mammy anything. With Mammy, she could be impulsive, she could be her real self, open and trusting. But with Granny, she was not so sure. How many times had she longed to curl up to her and tell her all her fears, fears that her parents might not send for her, that she probably had been forgotten? How she wished she could drop down dead, when Granny made her walk about the yard carrying her bedding, with all her friends watching and laughing at the back of their hands? How little Granny had made her feel when she sent her out to play simply because she and Uncle Johnny wanted to have an adult talk. And the most hurtful of all was when she started to suspect that Granny did not really believe that she did not encourage Uncle Johnny or that the whole thing was not her imagination. Childishly, she felt like reminding Granny Naomi of all this. But instinctively something warned her not to. First it would be unkind, second, since it was clear that she would be joining her parents, it looked as if Granny was weakening. And moreover Gwendolen still feared that Granny Naomi could stop her from going away. So, Gwendolen replied lightly, 'Oh, Granny, me never forget you. Ah write you as soon as Ah know how to write proper. You'll see, Ah promise.'

Naomi smiled. Her sunken eyes went deeper into her head. The white roots of her hair looked like a halo. She was thinner, and her hands were becoming palsied and bonier, with veins now showing in relief.

'You tell your Mammy about Johnny, eh, June-June?'

'No, Granny, Ah won't. They'll blame me, Granny, not so?' Gwendolen asked breathlessly as she stole a glance at Naomi; at the same time she smiled without joy.

Naomi did not reply. Maybe for that reason or for a reason Gwendolen could not understand, her mood suddenly changed. She became angry. She did not wish to be reminded of Uncle Johnny. She wanted to bury for ever the picture of Granny making a show of supporting her, believing her, then suspecting her of encouraging Uncle Johnny. Suppose Uncle Johnny should tell her parents, would they start blaming her too? She wanted to know if Granny would tell her parents, but was at first too scared to ask. Her mouth went dry. Why had Granny started talking this way? Then she swallowed hard and asked, 'Granny, you tell Mammy 'bout me and Uncle Johnny?'

Granny shook her head. She was in the shadows, sitting on her bed. The hurricane lamp threw light on the portmanteau. Gwendolen could not see Granny's face. Was she laughing at her, the way Shivorn and the others had laughed at her behind the back of their hands? Was Granny simply smiling? Was she speaking the truth? Did Granny never believe that she was innocent? She would never know. But she did see her shake her head. That was a promise not to tell.

Her anger against the adult world did not last long these days. Not since the day it became certain she was going to England. Somehow she was becoming faintly aware that the future belonged to the young. Shivorn's voice, 'Your Granny ol' nuh, she don talk crazy,' was becoming meaningful. After all, her Mammy sent for her and not Granny Naomi. Granny was even begging her to be remembered. As a younger child she used to be impulsive, but since Mammy left without her, a sense of rejection curbed all her impulsiveness. With the hope of going back to her parents now certain, she was beginning to feel almost fully mended. Before she had felt limp and lethargic like a damaged rag doll. She did not need to be too cautious any longer. Suddenly, she skipped over the portmanteau, over her jumble of cheap clothes, and dashed to Granny Naomi and hugged her. 'Me tell Mammy to send you letters, money and medicine.'

Gwendolen dashed back, crouched on her knees, buried her face into her clothes and began to laugh.

All such fits of lightheartedness were so unexpected that Naomi heard herself laughing with Gwendolen. They both had been so poor that worrying about everyday needs had made it almost impossible to acknowledge each other. 'June-June, what come over you? Huh-hun! You happy to go fer 'ngland.'

'Yes, Granny.'

Gwendolen knew she had felt betrayed when her Mammy was happy to go. Her Granny needn't feel betrayed because they would always take good care of her, by sending money, medicine and letters. She would remind Mammy, especially since Granny had promised not to tell anyone about Uncle Johnny and herself. She would rather carry that shame and guilt alone. She would not like to impose them on her parents. It was her guilt; it was her shame.

Uncle Johnny did not come to see her off at the airport. Everybody else came. Shivorn was sure she would soon go to the USA, when Aunty Monica's next letter arrived. Shivorn's mother, Roza, kept telling Gwendolen to be a good girl and not to mess about. Granny Naomi reminded Gwendolen of her promise to write. Shivorn wanted to know how Gwendolen, who could not write here, could write to Granny Naomi. Granny snapped at her and said that in England Gwendolen would go to a proper school, where she would learn very fast. They all agreed that anybody could be anything in England. Gwendolen mutely nodded at everybody and at everything they said. She could hardly wait to see this England, where she was going to live a new life, with Mammy and Daddy, her two young brothers and a sister. Life was not only going to be different, it was going to be fun. She would always remember all her friends, her Granny, the street markets and Granville. When she became rich like Shivorn's Aunty Monica, with fine clothes and fine manners, she would be kind.

She watched open-eyed as the plane took off and the whole of Jamaica danced out of view. She peered closer to the tiny glass window by her seat and could see nothing but clouds. It was comfortable inside the plane, with nice chairs and her own tiny table. When the air hostess gave her a tray full of different kinds of food, she was taught how to unstrap the tiny table. Everything was changing very fast. The toilet in the plane was fascinating. One of the air hostesses showed her how it worked. She was nice, this air hostess, and she looked like Shivorn's Aunty Monica. She smiled often and encouragingly at Gwendolen. Her mouth was wide and her skin pale, like Miss Peters, and her hair, which was pulled back, was very glossy and black. She smelt lovely. Maybe that was how everybody smelt in England.

Gwendolen soon fell asleep. It was hours before she was shaken awake by her new friend, the air hostess, who advised her to fasten her seat belt, because they were landing in England soon. She wanted to ask her what England was like, but shut her mouth because though she could understand the lady, yet she suspected that her village voice would sound strange to her.

A grey-green land full of houses and more planes danced towards them as their plane touched the ground. Gwendolen arrived in England on this wild windy October morning. The kind lady came and took her hand, helped her into the woollen hat Granny Naomi had knitted and asked, 'Gwendolen, where is your coat?'

'Gwendolen.' Was that what people would be calling her in England? Everybody called her June-June in Granville, in the county of St Catherine and even in Kingston. The nice lady was definitely addressing her because she was holding her hand and looking at her. Coat, coat, coat, yes, she looked around her and saw that everybody was putting on their topcoats. In reply Gwendolen shrugged her shoulders. She had no coat.

She had a beautiful dress made of the same kind of organza Mammy loved. She had white socks – long ones this time – and a pair of black plastic shoes. Mammy had sent money to purchase all these things. How she and Granny Naomi had suffered in the sun, the day they both trekked from shop to shop in search of white knee-length socks. Most children in the neighbourhood did not wear socks, and when they did they wore ankle ones, because of the heat. She and Granny failed to get a pair at first so they bought some ankle ones from Coronation Market. But then one of her cousins in Kingston came to wish her bon voyage and brought her a pair of knee-length socks which she was wearing. Granny Elinor and all her relatives in Kingston knew many smart shops from where they bought beautiful things. Granny Naomi had thought that with those socks and the tightly knitted hat, her beautiful dress with stiff petticoats, Gwendolen was well equipped for any place on earth, however cold. But obviously, judging from the layers of wrappings, the other passengers were piling on themselves, all her new clothes were far from sufficient.

'Maybe your parents'll bring your coat for you. It is cold out there,' her new friend said by way of assurance.

Gwendolen wanted to say that she did not feel the cold, but, remembering how different her Granville-bred voice would sound, decided to keep her mouth shut. Instead she smiled and nodded. But she could hardly keep steady the excited beatings of her heart. Just to think that out there were the members of her family was enough to make her skip out of the plane, coat or no coat.

But the lady, who could sense her excitement, took her hand and gently led her through some cream-painted corridors and channels. She talked to some officers in uniform and they checked her passport. One officer peered at the picture on the passport and looked at her all over. When the officer frowned, her heart leapt and she thought maybe Granny Naomi had told these policemen about her and Uncle Johnny. But eventually the officer gave the passport back to the stewardess and waved them on. They all smiled at each other without saying a word, these quiet dumb-like people.

They came out of the partition into another world. A world in which people were packed together and were talking and laughing like they did in Coronation Market at home. Some of them were carrying placards with slogans written on them. She did not, however, have much time to ponder over this human chaos, because a very black man with a felt hat, grey suit and pale brown shirt extricated himself from this thick mass of humanity and came forward, rather awkwardly, and said in an uncertain voice that stammered:

'June-June? You be big wo . . . man nuh . . . Me no . . . no . . . fit recog . . . nize you again. Lawd Almighty!'

That must be her Daddy. The faint image of his departure, that long ago, loomed in her mind's eye and it converged into this man standing before her with arms open in welcome. She rushed into the arms. She was like a child again. She was herself again, not a little girl who had to play adult. She could be herself now, she could show her emotion. She hugged the huge man. Her heart beat so fast and she was full to the brim with joy.

'Ho, ho, ho! You don' wan' to crush your . . . your . . . Daddy nuh, eh, June-June?'

Gwendolen watched proudly as he thanked the stewardess and gave her a box of what she later knew to be chocolate and thanked her again and again.

Gwendolen somehow did not wish the air hostess to go away. She had, during the past hours, assumed the epitome of her childhood, her Jamaica. Her presence in the plane was her assurance of the familiar.

'Good luck, little girl, this is England,' the air hostess said joyfully and disappeared behind the green partition. Jamaica was cut from her with that disappearance. It was the cutting of an umbilical cord; it was the burning of a drawbridge.

Putting all these feelings into words was not easy. Gwendolen smiled tearfully, then, with the new confidence that had come to her the past few weeks, she ran back and hugged the air hostess. At least if these sophisticated people did not understand her language, they should understand her action of love and trust. The love and trust she had learned as a child to give to many people at the same time, especially if those people were friendly. This lady had been her friend when they were in that huge tin sausage that brought them all from Kingston to London.

Moved, the air hostess kissed the top of her hat and Gwendolen ran back to her Daddy. She felt even at that early age that nothing, nothing at all given with love was degrading. She sighed happily, looked up to her Daddy and gave him her hand to lead her through the corridors of the airport to the future dreamland they called the 'Moder Kontry'.

4

Gladys Odowis

Winston Brillianton gave his daughter a coat. It was new and smelt so fresh. It was too long and too big but she swam into it. The coat gave her a warm secure feeling. The feeling of privacy – it was like walking about carrying your own house with you. You only showed that part you wished to be seen. She dipped her hands into the large coat pockets and could feel the elastic on top of her knickers without anyone knowing. This was great. She could keep her secrets in the big coat.

Her first taste of England was full of tiny discoveries. Here she was surrounded by a sea of pink faces, making Daddy and her own dark skin stand out. At home in Jamaica, it had been the other way round. She even noticed that people stared at them when they passed. Just as they used to stare at the whites who visited Granville. Anyhow, all that seemed so far away now. Granville, Shivorn, Uncle Johnny, all now seemed like another world. And since she could not imagine Granny going to the Indian letter-writer to write and tell her parents about Uncle Johnny and herself, she felt safe. She took one hand out of her deep pocket and gave it to her Daddy as if she was giving him her life to keep. She had never known what it was like to have a full-time Daddy, but from these first few minutes she knew she was going to like it very much. She was going to like saying my Daddy and Mammy, and not Granny Naomi and Uncle Johnny. She pressed her Daddy's hand and smiled at him. Winston was surprised and uneasy at the antics of this little girl, who was his daughter, and whom he was beginning to realize he had to work hard and wake up fatherly feelings towards. He tried to smile back, but gave a mechanical grin instead. He was uneasy with her, he was uneasy in these strange surroundings at the airport where there were so many well-dressed people who appeared to know exactly where they were going. His friend, Mr Ilochina, had told him to ask for the bus service from the airport to Victoria Station. It was easy when he was coming, because the buses were all there waiting. But here there were so many people. Like Gwendolen, he had to speak very slowly for people to understand. A man in uniform pointed to them where to go.

They went into the coach, Gwendolen still clutching at her father's hand. Though she was tired, yet she wanted to ask many questions. But there were so many new things to see and people around them were not doing much talking either.

The coach was white with blue curtains at the window. It was much bigger than the one they always caught in Ewarton on their way to Kingston. This was as comfortable as the plane. The difference was that the coach was running on roads. The roads were full of so many cars and the roads were so wide. Strange-looking houses sped by. There were no shacks and no trailers. There were no food-sellers or fruit-hawkers. And the sun seemed to have gone to sleep. The journey seemed to go on for ever because they kept stopping at traffic lights. She recalled when she went to Kingston alone, walking downhill from Granville to Ewarton where she took a minibus that took her through St Catherine to Kingston. She thought that the journey then was not as long as this one. In that bus, people had been talking; the driver sang and the journey was lively.

Daddy woke her when she was just about to drop off to sleep. 'We soon be . . . be . . . home nuh. You tired, June-June?'

Gwendolen shook her head. 'No, me no tired, eh, Daddy.' The word 'Daddy' sounded so reassuring to her that it felt like she had just acquired a new toy.

They left the bus depot at Victoria and queued for a taxi, just as Mr Ilochina had advised. When inside, Winston Brillianton gave the driver the address written on a piece of paper.

'Off Stroud Green?' the driver asked.

'Dat's ri . . . ri . . . right.'

Gwendolen was wide awake now in this black car. She looked out of the window and saw more neat houses in rows on both sides of the road. There were trees, but they did not look so green. Some of them had leaves that were yellow-brown. Everything and everywhere looked tidier, but grey. And now she was beginning to feel the cold everybody had talked about.

'We home nuh,' Winston said as they turned into a smaller road.

'Where?' Gwendolen asked with expectancy.

'Dere.'

Gwendolen wanted to rush out as soon as the taxi stopped, but her father's hand steadied her. She looked at the hand, strong, stumpy and black, and she knew it was the hand of authority. Her father led her out slowly. He then thoughtfully counted out the money for the driver. The driver touched his hat and thanked Winston. This impressed Gwendolen a great deal. She did not know whether it was right or wrong, but a white man thanking a black man was a sight she had never seen. Granny had always said that people with pale skin colour put on airs as if they had two heads. Gwendolen had accepted it as natural especially after her encounter with Granny Elinor. But here, a real whitey thanked her Daddy.

'The whitey, him thank you, Daddy,' Gwendolen remarked in astonishment.

'Some o' them nice, June-June.'

Her father even had his own key! He did not have to call anybody to open his door for him. She wished Shivorn were there to see how important her Daddy had become. Was this his house? Gwendolen wondered. This big house. Inside they climbed so many stairs. When her Daddy opened the door on the top floor, it led into a nice warm and colourful room. Her little brother was about six, there was another who looked a bit younger, and baby Cheryl was in a cot looking at her. Mammy Sonia came out of another room and shouted, 'June-June, you big woman nuh!'

'Mammy, Mammy,' Gwendolen cried as she rushed into her mother's open arms. She felt reborn. She felt as if she was entering into her mother's womb again: new June-June, a new her. She looked around her excitedly and saw herself surrounded by warmth, love, curiosity and pride. She suddenly felt as rich as her African ancestors who firmly believed that it was always better to have people rather than money. She had now arrived in the warm womb of her family, that family consisting of her father Winston, huge, black, with halting speech, her Mammy Sonia, with a scarf on her head, in a dress with a full skirt, and a yellow cardigan on top, her brothers Ronald and Marcus and baby sister Cheryl. What else could a girl of twelve want! But what she did not know was that at that moment, her destiny had become entwined with that of 'de Moder Kontry', Britain.

In the morning Gwendolen was exhausted from all the excitement of the previous day, but not too tired to hear her Daddy leave for work, her mother getting baby Cheryl from her cot and preparing breakfast. She wanted to get up and start helping Mammy straightaway as she knew she had to, but felt too tired. Added to that was the fact that she did not know where to start. She moved about the bed she was lying in and, unlike her bamboo bed in Granville, it did not squeak. She studied the room. She shared the same room with Ronald and Marcus. Those two shared bunk beds. Gwendolen had never seen a bed like that before, and for a while she thought that Ronald would fall and break his neck. But he slept soundly. Marcus slept soundly too. They all slept through the parents' talk. Gwendolen knew that baby Cheryl was sleeping in another room with her parents, because she'd heard her crying in the middle of the night and her mother hushing her.

What a contrast to her life in Jamaica where she and her Granny slept in the same room. Her bamboo bed used to squeak and Granny's used to make a kind of whining sound. Each of them almost always knew when the other moved. Here it was different. The room was cosy, and she was lying on a real solid bed and it was dry. And there were these new domestic sounds of her family all around her.

She took her hand out of the blanket and could feel the cold. That cold, the strangeness and the exhaustion made her shrink deeper into her blanket. She drifted off to sleep again. When she woke this time, she knew she had to get up. Marcus and Ronald were having a pillow fight. They were rocking the bed and making so much noise. She stared at them, marvelling at their freedom. She wanted to tell them to stop their noise, but she kept quiet, because though she was much older, she sensed they had a kind of confidence she lacked. On top of that, they were speaking with that kind of voice similar to the air hostess's. And she knew that these two brothers of hers would laugh at her if she opened her mouth. She could see that they were mischievous. Maybe here children were not told off by their parents.

'Maaaarcus . . . Roooonald, come for your breakfast. Wash your faces first. June-June tired, let her sleep.'

'Me awake, Mammy,' Gwendolen cried, jumping out of bed and at the same time trying to find out where her mother's voice was coming from. Sonia was preparing breakfast outside their door in the corridor. A kettle of hot water was screaming on the cooker. On another burner was a milk saucepan. The noise from all this bustling domesticity attracted Gwendolen to the door. Her quick and inquisitive eye soon took in what was going on. 'Good morning, Mammy.'

'All right, June-June?' Sonia replied without turning from the porridge oats she was stirring.

'Yes, Mammy, me all right, but me cold though.'

Sonia laughed. 'You get used to it, no time. Put hot water in dat blue bath and wash yourself.'

Gwendolen stared. How could she wash herself in a room in a large plastic bowl shaped like a boat? Her mind sped back to Jamaica where she used two round bowls to wash plates in the backyard. She was taught to wash the dishes in one and rinse in the other. But to do all this including washing oneself indoors, she found fascinating. 'What of the backyard, Mammy?'

'Hm . . . June-June, backyard too cold here. We do everything indoors here. Wait, me show you.'

Mammy was a busy person. Gwendolen could see that. She watched in contemplative fascination as Mammy poured some hot water into a blue plastic bucket, then diluted it with the cold water she had collected from a corner sink downstairs. She then dragged the boys back into their bedroom, and with a towel she'd dipped into the bucket containing the warm water, she washed them all over. The room, the boys, all started to smell lovely, because of the sweet smell of the soap. Gwendolen, who had never thought anything like this possible before, opened her mouth in wonder. How could Mammy wash two noisy boys, boys who never stayed still for one second, without spilling the water on the linoleum?

Mammy was almost Granny's lookalike, but not so wrinkled. Both women were small, both had scanty hair and bad teeth. In fact Granny Naomi had very few teeth left and even those few were always giving her pain. She had been used to still greater agony until she had most of them removed. In the old days, when Gwendolen was a little girl, Granny used to have a golden tooth just like Uncle Johnny. She could not remember what happened to it. But then Granny had stopped being particular about herself, especially

54

after Sonia left and when Uncle Johnny had stopped coming to their house.

'June-June, see, this is how you wash yourself here. Soon you'll help me wash them every morning,' Mammy said, cutting into her thoughts.

Gwendolen nodded. She would like to help very much. To her all that was nothing. At home in Granville, she had to fetch wood to make the fire, whenever Granny ran out of kerosene. And this happened almost every other day. But here, Mammy cooked on a shiny white cooker. The greatest bonus of all was water. It was downstairs on the first landing, so she would not have to go into the street to fight for water. This was something. The only bad thing was the cold. She was still shivering.

'You very cold?' Sonia asked purely out of concern and sympathy, because not only did her body shiver visibly but also she was hesitating about removing her night-clothes. Gwendolen even clung to the top blanket from her bed.

'Yes, Mammy.' Her voice was small. She liked this new feel. The fact that it was her real Mammy and not Granny who was asking her these questions.

'Yes, Mammy,' mimicked Ronald. 'She's not Mammy, she's Mum. Yes, Mammy!'

Marcus laughed so much that he spluttered the porridge all over his face. He was very black and stocky like Winston and when he laughed like that he looked like his miniature. The resemblance was startling.

'Stop laughing with yuh mouth full,' Gwendolen said without thinking.

Ronald stared at her as if to say, 'So she can speak.'

Gwendolen watched her mother take a clean cloth and tie it round Marcus's neck, just in case he decided to laugh again.

'Dirty Marcus,' Sonia said indulgently.

Gwendolen laughed out loud. Her first real laughter since her arrival. She was feeling confident. She too could tell her younger brothers off just like their Mammy was doing. So just for a good measure, she echoed her mother, 'Dirty Marcus.' Her mother's voice was not that different from the Granville voice, but she noticed that the others did not refer to her as 'Mammy' but called her Mum or Mother. She would have to remember that, otherwise the boys would laugh at her again. That did not stop Marcus, now subdued, from making funny faces at her, and Ronald saying in whispers, 'Yes, Mammy, no, Mammy.'

In no time at all, they were all washed and breakfasted, and Sonia had said they had to take the boys to school.

Gwendolen marvelled at the number of clothes her Mum piled on her. As well as the woollen underclothes, she had on an extra vest, woollen tights that stretched up to her navel, a heavy dress, a cardigan and then the deep blue topcoat Daddy brought her at the airport the day before. Then on top of all that she put on the white woollen hat her Granny had crocheted for her. She now had gloves as well and her feet were thrust into plastic boots with warm lining inside. She wondered how she would be able to walk in all this gear which made her feel not only heavy and cumbersome but also like a walking wardrobe. But she used the corner of her eyes to spy at everybody and she knew that that was the way they dressed in England.

'We take Marcus and Ronald to school and me show you my friend, Mrs Odowis. You hold Marcus's hand and I put Cheryl in the push chair,' Sonia announced for the third time, more to reassure herself than for her children. She was already getting tired that early in the morning, but she had learned from experience to take little rests in between her daily routine. She knew the day would slow down as soon as the boys had been left with their teachers. But before then there was the mad rush not to be late for school. Slowly they descended the stairs and on their way out they met their Nigerian landlord.

'Dat's the landlord man,' said Sonia. 'Good morning, Mr Aula, this me daater, you know.'

'Hallo, little girl,' said Mr Aliyu who had given up the task of teaching Sonia how to pronounce his name properly. Being a Nigerian, with a deep family meaning to his name, he used to be annoyed when his name was badly pronounced, thereby rendering it meaningless. He could appreciate when white people would not bother to make the attempt, but when it came to black people like himself, the pill became very, very bitter indeed. But by now he had learned to regard it as one of the dehumanizing processes of existence you have to go through in a country that is not your own.

'What is your name?' he asked Gwendolen in his heavy Nigerian voice, quite unaware that Gwendolen had not heard English spoken that way. His voice reminded her of the voice of a man chewing coconut and talking at the same time. But before she could answer Mr Aliyu, Sonia said quickly, 'Grandalee'. She too was trying to remember the right way to pronounce her daughter's name.

'Grandalew?' asked Mr Aliyu. 'Is it a Barbados name? It is lovely.' He grinned.

'Me from Jamaica, you know, Mr Aula,' Sonia said smiling a little. She was amused that this Nigerian 'know-all' man did not in fact know all at all.

'Oh!' cried the Nigerian who, to be candid, did not know the difference between the islands in the West Indies. All he knew was that they were all West Indians. His Nigerian education taught him the names of all the important towns in Britain and America, but little about his own country or about his brothers living in the Caribbean.

'Grandalew, is that right?'

'Me no know, man,' Sonia snapped as she strapped Cheryl to her chair and made for the door, her children right behind her.

Mr Aliyu chuckled and said, 'Welcome to London,

Grandalew,' making it sound like the meaningless sign-boards a traveller reads on arriving at another country's airport.

When they were safely on the pavement and about to rush off, Ronald asked, 'Mum, is her name not June-June any more?'

'It's June-June and it's Grandalee,' Sonia replied as patiently as she could. Ronald wanted to ask more questions, but decided against it because he had to wipe his already watery nose with the back of his mittens.

As for Gwendolen, she kept completely quiet. She was baffled though. She had in the last few days started to be confused about her name. It was beginning to look as if different people had different ideas as to how it should be pronounced. She did not know which version to use or which was right. In Granville everybody called her June-June. Even Miss Peters and Granny Elinor called her that. She would have to get used to these new versions of her name, just as she would have to get used to waddling in heavy clothes and not complain too much about the cold wind. Neither her Daddy nor her mother could do anything about the cold weather. After all, did Granny Naomi not warn her about it in Granville? But she did not imagine that it could ever be this cold. She sniffed, holding Marcus tightly, and tried not to cry.

And there was no sun: it was misty and grey. But Gwendolen held on to Ronald since Marcus had suddenly decided that he was going to hold a side of the push chair. They soon turned a corner and then saw other mothers with their children. They had to wait outside the school gate because they were a little early. The school did not look like any school Gwendolen had seen before. School buildings were more open, but this had a big grey wall that separated it from the road. In the middle of the wall was wedged a formidable-looking iron gate painted black. They like others before them had to wait in front of this gate. Opposite were more houses looking like their own. Everything and everybody had a clean, cold, greying air about them. Gwendolen noticed that her mother did not speak to the other mothers and they did not talk to her. They did not even give her a look. They all behaved as if the family was not there. Everybody seemed to be standing in their little vacant islands, not touching, not talking, just waiting for the gate to open. And it looked as if that was the most important thing to do at that moment in the whole wide world. Just standing there for the gate to open. Then slowly at first, as if it was against their wishes, a few children started to run around, but still not making as much noise as Gwendolen knew usually came from schoolchildren. Like the mothers who in disciplined readiness stood for the gate to open, the children's play seemed calculated. Maybe it was too miserable for the children to completely let go. Gwendolen was about to ask her mother if a teacher would tell Ronald and Marcus off if they ran around like other children, when suddenly Ronald let out a whoop of joy and struggled himself free from Gwendolen's grip and ran to another black family turning into the street. The mother looked as if she thought she was late, so was hurrying her two kids along. Ronald met them and cried, 'Hallo, Ozi, this is my sister June-June!' He was breathless with excitement. His voice was loud and he was jumping up and down as he shouted this news.

'And sometimes they call her Grandalew,' put in Marcus in his equally big voice. Many heads turned at this information, and some mothers even managed a smile, all of which made Marcus hide behind his mother.

'Sonia!' cried the woman. 'Your daughter is here at last. I thought she might be arriving yesterday. Good for you.' She came closer to Gwendolen and embraced her. 'Welcome, daughter. Your name is June-June, is it not? You see, I know your name because your mother never stopped talking about

59

you. Gosh, you must be so relieved to know that she is here safe. Gosh, all those paper fillings and bureaucracy.' She stood Gwendolen at arms' length and declared in a lower voice, 'She looks exactly like you, Sonia. Your carbon copy. Congratulations.'

Sonia laughed. The laughter started a bit loud and ended up in giggles, during which her hand went to her mouth covering it. She smiled into her hand, a habit which Gwendolen could not remember her mother having.

Now everybody's head turned slightly, though many pretended to be staring at something else right on top of the browning trees which stood outside the school gate. Sonia was not unaware of this minor hypocrisy. So she agreed with her friend in a low voice, 'Ah proud of 'er. She's a grown 'oman nuh. Winston still no fit believe he eyes. She grow so quick.'

Mrs Odowis nodded. Hum . . . hum. She'd just become aware that her voice was unnecessarily raised before. Though she'd lived in England for over four years, yet she still could not cope with this type of solid wall of indifference in which people look past you, or on top of your head, or stare at your shoes, actually look beyond you so as not to look at your face, all of which was to tell you that as far as they were concerned you were not there. And like a child begging to be noticed, she'd invariably caught herself talking in a rather exuberant way, a way which she hated and which was against the very grain of her nature. She hated herself for it afterwards, and had to hold herself very tight to prevent her exploding and attacking those who with their uncaring attitude were reducing her to the level of a child begging for attention. She knew that her friend Sonia must have been standing there, and the other mothers must have noticed Gwendolen, but they would rather die than ask politely, 'Is this your daughter?' They could see that Gwendolen was her mother's picture, down to the bow legs. It would not be

60

proper for other mothers to ask a human question like that; it would be interfering, it might make Sonia Brillianton think that they actually cared for her. They could not even afford the pretence. Even some time ago when Sonia used to go out of her way to say a breezy 'Go . . . marning all', they used to ask her what she meant. Sonia had become wise now. She did not talk to them and they did not talk to her.

Anyhow, Gladys cared. She had to. Sonia did not give her any choice. Sonia had talked about this daughter of hers for so long, that Gladys Odowis knew what to expect. Even the night on which she was so desperate and did not know where to turn, the night on which her husband Tunde had knocked her about almost unconscious and had called in the police claiming that she was mad, and she stared not believing what she was hearing when it looked as if the police were going to believe Tunde and not her cries, she had run out of the house. She took her two frightened children with her. The only friend who believed her was Sonia Brillianton. Tunde had beaten her so much that she was incoherent even to herself. Her face was swollen in places and her hair stood out in spikes like the back of a hedgehog. Gladys Odowis knew that Sonia could not understand her BBC Nigerian English at the best of times, to say nothing of when she was tired and incoherent, yet Sonia could feel what she was feeling. Sonia hid her and her children from her husband for three days. Her husband Tunde did not dream of looking for his well-educated wife and their two children at the house of their 'Illiterate West Indian daily minder and her equally bungling husband'. But Sonia calmed her and her children for three days, before she could go to her doctor to report that she was not mad, that her husband Tunde only wanted her to be locked up, to teach her sense. Sonia was with her all the way, pushing the children up and down Crouch Hill, and all the time she was saying, 'If June-June here, she for help with the pikneys . . .When June-June come Ah go a work . . .

When June-June come, life easy for me, you know, Mrs Odowis.'

Gladys smiled at her Jamaican friend. She had never had a sister in her native land in Nigeria, but Sonia Brillianton was the nearest sister she had. Gladys was grateful and valued this friendship that did not ask her to be anything else but herself.

'She's Mrs Odowis,' said Ronald, dancing around the two mums enjoying this feeling of importance.

When the school gate opened and they took the children into their classrooms, Gwendolen was struck by all the colourful teaching aids. There were pictures on the walls; there were paper kites and paper aeroplanes hanging from the ceiling; there were piles of books in low shelves and there were low chairs with wide tops. It was fascinating. Gwendolen had never imagined any place like this before. It looked as if all these colourful things were piled here just for children to play. She did not know what to expect in a classroom, but definitely not this that looked like a carnival room. Granny Naomi had told her that she would eventually go to school in England; she was not looking forward to it, not after seeing the village school in Granville and after Miss Peters. But this classroom looked warm and inviting, a welcome contrast to the greyness outside. She would not mind coming here to study for a few days.

She was still staring about her and touching things when her mother and Mrs Odowis who had been hanging up the children's coats called her. They had to go and leave the younger kids at school.

'You like the classroom?' Gladys asked kindly.

Gwendolen smiled and nodded shyly.

'This is a junior school. You'll go to a bigger one for girls of your age.'

Again Gwendolen nodded. In the last couple of days, she had had to listen to English spoken in so many different ways.

Mrs Odowis used words differently. The good thing was that her voice was slower but it was none the less different.

The two women were walking very fast, and Gwendolen was bringing up the rear. She could hear everything they were saying, but she concentrated on the pavements, the cars rolling down the hill and the grey sky.

'You're really lucky now, Sonia. Girls raised at home are very useful, you know.'

'Yeah, man. Me know. Dat's why she come. Ah fit go morning job and she look after the kids for me, you know. She fit look after dem, you know,' Sonia added with an energetic nod.

Mrs Odowis looked at her friend rather curiously. Did Sonia send for her daughter just because she would help her in the house? Knowing Sonia, Gladys suspected that she wanted to raise her daughter herself as well. 'She will have to go to school, won't she? It's illegal here to keep girls at home, you know.' Her voice was not quite able to mask her curiosity. She knew also that she had to be careful not to sound patronizing. She too wished she'd had a daughter who could stay with her younger ones in the evenings so that she could pursue her course in Community Studies. But the girl must go to school. Not that her own long years at school had done much for her, but at least she could communicate, and she could enjoy a good book. She would not like her friend to deny her daughter that.

Sonia sighed, showing her boredom on the subject. 'Me no know. Maybe after Christmas. She no like school, anyhow.'

'Mammy, me no like school.' Gwendolen felt that loyalty was called for here. She'd also forgotten to say 'Mum' as Ronald and Marcus taught her in the morning.

'School is nice here. No cane, lots of fun. I am sure you'll come and tell us all the things you've learned. You'll see.'

They crossed the busy road and proceeded into a narrow one in which nearly all the houses had growing shrubs in front. They were not flowering, but had autumn leaves with some already browning, readying themselves for the winter that was to follow. Sonia and her friend pushed their buggies with their babies in them and talked as if the cold that pickled the top of Gwendolen's ears and the tip of her nose did not matter. Maybe it did not matter to them, she thought. However, she pulled down the knitted hat her Granny gave her with so much careless determination that she almost covered her eyes. But she still felt the chill.

They cornered into another street with shops. The front of the shops had no shrubs but plenty of foodstuff displayed on tables placed on the pavements. Gwendolen saw men who looked like Indians she used to see at home in Jamaica, putting out plantains and yams, okra and sweet potatoes, some vegetables she was quite familiar with.

'Your mother will miss her,' Mrs Odowis persisted. Somehow it looked to Sonia as if Gladys was keen to puncture her new smugness. She did not understand why Gladys should continue to question her this way. One would have thought that she'd hidden the fact of Gwendolen's arrival from her. But she knew all about it. Or did Gladys think that she and Winston were so stupid they would not be able to carry through their plan of bringing Gwendolen into England? She had no way of knowing. And she knew how wrong suspicion was. Anyhow, they were friends. And friends who did not forgive each other, would not remain friends for long. They needed each other.

None the less, she sighed and replied, 'Yeah, me know. But what to do. We come here, come work, no work at home. To work for a few days in the harbour way back home, Winston had to live in Kingston and me on the hill in Granville. Life 'ard, me tell you. Ah feel for me Mammy some time, but what to do.'

'I know,' Gladys Odowis said, smiling apologetically. 'If things had been different, I would have gone back home too. But, well, here am I in this terribly cold place, pushing my babies like a crazy woman pushing junk furniture. Hm. There is work in Nigeria you know, but too many family pressures; I mean my husband's people, they're bound to make trouble. They would gladly interfere in my upbringing of the children . . .'

'You mean they fit take the kids from you, that 'tupid. Their son, not a good man at all, 'tupid man. Ah no like that man, you know.'

Both women laughed, clutching at their buggies for support.

'Men like that should be sent to prison, Ah tell you.'

'Well, his people won't see all that beating and harassment. They'll say he's your husband, stay with him. And in our culture, it's bad to talk about the beatings you receive from your husband outside the family. Many people think a wife who is beaten deserves to be beaten. And you know that I talked to social workers and the police. All that had stamped me as a bad woman.'

'It's like that back 'ome, you know. But me, if Winston mess up with me, Ah do exactly what you did. Pack and go. See your kids nuh, dem look happy and cheeky, just like other kids. Before, them too quiet. But if Winston come nasty to me Ah show him . . .'

'Shush . . . Sonia, your daughter is here. She's too young to understand. We don't want to scare the next generation, do we?'

Sonia looked furtively at Gwendolen who was trying very hard to follow their drift and to keep her ears warm. Her nose was running shamelessly now. She sniffed and placed the palms of her hands over her ears. As far as she was concerned, the women could rattle on as long as they liked, she'd stopped trying to make out what they were talking about, Mrs Odowis in a kind of voice she'd never heard before, her mother in a new kind of Granville tone. There was too much to take in in such a short time. She wanted to see and hear everything, yet she wanted her new nice warm bed, with fluffy blankets.

'What next generation, Ah no understand. You mean June-June?'

In reply Mrs Odowis laughed. 'Oh Sonia.'

They walked towards one of the tables groaning with ethnic foodstuffs of so many bright colours.

'Must buy some plantains. Did your daughter bring any from home?'

'No . . . she too small to carry food. Me get small honey though. You like honey?'

'You know honey and milk are things I never really like. I coughed a lot as a child. And they always asked me to take Nigerian honey, you know, the real thing. So I always regard honey as medicine. I force myself to drink milk when I'm pregnant. No, thank you.'

'Well, neber mind. Sometimes our food cheaper here, you know.'

Gladys laughed. 'That is true. Foods imported from Nigeria are sometimes cheaper and better here. Our people send their best outside the country to make money.'

'Ah know, the nigger race 'tupid.'

'It is not the ordinary people. It is the politicians who are to be blamed. They are so greedy, they make us all economic refugees.'

Sonia stared. And Gwendolen who at that instant had removed her hands from her ears gaped.

'God died for the truth, Mrs Odowis. You sometimes so clever with them big big words you know. But me go nuh. Come on, June-June.'

Gwendolen panted beside Sonia who was walking very fast to get home and warm herself and the girls.

'She your friend, Mammy?'

'Huh-huh, we good friends. She Nigerian, you know. But she a nice 'oman. We good friends.'

5

School

Gwendolen would never forget her first day at school in England. Hers was a different school from Ronald and Marcus's, because she was twelve. She was to go to a secondary school and the boys were still in a junior. 'Secondary and Junior' were words Ronald and Marcus seemed to know very much about. They seemed to talk of nothing else. It was, however, decided that her father and not Sonia should go with her.

She felt conspicuous in her new wine-coloured gaberdine skirt, cream blouse, wine-coloured tie, vee-neck jumper and brown shoes. These new things really thrilled her. Her parents had been awfully nice to her, buying her all these things. Still, she worked hard at home though, cooking and helping her Mum look after the little ones, whom she minded during the day. All these things were giving her a sense of being really needed, a new kind of importance.

Despite all that work, life was slightly easier than the one she had in Granville. She could never put a price on having her Daddy and Mum, and her brothers and Cheryl around her. She'd now become used to the sounds of the breakfast rush, the quick baths, and the fights between Marcus and Ronald. They were new sounds of security. Once in a while her thoughts went to her Granny Naomi and her childhood playmates, Shivorn and Cocoa. Would she ever see them again? She wished Shivorn could see her in her new school uniform or the new grey dress Mum made for her at Christmas. When Mrs Odowis advised her Mum to buy the material, Mum was at first not interested. She said it was too dull for

June-June. And Mrs Odowis said that bright colours look cheap in England. She said her Mum could wear what she liked, but June-June was going to grow here in England, so she should start wearing dull colours like white girls of her age. But when her Mammy made it into a pretty dress with white collar and white braid trimmings, it was beautiful. She now wished Shivorn and Cocoa would come and see her family all dressed up on their way to church on Christmas morning.

Her Daddy was in a navy blue suit; the jacket had shrunk a little, because Daddy kept getting bigger as her Mum had said, but his white shirt sparkled, and Mum put a flower they called a carnation in his button-hole. Ronald and Marcus had new suits too, suits which Mum had bought from a big shop in Holloway Road. And her Mum made her own dress and Cheryl's too. Oh, they looked so smart and she felt so proud. And now she was beginning to see how hard they had to work for all the good things they now had. They had so much that Uncle Johnny with his smart jaunty clothes would have been green.

The only confusing thing about church-going here was that she had no idea what it was about. She knew her parents were none the wiser. They stood up when others stood up and sat down when they did. They always sat at the back because when it became too boring, Cheryl would start her screaming, and all eyes would turn and look at them. Those stares made her feel she and her family were doing something wrong, but she did not know what. She was not surprised her family did not go to church every Sunday, definitely not as frequently as she and Granny Naomi used to in Granville. After the church service the Preacher stood at the door, and shook their hands and smiled only with his mouth, whilst the rest of his face remained rigid. The only good thing in going to church here was in the dressing-up. The rest was just too cold. But on Christmas morning, Ronald and Marcus showed off because they knew some of the songs. She knew Christmas songs too and she liked to sing, but with all these white people around peeping at them from behind their hymn books, singing to the Lord would be inappropriate.

For the moment, school meant putting on these nice new clothes. She did not wish to think of what would happen when she got to school. They said it was illegal for a child not to go to school here. Her parents would be in trouble if they arranged for her to go for lessons with Mrs Odowis. Mrs Odowis said June-June needed friends of her own age any-how. Gwendolen did not mind either way, but from the way people looked at her family in the church, the way nobody talked to anybody at the laundry, she feared the white chil-dren. She missed friends like Shivorn, and she was beginning to miss the backyard where they gossiped and laughed at the adults. Maybe she would get friends like Shivorn and Cocoa at school. But would these white girls make fun of the way she spoke? Would they like her? Anyhow the school uniform was nice, she could always keep it even if she did not like the school. Could they force her to go to school if she refused? she wondered.

Her father asked people where the school was. To get to her classroom, they had to go through a shabby building with rubbish spilling from the dustbin. Her Daddy had had everything written out for him on paper. And when he showed this paper to a man who was rushing across the school compound and was very impatient, he directed them to a classroom and dashed off on his own business.

They eventually entered into this classroom full of girls of her age. The teacher was calling out names from the register when they came in. On seeing them, she stopped and asked, smiling that kind of smile the church Preacher had, that kind of smile that stretched the corners of the mouth but the eyes remained cold like those of a fish and Gwendolen's heart started to beat very fast, 'What can I do for you?'

'Did . . . diddd . . . June-June,' Winston Brillianton stammered.

The teacher's eyes swept from her table and rested on Winston, a six-foot-three black man, with a body that mainly consisted of bone and muscle, yet somehow ungainly. With close-cropped hair, a tight Sunday suit, white shirt and a black bow tie. Her eyes shifted and rested on Gwendolen for a while. Gwendolen felt like melting and completely disappearing from the scene, because she knew her Daddy could not speak the teacher's type of English properly. Coupled with this was the fact that Daddy was a natural stammerer. The stammer got worse when he was nervous. This was what happened when the teacher asked her name. Then the teacher directed the question to her. She was not sure whether to say 'June-June', her pet name, or, as her mother said, 'Grandalee', her official name, but she knew that neither sounded anything like that version used by the air hostess on the plane that brought her from Jamaica over eight weeks ago.

'You are the new girl?' the teacher asked, her voice losing its former oily smoothness and Gwendolen knew that she was becoming impatient.

'Da . . . da . . . t's so,' Winston said and Gwendolen nodded rather exaggeratedly.

'Now let me see, you must be Gwendolen Brillianton.' Gwendolen nodded again, this time with her warm sweet smile. A smile that embraced them all. The relief that Gwendolen felt was so unashamedly perceptible that the teacher felt as if she was being invited into the privacy of this little girl's world. A world in which Gwendolen was beginning to doubt the sense of parents giving their little girls names they could not pronounce. One thing she was determined to do on her first day was to learn how to pronounce her name right. This teacher, being white, she felt would definitely get it right. The air hostess did get it right, but that was months

70

ago and she could not remember exactly how the letters were formed. But here in this class, she knew she was going to have opportunities to pronounce her name correctly. Like most people who are used to handling and moulding the young, the teacher seemed to be reading the workings in Gwendolen's mind and then she smiled. This time her eyes smiled too, because somehow she felt privileged.

'Your name is Gwendolen, Gwendolen Brillianton,' the teacher said slowly.

The briskness soon returned to her voice when she called, 'Amanda, please show Gwendolen where to hang her coat and bring her back to her seat. Don't take all morning about it, Amanda.'

A very pretty black girl got up shyly, came forward and said, 'Come on, Gwendolen.'

Gwendolen followed Amanda to the cloakroom, mouthing her name slowly, 'Gwendolen. Gwen – do – len.' Amanda showed her where to hang her coat. She smiled at her but did not utter a single word, much to Gwendolen's relief. She would not know how to reply properly. She knew she no longer spoke the full village English, because Ronald and Marcus had stopped mimicking her. None the less she had to concentrate on her name and how to pronounce it correctly.

Back in the classroom, the teacher asked if anyone would volunteer to look after Gwendolen for a week so as to show her the routine, because she was new and had never been to school in this country.

To Gwendolen's surprise, many hands shot up, including that of Amanda. At this gesture, the teacher gave Gwendolen and her Daddy a smile of reassurance. This confused Gwendolen for a while. Granny Naomi had said that most people with pale skin colour thought they had two heads instead of one. So Gwendolen had come to be wary of them. Her experience of Granny Elinor and her family buttressed this belief. Since she came to England, she had noticed that many white people did not actually insult her parents, but they treated them as if they were not there. And whenever her mother tried to communicate with any of them, they made her repeat herself several times. Consequently, she clamped her lips whenever they were outside their flat. Her mother, however, did not mind the whites' indifference. She was used to it. Gwendolen was still learning. But in this classroom, it looked as if things were going to be different. The girls really took notice of her, they listened to what the teacher was saying about her. Mrs Odowis had said that she would soon make friends of her own age. She could not imagine herself having a white girl as a friend. But it was beginning to look as if this would be possible.

'I am glad to see so many volunteers. Amanda, since you've started taking Gwendolen around, you might as well continue for the rest of the day. Then tomorrow it will be Roberta's turn and the rest of you can have Gwendolen one day at a time. That way Amanda would not monopolize her!'

The girls cheered and Amanda smiled. Then showing off she called, 'Come and sit here, come on, Gwen.'

Gwen, Gwen? Was that her name too? Gwen?

Luckily Amanda shouted this invitation with loud gesticulation, so that Gwendolen knew that her name was 'Gwen' too.

As soon as all this was settled, the teacher smiled at Mr Brillianton, who still stood there, hat in hand, his bow tie showing on top of his dark topcoat. Gwendolen knew that her Daddy looked smart, for she had polished those shiny shoes herself last evening.

'She'll be all right. Your house is not far from here.' Then she looked in Gwendolen's direction and said, 'You know your way back from school, don't you?'

Gwendolen stared. She could not understand her teacher,

not when she talked so fast. The situation was more complicated now because the teacher had put her glasses back on and though she looked in Gwendolen's direction, the girl was not quite sure who was being addressed. The teacher repeated herself and added, 'Gwen, I'm talking to you.'

Yes, Gwen, Gwen, she's Gwen too, Gwendolen thought quickly. But Amanda gave her a not so gentle nudge. Gwendolen shot up. 'Yes, Miss.' Good thing Ronald had taught her to say, 'Yes, Miss, no, Miss,' and not 'Yes, Marm' or 'Mammy'.

'Can you get home by yourself?' the Miss asked with that exaggerated slowness of tone one used for the very stupid and simple. Her patience was spent.

Having settled all this, Winston bowed to the teacher, behaving gentlemanly the only way he knew how. He belonged to that race who believed that all teachers were committed and should be treated with the respect they deserved. It would never occur to Winston and Sonia to question a teacher, and a secondary school teacher for that matter. He felt sure he had left his daughter in capable hands. He felt sure they had done the right thing, bringing Gwendolen to Britain. He gave his daughter a last smile of reassurance and encouragement, and then left the classroom.

Gwendolen followed Amanda from classroom to classroom like her shadow. There was a lot to take in and learn that first day. But how she enjoyed the physical education and games. She had been cooped up in their two-bedroom flat on the top of a terrace house for so long that the large open hall and all the gym equipment were welcome. She did not realize how much she needed this freedom, freedom she had in Granville when running up to the bee hill in the morning, or when calling over the fence in the backyard to Cocoa and Shivorn to see a hen that had just laid an egg. Or to gossip and laugh over Granny Naomi's latest grumble. Here, people did not talk to her much, not even Amanda. Somehow

Amanda was shy when there were only two of them, but maybe people did talk to her, and since she could not understand most of what they were saying, she abandoned herself to enjoying the physical freedom of the exercises provided.

At mealtime, there was a minor problem. Amanda wanted to know whether she was free dinner, packed lunch, or money dinner. Gwendolen had no money and no packed lunch. Amanda, who was hungry and hated cold dinner, was now exasperated. Gwendolen had no idea what she was asking her about. A senior girl who wanted to know why the two girls were holding up the queue, came to the rescue. The big girl told the dinner ladies to give lunch to Gwendolen and promised to see that the paper work would be solved the next day.

'Suppose she is not a free dinner?' one cheeky first year asked of her senior. The big girl looked at the tiny girl and replied without malice, 'Most of them are.'

Happily the innuendoes were all wasted on Gwendolen. The situation was a wicked irony because Winston Brillianton normally came home with good wages and Sonia made a lot from her daily minding and the parents would have been delighted to pay for their daughter's meals, but one look at Gwendolen, her inability to understand London English and Winston's stammer, and they were automatically regarded as ignorant poor. Mr and Mrs Brillianton, who were never given to complaining, accepted whatever the teacher said. Gwendolen became free dinner because she looked like someone who would be on free dinner. What nobody realized was the price her dignity as a person was paying. Those who made society's laws are still a long way from knowing that Gwendolen's inability to speak or understand one brand of the English language did not automatically condemn her to be an imbecile. But to keep a school like hers running smoothly and with less friction for all concerned, it was easier for her to be regarded as one. All the same, Gwendolen enjoyed her shepherd's pie, followed by rice pudding with jam.

The last period of the day was reserved for singing. This was because the school's Open Day was not too far away. For Gwendolen, this was a bonus. For on her first day at school, she had physical education, dinner, and singing. The class had other subjects like combined maths and literature, but all those went through Gwendolen. It was difficult enough to follow the teachers' voices, to say nothing of what they were talking about. Her class teacher Miss Rawbottom called her when she was following Amanda into the music room where the girls practised all the anthems they were going to sing on Open Day.

'Gwendolen, Gwendolen Brillianton!'

Amanda turned and said to Gwendolen, 'The Miss is calling you. Why don't you ever answer to your name? Anyone would think you didn't know what your name was.'

The teacher gestured her to come. Gwendolen followed her teacher back into their own classroom.

'These are your work-books. The textbooks are in short supply at the moment, but take these home. I know you'll keep them clean,' she added encouragingly.

'But why don't you talk to us, though?' Miss Rawbottom asked after a while. She had expected Gwendolen to say, 'Thank you, Miss.' Gwendolen wanted to thank her, but somehow her words of thanks got stuck in her throat. Anyhow, she smiled, getting used to the teacher's voice gradually.

'You understand English though?'

'Yes, Miss, Ah do.' Her voice was Caribbean, the teacher noticed. So that probably was it. And she was undoubtedly sensitive about it. Well, most girls tended to be self-conscious on their first days in a new school. All that would change with time.

'I've put your name on one or two of your work-books. When you get home, write your name on the others, OK?'

She turned away from Gwendolen and looked at the window. 'Gosh, what a day! Have you ever seen snow in Jamaica, Gwendolen?'

Gwendolen was too dumbfounded to answer. She followed her teacher's gaze and saw what looked like white feathers falling daintily in the school compound. She'd seen snow on the Christmas cards her mother had bought and used in decorating their flat. She'd also heard Mrs Odowis say, 'This winter is mild. With luck we may not have snow.'

'Dat snow?' Gwendolen gasped eventually after watching mesmerized for a few minutes.

'Yes, Gwen. This is your first snow?'

'Yes, Miss.'

'When it settles, it is beautiful. You must have seen snow on cards before.'

'Yes, Miss, and on television!'

'Good, now here it is. This one may not settle. Run along now to the hall at the end of the passage and join the others. You like singing? Girls like you usually have good strong voices.'

Gwendolen thought, what a nice compliment and smiled.

The Miss watched her put the new books carefully into the new plastic case her Daddy had bought her for Christmas, 'for take to school', he had said. Though made of plastic and coated in black, it looked very expensive, and Gwendolen was proud of it. She'd seen many girls in her year carrying identical cases, during the day.

Gwendolen was too scared to enter the hall. All the girls of her year were there, not just her class. Some giggled as they saw her standing by the door, uncertain. The music teacher glared at the girls and waved Gwendolen inside as if she was a piece of music. Gwendolen kept her eyes on the music sheet even though she did not know the tune. She could only recognize a few words on the sheet anyhow. She found the melodious tunes unintelligible, just like some of

76

the songs in their cold church. But when it came to one or two rhythmical ones with catchy words, she found herself singing with the others.

Miss Rawbottom was wrong. The snow was falling thickly. The school compound that was grey in the morning, was now covered in white. Her heart started to beat very fast. Amanda had disappeared, because Gwendolen had indicated in the morning that she could find her way home. But then nobody had told her the landscape would change so suddenly. She knew she would have to find her way, because many of the girls seemed to be infused with excitement on seeing the snow. She watched, alarmed and fascinated, as some slid and danced on the snow. Others rushed into the compound, made snowballs and threw them at their friends. There were shrieks of laughter as some girls fell, got up and chased their friends. They seemed to enjoy falling. It was a kind of game.

The thought of joining them did not enter Gwendolen's head. What she was thinking was: How Ah fit get home today! She tentatively put one foot into the now dirtied snow and started to walk carefully. It was slippery. She spread her arms wide like a bird spreading her wings to balance herself, because there was nothing to hold on to. She did not fall, but then she had not learned how to avoid the areas where the snow was thicker. In no time, her socks were wet and the water soaked into her shoes. 'Tomorrow, Ah wear me boots,' she told herself mentally.

People and cars were moving as if nothing was happening. She scooped some snow into her hands out of curiosity and because she was breathless. She squashed it and it melted into water like sugar ice she'd licked at home in Jamaica. She looked this way and that and, when she knew no one was watching, she tasted it. It was just water. It had no taste. God died for the truth as her Mammy would say. This was experience. She now wished Shivorn was there to see all this.

She remembered the promise she made that she would write. But she still needed to know how to write letters. This was only her first day at school. When she knew how to write, she would tell them all about this cold, snowy experience. Her mind conjured up the image of Uncle Johnny reading her letter to Granny Naomi by the hurricane lamp whilst Shivorn and Cocoa envied. Her mind was in Jamaica and she momentarily forgot that her body was in the snowy slope of Tregaron Avenue, and she slipped and fell. She fell hard on the snow. Nobody asked if she was all right. People just looked away. They did not even laugh or mock. They just turned their faces the other way.

She picked herself up. Her coat was now wet, and the cold that was biting her fingers seemed determined to meet the one that was creeping into her body from her near-frozen feet. She suppressed a sob. For the first time since she'd arrived in England, she longed for Jamaica.

She walked more carefully after that, putting her thoughts into every step as she squelched through the muddy snow. But as she turned into her street, her heart was elated, because the snow here was still very white and untrodden and she thought it would be easier. One big stride sent her rolling into the muddy bits at the bottom of her street. Their house was on a slide, and she kept sliding back each time she tried to go forward. In desperation she called out, 'Mammy, Mammy!' in her emotional Jamaican voice. She could not help being natural.

Her mother was too far away to hear her call. But a man who was returning from work, and whom she'd seen a couple of times in their street, saw her.

He crossed the street in a few huge strides and said, 'All right, just hold my hand.'

The man led her to her door.

'Thank you,' Gwendolen said breathing hard. 'This my first snow,' she volunteered, trying to copy her teacher's voice.

The man smiled. 'Your first day at school as well?'

'Yeah,' replied Gwendolen wondering how he knew.

'Oh, oh, was it nice? Are you going to like school?'

'Yeah, but Ah don' like dis snow.'

'Never mind, you'll soon get used to it. It's beautiful when it's settle though.'

'Everybody kept saying that to me. "It's beautiful when it's settle." ' Well it had settled in her street and all that its beauty did to her was to send her reeling backwards down the slope. She would have to look at it again on a Christmas card, maybe then its beauty would become more real to her. But she would never forget that snow could be beautiful to look at, yet it could make you break your neck in a fall.

Inside her doorway, she turned and looked at the houses opposite. Yes they were very beautiful. Even the bare trees were all clothed in white and glistering. But the cold was eating into her body. She rang the bell firmly.

Ronald opened the door. One look at her tear-stained face and he howled in laughter. 'Oh, you cry in the snow! Cry-baby, June-June cry in the snow . . .'

'No, Ah did not! And my name not June-June. My name is Gwendolen, or Gwen. Don't call me no June-June no more.' Gwendolen wagged her forefinger in Ronald's face. She used her other free hand to wipe her face furiously. She was not going to let her family know that she had cried when she fell, and definitely not Ronald and Marcus.

'You hear, my name Gwendolen or Gwen nuh! An' the snow is beauthiful when it done settle.'

Ronald watched his sister open-mouthed. You would have thought she was making all this emphasis about herself and not the snow. You would have thought she was saying, 'I'll be beautiful when I'm settled.'

'You're not going to close dat door and come in? Or you just standing dere, staring at me?'

'I did not know your name is Gwen. I have a girl called Gwen in my class, but nobody called her June-June. Why didn't Mummy and Daddy tell us your name?'

'Because them no fit say it right.'

Ronald was now more than confused.

6

Education

Gwendolen was adjusting so well that one could hardly believe that only six months previously she was living with Granny Naomi in Granville. She'd grown more confident, taller and slightly rounder. Though she still suffered from bouts of cold, yet she looked healthier. The weather was getting milder and she noticed the unfolding of the early spring tulips in front gardens and window-boxes.

She enjoyed leaving home for school, at least to escape the housework. The glamour of being indispensable to her mother was slightly wearing thin. The work she had to do in England was very different from that she was expected to cope with in Jamaica. But in Jamaica, though there was a law that said she should be at school, nobody forced Granny Naomi into keeping it. Here, her parents had to respect that law and she was expected to keep up with schoolwork as well. As things were, there was no way she could catch up with the rest of the class. She could not read for a start, so she had to spend most of her time in the remedial class. The school authorities thought that would help her, instead she felt degraded. Her colour, which was in the minority, was not helping her very much.

There were four other black girls in her class, one of them of Indian origin. Apart from the Indian girl, the rest of them were on free dinners. One of them, Ravi, went to the remedial class with Gwendolen. About half the class were white, the others were of Mediterranean origin. Almost all the girls from the latter group belonged to families with businesses in the rag trade with shops around the local area. Some of the girls' fathers owned a bank or two, or so Amanda told her!

Amanda was black and clever, but she stuck up for her friends many a time. She understood all that the teacher was saying and asked so many questions that she made Gwendolen envious at times. How did she manage to get so much from all that the teacher was saying? Gwendolen listened carefully, but she was always lost. However, she helped Amanda with her needlework, which she was good at. Gwendolen was not perfect at sewing but making blouses, dresses and little trousers were things her mother Sonia did whenever she had the time. So, she was quite used to the sewing machine. Unfortunately the subjects she was good at – needlework, cookery, sports and singing – were not regarded as academic. As for the likes of mathematics, science, history, she simply slept through them. She would have liked to learn how to read, so that she could read her stars and stories as Amanda did. If only she had the time to study a little, she knew Ronald would have taught her the basic rudiments of reading. She knew she could learn more from him than from the remedial teacher who treated her as if she had nothing in her brain. As for homework, her mother did not understand why girls should do any, especially when there was so much work that needed doing at home.

'Hi, dreamer,' shouted Philipa when she caught up with Gwendolen on her way to school that early spring morning.

'Hallo, Philipa,' replied Gwendolen in her new slow English.

'Yeah, today is Friday. I like Fridays. No school tomorrow and the day after so I can sleep late, watch all the programmes I like on the television and do my homework on Sunday night. Ha, ha, ha.'

'Don't you help your Mum at home?' Gwendolen asked.

'Help my mother? Well, I do sometimes, but she prefers to

do most of the housework herself, because she said I'm too slow. I don't like housework. My Mum knows that.'

'But you are a girl,' Gwendolen protested with heat.

'So?'

'What do you do then?'

'What a silly question. Well, since you asked, I'll tell you. I lay the table sometimes and occasionally I help in washing up. Satisfied?'

Gwendolen's mind went through all the little chores she had to do in the morning before coming to school. 'I mean, what do you do before coming to school?'

'What can one do in the morning for Jupiter's sake? I have to eat my egg and cornflakes and get ready for school. What else can one do in the morning? What do you do in the morning then, clever Dick?'

'Well, I make the beds, wash my brothers, cook our porridge, sweep out the front room for the babies . . .'

'Eh, just wait a minute. What does your Mum do then? It's not your fault she has so many babies.'

'They not her babies, you know. She minds other people's.'

'Oh, I see, your mum is a child-minder. Then she should not take the job if she couldn't do it. After all, you're on free dinner, so she pays nothing for you. It must be really awful to do all that work and be on free dinner. I'd die . . . Hallo, Allison . . . Allison, wait a minute.'

Philipa ran to another girl from their class. Gwendolen walked slowly into the classroom wondering why some mothers allowed their daughters to do little or no housework. They could not be right because even in Jamaica girls did a lot of work at home. Some of these white girls were spoilt silly, she thought viciously. She must tell her Mum about it.

She did not ask Sonia that very day but on the following Saturday. Even though they did not take in babies on Saturdays, yet they were equally busy. Gwendolen had to take the washing to the launderette, whilst her mother did the weekend shopping.

'Mum, me happy here, so much work fe do though.'

'Yeah, me know,' Sonia said laughing. 'You have to thank me nuh, you speak with so much education.' She laughed again.

'Them say me have to do more studies at home, otherwise me stay for ever in the remedial class. And me feel shame, Mum.'

'What you talking 'bout? What's bad with remedal class? That na special class, to help you learn quick quick. Hear me nuh, just hear me. You stay all day at dat school doing nutting, and when you come home, you have to help. You understand me? Dat's why me send fe you to come, not just for education!'

Gwendolen wanted to ask her mother why it was necessary for her to do all the extra jobs she was undertaking but kept quiet for a while. She thought of asking about it in a roundabout way.

'Mum, don't Daddy bring enough money for all of we?'

'Course 'im does, gal, but we come fe make money here, you know. What point coming all the way from home to sit around on your backside, eh, gal?'

Her mother, like Granny Naomi, had a subtle way of making her sound silly. Now she felt awfully stupid. Making money was good, but her mother was always dashing about. The only time she was still was when she was lying down in bed ready to go to sleep. Gwendolen thought that before long her baby sister Cheryl would have a younger brother or sister. She had believed everybody lived like that until Ravi, Amanda and Philipa started talking to her.

Maybe all those people Amanda talked about were rich, but what of Mrs Odowis? She too had three children and was expecting her fourth. But they lived in a big flat. The boy Ozi had his own room and the little girl had hers and there was another room which they kept for visitors. She was not even living with her husband, yet somehow she seemed happier and more relaxed than her mother. Why was it her parents could not have accommodation like that?

'Some black people buy dem own houses up the road, don't they, Daddy?' Gwendolen asked her father one Saturday afternoon, when she knew her mother was not there to shush her.

'Yeah . . . me . . . me friend Mr Ilochina, him don buy 'im own house. Dem . . . dem have money, you know.'

'Be nice to have a house of we own,' Gwendolen said wistfully.

Her father laughed. He stammered and that made him lower his voice when he talked. But when he laughed, it was different. He usually threw his head back and opened his mouth to the ceiling and gave out a humorous bay and then slapped one of his legs. Sonia, when around, often joined him in this loud humour.

'Look, look . . . look . . . the lill gal me paid fe bring from Jamaica the other day. You wan' make Ah buy a 'ouse, huh? Nice . . . nice. But 'ouses cost . . . cost money. Plenty money.' He rubbed his two thumbs together to emphasize how expensive houses could be.

'Well, Daddy, can't we have one like Mrs Odowis? It's nice and she don't have much money.'

'Ah, da . . . dat's council flat. Her 'usband nasty to her, so dem gobermint give she a new 'ouse.'

Gwendolen stared, uncomprehending.

'You . . . you wan' make your Mammy part with me be . . . cause of a 'ouse?' Winston asked humorously.

'No, Daddy, me just ask.'

Winston narrowed his eyes and studied his daughter more. She was growing into a pretty young woman. She had a smoother skin than Sonia. She had the alluring hesitant attitude of the disciplined young, still unsure of her steps and frightened of making mistakes. Then it struck him. Gwendolen was going to be a beautiful and stimulating woman. But when exactly did she grow up? It was only like yesterday that he was kissing a little girl with bare legs goodbye at the harbour in Kingston. And the next thing he knew was this young woman coming to live with them. And she was already having big ideas. Sonia was different. As long as he gave her his pay packet, she felt happy. What she never guessed was that he always kept a little for himself, just to buy that extra lunch he needed when he was tired of his wife's soup and bread roll lunch. In their private life, she accepted him without a murmur. The only thing that happened to alter the monotony of their life was the arrival of babies. On the whole, they considered themselves really lucky. If they had stayed in Jamaica, he would have asked Sonia to come and join him and the best accommodation he could afford, on the odd jobs he was doing, would have been one of those barrack-like shacks in a cheap shanty district. If one was white in Jamaica, one could coast along, if one was brown, life could still have a meaning, but if one was black and uneducated, life was a steady downward pull to Hades. And it would not have ended with himself, but with his children too. Now his daughter wanted them to move up, because unlike her parents, she saw only part of the poverty of the Hills, she did not taste the stink and degradations of the shanty towns. In a way, he was happy about it, because sometimes he thought they had left the girl too long at home. This one was going to demand more from life than his Sonia.

Gwendolen had her mother's small frame, but she tilted her head to one side as if to get a better view of life. She had inherited Sonia's rickety legs and, when she walked, this tendency to tilt to one side looked like an affectation. And she had changed so rapidly within a few months. Women grew so fast huh?

'Pay me no mind, June-June, when Ah . . . Ah win the pools, we buy big, big 'ouse.'

Winston, Gwendolen and the boys laughed loudly and happily at their father's joke. A kind of family bond was growing, despite the fact that Gwendolen had only joined them less than a year ago. Father was looking at his long-lost daughter with a new eye and Ronald suddenly seemed to realize that he had a new sister. The idea of their father ever winning the pools was to them not only remote but impossible and as for that of buying a house, Gwendolen must have been dreaming. Winston Brillianton lifted his thigh again and let out one of his bays. 'Lawd God Almighty, whar . . . rr . . . is this?'

Suddenly Sonia was there, taking in the whole scene in one angry glance. The laughter ceased abruptly. They all felt guilty for no reason whatsoever. She dragged in the large plastic trolley, which was filled with food and cheap market junk, a physical proof of the last week's hard work.

'June-June, why you sit dere laughing with your Daddy and Ronald? Me give you work fe do, before me go to market. You sit dere laughing with men, eh, Marm?' Anger blazed in every word.

Sonia sat down with a bump. 'Lawd, Winston, what is dis, huh? You encourage the gal to sit down and do nutting?'

'Me washing the window, Mammy,' Gwendolen said in a small voice.

'Windows, windows, eh? You fe finish them long time ago. Whey Cheryl, huh? Whey your baby sister, June-June?'

'Cheryl sleeping.' Gwendolen's voice was despairing.

'Look, look, Sonia, we just laugh. We . . . we just taak and we laugh. Wharr . . . wharr wrong with dat? Sit down, woman.'

'Sit down, sit down! Hear me nuh, just hear me. If Ah sit down who fe get ready your church clothes for Sundays? Who fe clean the 'ouse and cook the dinner? If the place

87

dirty, Ah don' get no baby to mind. Ah have to clean in de evenings too.'

'You know wharr killing you . . . you? Greed. Me give you enough money fe . . . fe anything you wan' but you put money fe big padner . . .'

'Me save money fe we all. Me go a work . . .'

To the surprise of Gwendolen and Ronald, their mother started to blubber like a child. Sonia herself did not know why she was crying. Winston was a nice man, but he and she seldom laughed together, the way she caught him laughing with Gwendolen and Ronald. Winston had never laughed like that with the boys. There was something new and she guessed it was Gwendolen. She could not put a name to what exactly it was that suddenly made her inadequate. But she felt it. It was there.

She could not believe what she said. It sounded as if it was coming from somebody else's voice. But she said it. She said, 'To think me tell Winston to let we save money for bring you here. I hope you're grateful, gal. Ah sincerely hope so.'

Something coiled inside Gwendolen. The picture of her Granny Naomi in her off-white dress and scarf, hinting that she had sent Uncle Johnny away loomed in her mind's eyes. Her young chest cried: Oh please God, don't let me be blamed for laughing with me Daddy. She could foresee the same play rolling on again, and she did not care very much for the repeat. This was bound to be different. After all, this man was her Daddy. But why did her mother give her the eye of suspicion Granny Naomi gave her a long time ago in Granville? She wished to bury that past, just as if it had never happened, as if it were a bad dream which must be forgotten at the dawn of the day. Or like the body waste that must be flushed out in the water closet. She so hated that past, and hated even more the idea of being reminded of it. Her mother was wrong. This was her Daddy and Daddies did not hurt their daughters. Her laughter with him was innocent.

She knew what her mother was suspecting, because she had grown older than her years in such matters. Pity she could not tell her mother. It would only do more harm than good. See what happened in Granville.

'You tired, Sonia,' Mr Brillianton said solicitously, as he adjusted his braces and clamped his cloth cap on his head and stumped out. Ronald, on deciding that it was better outside, called his brother Marcus and they went out into the small open Green nearby to play football.

When they had gone, Gwendolen thought her mother was going to beat her, but she did not. Their parents never laid hands on any of them. They did shout and bully Ronald and Marcus, but they did not beat them.

When she finished the windows, she went to unpack the shopping bag. There was the usual offal, green bananas, black-eye beans, rice and then window net; shiny tea-cups and saucers, plastic flowers and their containers, another plastic table runner, more plastic flowers, these in orange and those in blue, and more cloth remnants . . .

Oh, Mum, we don't need all these, her heart cried. There was scarcely any space in their front room for any more decoration. But she knew that that was where most of the money they all worked so hard for during the week went. Sonia liked their flat to be clean, bright and shiny.

Gwendolen became very cautious after that day. That feeling of belonging which had engulfed her when she first came, became slightly tarnished. Not that she ever confided in her mother that much, nor in any other adult, but that slow trust that she had begun to nurture towards Sonia began to waver. She now knew that she had to tread warily.

She watched with the corner of her eye when her mother picked baby Cheryl up, felt her nappy to know whether it was wet, but found it to be dry. She picked up the glass mugs, mugs which were ordinarily meant for drinking, but which the Brillianton family used as decoration, and looked inside all of them one by one, but found them to be clean. She was looking for a fault. Her movements were jerky, mechanical, as if she was not thinking of what she was doing. Gwendolen felt so hurt that she did not wish to calm her mother by saying something nice, because she felt Sonia was going to misjudge her like Granny Naomi and because these two women were hurting her by not trusting her. Her mother had not said it, the thought of it had probably never entered her mind until now. And Gwendolen felt that it was a question of time before her mother would accuse her of the same sin Granny Naomi had blamed her for when she was a child in Granville. Or maybe she was imagining it all. That mental bruise she had at ten years of age had coloured her image of her mother. After all, she was only laughing with her Daddy.

Sonia worried that probably she was too harsh on Gwendolen. She was not that educated but she had always lived among other people and that native West Indian sense had taught her so many things not found in books of psychology. She knew she was wrong, but how could she apologize to her young daughter about the uneasiness 'me feel in me bones'? It was so ridiculous, that she did not wish to give it another thought.

Sonia pushed it all to the back of her mind. It was all due to the fact that she wanted Gwendolen to come to England and help her with the housework and looking after the others. But she did not take into account that in doing so, Gwendolen would become confident and free like the English girls she saw in the streets and those she met at school. That freedom seemed to be eroding her power over her daughter. When she had been little, though her parents spoiled her, yet it was always, 'Yes, Mammy, yes, Fa.' She had never challenged her parents. She had never given them the feeling of not having authority over her. She could understand Marcus and Ronald, demanding their freedom early because they were boys and were born here. But Gwendolen was supposed to be her ally, and to be hers, and to be under her. She had not allowed herself to think too far into the future of her children. All Sonia cared for now was that they were clean, well fed and kept healthy.

Sonia had a thing about nice clean net curtains. She had net curtains with frills on all her doors. She had lacy ones for her windows and some frilly ones on her coffee table instead of runners. She still favoured frilly petticoats under wide organza skirts and wore beautiful hats of different colours. And as for plastic flowers, she could never have enough of those. If anybody asked Sonia about tomorrow, she would quote from the Scriptures, 'Enough unto the day, man, just enough.'

She had not failed to notice though that sometimes Gwendolen did not jump at the housework she was asked to do. And if anyone had asked Sonia whether she did not think she needed some time to herself, she would say, 'But a woman's job neber finish and she growing into a big, big 'oman.'

Gwendolen started going shopping with her mother on Saturdays. She loved going on buses and roaming from one market stall to the other in search of bargains. Most stall owners in that part of the Holloway Road knew her mother. They always spent more time in the material stalls. Her mother fingered this one and that one, and as soon as she saw a new net curtain design, she became almost excited. She bought and bought. Their shopping trolley was full of frothy white remnants. She was going to make new door nets for their door and flounces for their bedroom. Gwendolen's arms were full of gaberdine remnants that her mother was going to make into shorts for everybody one day. It struck Gwendolen that they had so much money to spend and not to save to buy their own house like Amanda's family and the families of her other schoolfriends. But her friends' homes were bare compared with theirs. Theirs was always crowded.

'Mum, we have money.' Gwendolen had learned very early to start a conversation by stating the obvious.

Sonia laughed. She almost laughed like Winston now. The two of them had lived for over seven years together and tended to behave alike, though neither realized it. They reacted similarly to events. Her father too liked to be told they had money.

'Why can't we move to a bigger house? There's not much space in our present flat.' Her face now was almost level with her mother's as she was nearly as tall. She screwed up her face, ready to hear her mother say that she was talking nonsense. But was surprised when Sonia said, 'Houses cost money, but me want one of those council places. They no cost much, but the landlord man will be in big trouble if we ask the council to give us a house.'

'Oh, I know. The type Mrs Odowis have, council house.' Her mind went to the four-bedroom flat their friend Mrs Odowis and her family had. They had a kitchen, their very own toilet and did not have to boil their hot water.

'Why the landlord man be in trouble, Mum?'

'Because him not suppose to let the flat in the first place.'

Their bus came and with so many other shoppers they rushed in dragging trolleys and packages. There were many mothers with babies and buggies. Buses that plied that route along Seven Sisters Road were wont to be noisy especially on Saturdays.

When they came out at Finsbury Park to change into another bus, Gwendolen gave her mother further glances to continue the conversation, but Sonia's stiff face told her that her patience was now exhausted. She dared not ask any more questions. Here she envied Ronald and Marcus. They would ask their mother unanswerable questions, they were not even afraid of offending their parents. Gwendolen, though she loved both parents, knew somehow that she could never reach such deep understanding with them.

The same situation was repeating itself at school. She was not academic. She could never be. She'd started too late. But she was fast mastering the language. Although English was her mother tongue, this type of school English was different from her emotional brand. With constant teasing from her brothers she was beginning to get the drift. They were still trying to teach her to read and write. She could print her name and was beginning to recognize words, but she never let her teacher come close enough to see her ignorance. When asked to write she would say she had no pen, or that she had a bad hand. Reading aloud in the remedial class used to be hell, until she learned to shout back at the teacher. Sometimes she would use to her teachers the new swearwords she'd heard her friends use in the playground. She knew she could scare them into silence. They probably put all these things into her report, but as neither parent could understand written English, she had nothing to fear there.

She learned a great deal during the current affairs discussion time. It was from here that she knew of overcrowding. It was here that she learned that she was old enough to need her privacy especially during her monthly when she would rather just lie in bed and be alone. It was here that she learned from Amanda and Marie that one could question one's parents.

Marie came to school from a Home. It did not take her long to identify with the dregs of the class like Gwendolen. The clever ones stuck together and their circle was very tight. You could never belong unless you were clever and had parents who visited the school and talked intelligently to the teacher. Gwendolen knew her parents were actually shrewd with a lot of common sense, but did not have the posh voice to show these attributes to the likes of her class teacher. Their intelligence was enough to make them live and be happy in their own world. But a new world which her parents did not know was being opened to her and her brothers. She was going to let her family share from her experience.

Gwendolen would have liked to be one of the clever ones in her class. They were always in stream 'A' or Group One for most subjects, but she could hardly read, to say nothing of knowing the whole contents of a book. None the less, school meant getting away from their two-room home, getting away from cleaning other mothers' babies; away from cooking and away from washing.

'Why don't we have a council house?' Gwendolen asked Amanda suddenly in a harsh stage-whispery voice a few days later during a needlework lesson.

'Because your Dad is too dumb, that's why,' came the wicked reply.

'Lawd Almighty, Amanda, you've no right to say things like that,' protested Gwendolen in her now diluted Jamaican voice.

'Then you have no right to ask such daft question,' Amanda replied, her voice rising.

'If you two don't keep quiet, you'll go out and have your shouting match there,' the supply teacher who was with them during this lesson said in an equally loud voice.

The two girls looked at the teacher as if to say, 'How dare you intervene when we talk.' She was only a supply teacher after all. But they kept quiet so suddenly that its abruptness made the other girls giggle.

Gwendolen told herself that when next Amanda invited her to her house, she wouldn't go any more. Just because Amanda's family had a three-storey house with a garden; just because she had her own room with a television and a record player. A needle pricked her finger and she shouted, ' 'Ow, now see what you have done.' There was more laughter from the other girls. Suddenly she laughed too. It was nobody's fault. But whose fault was it? Anyhow, I won't pay no mind to Amanda, she's a friend.

Less than a year ago, she was in Granville in Jamaica where she shared the same room with Granny Naomi. All her prayers had been for her to have enough to eat and to have enough energy to go to the farm to collect some honey for sale until her mother Sonia sent them money. Despite everything, she did not wish to stay there, get married and raise babies. She dreamed that one day she would go to England or to America like Shivorn's Aunt Monica. When they played, Shivorn, Cocoa and herself, they all talked about going overseas. They did not know in which direction overseas lay. They had no idea what they would do when they got there. All they knew was that they wanted to live in solid houses and not in the likes of her grandmother's shack. Shivorn had scared the living daylight out of her when she explained to her that Uncle Johnny's intrusion into her privacy could make her pregnant. Because she had seen a girl who had a baby at the age of eight! This had scared Gwendolen the more because she'd seen one of the women living in the trailers in labour, she was waiting for a taxi to take her into hospital. Her screams haunted Gwendolen. It was more frightening when they heard a few days later that the woman and her child did not survive the ordeal. How that incident had given her sleepless nights for days. Shivorn, she had a way of scaring you so!

But all that happened in the time of long ago. She ought to put all that behind her now. Now she had everything she thought she wanted – until she visited Mrs Odowis's house, and until Ronald started peering at her whenever she wanted to change her clothes. Once he was so baffled and exclaimed, 'Gwen, you know you're a girl.'

'Yes, I know I am a girl!' Gwendolen retorted. 'Everybody knows I'm a girl. You're stupid, Ronald you know that.' And this made Marcus who was there in the room laugh so much that he started to cough.

'Yes, choke yourself. You boys don't know nothing.'

The church which they attended occasionally preached against greed. She was greedy. Her Daddy always said her Mum was greedy. Then she must be greedy. But having to wait for the tenants on the ground floor before using the toilet was no laughing matter. She'd seen Ronald doing a water dance one day because he was waiting for one of the landlord's innumerable guests to finish with the toilet. Sometimes Sonia allowed Marcus to use the bucket inside their bedroom when he could not wait any longer, because he was young.

Her mother sent her to Mrs Odowis in the evening to give her some left-over remnants she'd bought.

'Gwendolen!' Mrs Odowis exclaimed. 'Honestly, you shoot up so fast and you look so pretty. Children, children!'

She spoke good English, Gwendolen thought, but with a different kind of music in her voice. Gwendolen could not always understand Mrs Odowis, but she was nice and looked really educated. Her life surprisingly did not look as busy and cluttered as her mother's. Her flat felt so spacious that Gwendolen wondered whether it was out of choice or because she had no money. She knew Mrs Odowis genuinely liked her so she felt confident enough to say, 'Our place is too small for us now I'm living there, too, and my Daddy said he does not wish to upset the landlord. And here the backyard is so cold, you do everything inside the rooms. It feels like a prison.'

'Oh, I know you're overcrowded. Your parents are nice people and they never forget that the landlord gave them those rooms when they had no other place to go. Do you know that at one time they allowed me to stay with them when I was having difficulties with my husband? Oh, your parents are nice. But I still think they should talk to the landlord. He will understand. And it takes a long time to get an accommodation from the council these days.' She did not wish to expand to the girl the main reason why she was given a flat. The phrase 'battered wife or mother' was scary enough for grown-ups, to say nothing of a young teenager. After all only a minority of men were insecure enough to batter their families.

'Mrs Odowis, you don't like furniture?'

Gladys Odowis looked round her flat and did not understand what she meant.

'I mean, Mrs Odowis, you no like lots of nets and flowers and chairs and baby things?'

'Oh, I see, you're a very observant young woman. I like openness. It's no use buying all those things with my children. They run around and knock everything down. And I think it's easier to clean when you have less things around.'

'When I have my own flat, I am going to have an "openness" – is that what you call it?' Gwendolen asked, spreading her young arms wide to include the whole room.

Mrs Odowis laughed and agreed. 'And you will have a nice hard-working young man to help you paint your walls. I never get used to flowery wallpapers. They seem to clutter a living room somehow. I don't mind them in bedrooms. Maybe that is why your place looks so close to you. Your parents did not hang those wallpapers, the landlord Mr Aliyu did.'

'And we have a lot of birthday and Christmas cards on the walls.'

'And don't they make your walls look so nice and colourful?' Mrs Odowis said with tact. She was a mother too and was not going to encourage Gwendolen to criticize Sonia behind her back. It was a thing not done in her culture. You stand by your family, no matter what. But she wondered if Gwendolen had not started talking to her friends and teachers at school. Should she warn Sonia that her daughter was not only growing very fast but also that she was absorbing all her surroundings including the culture of this place? This place where it was not considered bad manners to talk of one's family outside. She could not imagine a conversation of this kind taking place in Nigeria. But how would Sonia take it? Suppose it is permitted in the Caribbean.

Gwendolen turned it all in her mind. People were the same and yet different. Her mother and Mrs Odowis had several things in common, they were both black women, and they both had young children, yet they were so different. She wondered why this was so. And the painful part of it all was that her family worked so hard. And for no reason at all, she was shy about her home. Telling her mother about it was out of the question. She could not bear to hurt her, because her mother thought she was doing the right thing, things like buying very expensive and colourful Christmas and birthday cards and sticking them on their walls. They never sent Christmas cards to any of their friends . . . Well, she simply would learn to accept it and not ask too many questions, otherwise people might start thinking she was simple. What was the word Amanda had used? 'Daft', that was what she said, and she also said that her father was 'dumb'. What did it mean to call somebody who could hear perfectly well and who could speak, 'dumb'? 'So many tings fe learn for dis England,' she concluded.

She shied away from reading aloud. She pronounced the words wrong and she felt stupid at failing to do such a minor thing as reading, which her brothers could do with ease. Nevertheless, she observed acutely and listened and reasoned. Yeah, it was not so bad in England after all. On the one hand, her physical needs were mostly satisfied. But on the other hand, she felt reduced as a person.

She and her Granny had lived in a shack made of corrugated iron sheets. She slept on a bed made from bamboo sticks and so did her friends Shivorn and Cocoa. They all lived in similar shacks too and were always referred to as those who lived on the Hills. She had not learned to envy those who lived down the coast because she had no friends amongst them. But here her friends lived in proper houses. She lived in a house too. But it was a different kind of house, part of a house with no backyard and no garden. In England, there were homes and homes. They were all homes, but they were different. What a complicated place. Made more complicated by friends who knew and yet were too 'nice' to say it to your face. Did all her friends feel like this and still pretend it did not matter? She dared not ask Amanda, or Ravi, or Isabella, or any of them. They would only say, 'You're daft, Gwen, you know that.'

But all these things were making her feel as small as a titch.

She could not fight against all this. She was helpless. Just as helpless as when Granny Naomi was hinting that she was walking in a strange way, leaning to one side, and that it was this walk that lured men like Uncle Johnny into troubling her. Gwendolen knew now that whenever Granny Naomi found faults in everything she did, food was running short. She was the scapegoat. And but for her, Granny could pop in at Uncle Johnny's for salt fish and beans. Her speaking-out closed this channel. But one thing was certain, Granny Naomi had stopped being friendly with Uncle Johnny for a while.

' She could not force her parents to change the way they lived. They were happy, and she was happy until she started comparing their life with that of others around them. She had to get this feeling of helplessness out somewhere. She was not conscious of this, but that was what was beginning to happen.

Gwendolen started fighting her teachers. They stood for authority and everything that was right and proper, things the likes of her family could never get. Things her parents were not even aware belonged to them by right, things they did not even know existed, things they had not even acquired the taste for, but which had now been thrust under her nose. It looked as if the Authority was saying to her, 'Look, but do not touch.'

Gwendolen became disruptive, so much so that soon

teachers learned to ignore her and even warned her that she could be expelled from school. She soon learned just how far she could go, how far she could use her knowledge of Granville swearwords to shock her teachers and classmates, because she needed to get out of the house.

This was a pity, because if anyone needs education it is the Gwendolens of this world.

7

Mr Ilochina

The weather was so bad in February 1971 at the start of Gwendolen's second year in school that it looked as if it would never get better. Azu Ilochina hated Februaries in London. He'd noticed that with the passing of January his heart would leap in hope that they would at least have a few warm days to allow their guv'nor to fit in some outside work for them. But no, this cold and wet dragged on and on.

He was thirty-nine now. His wives quarrelled all last night because the senior one caught him playing with the younger wife. Cecilia, his senior wife, was much more masculine and, as a result, she believed in fighting her way through life. Azu Ilochina knew that the fault was all his. He had sneaked into England, in the late fifties, with a young and beautiful student of his, leaving an older girl-friend at home. Unfortunately the older and plainer girl had become pregnant. And as if that was not enough she had a set of identical male twins and they were the picture of the father. To put her aside was an abomination. He could imagine the joy of his parents at home and also their sorrow when they learned that he was in England with another girl. He was an only son, so his mother made sure that the plain woman was in England too with her two sons. This woman had now become the queen bee. If she caught him having sex with the younger woman, she would demand hers however tired he pleaded he was. And if he refused, there would be no peace and her children would howl. The older one kept having boys. It looked as if God was on her side. Trouble was, he would have liked Maureen to have at least one son, but how could she hide her pregnancy? For as soon as she became pregnant, Cecilia would want to be made pregnant too and she would have another boy enhancing her position the more. Maureen had five girls now and Cecilia six boys and a girl. The house he was struggling to pay for was like a zoo.

He did not mind it very much in summer when he could get enough well-paid outside work to cover the mortgage and the food bills. But in winter, and this type of prolonged winter, there were few indoor jobs. He had done everything he could. He and his large family occupied only a floor of their three-floor terrace house. They sublet the other rooms, but still he was short of money. And damn it all, should he not be studying for his law degree as he'd intended instead of sitting here worrying about the lack of employment on a building site.

His mind was so full of his own woes that he did not hear Winston Brillianton's greetings.

'Goo . . . gooo . . . good morning, wharrr happen to you?' Winston stammered loudly in protest.

'Hmm, hmm, sorry, Winston, I did not hear you come in.'

Mr Ilochina did not need much prompting for him to pour his heart out to his friend. As the day was freezingly cold, and they could see that there was no hope in hell of their getting an outside job, they made themselves comfortable by building a small fire in an old tin drum. Some of the workers spread their hands over the heat hoping that their guv'nor, who had gone out earlier on a call, would return with some good news about an inside decorating job.

Winston Brillianton and his African friend looked so grotesque that if the devil himself had seen them, he would run for shelter. Both men were big and tall and this morning it looked as if they had on twenty layers of old clothes instead of the usual two. They each wore two pairs of socks and two thick jumpers. All these had been smothered with the usual London grime, which outside workers have a knack of collecting in cold weather. Their gloves were originally made of yellow suede, but one had to look really close to see the traces of the original yellow leather, for they were all now covered in murky brown. The only difference in their turn-out was their head-covers. Winston still wore his cloth cap, but he now pulled it lower down to the bottom of his ears so that it looked like a beret rather than its original shape. Azu Ilochina wore a woollen hat with external flaps for his ears. The way both black men turned out every morning, one would have thought they were going to have a fight to the death, a battle with the devil, and not just going to work for their daily bread.

Winston listened to his friend with patience. One of Winston's attributes was that unlike most black men he was a good listener. Maybe this was due to his stammer which had a way of surfacing whenever he allowed himself the indulgence of over-excitement and rushed his words. Somehow he was able to view his friend's problems dispassionately. That today's babies would still depend on their parents in ten years' time and that they would have to be fed and nurtured for at least six years after that, made Winston frown. Winston seldom frowned. His face was always full, shiny and placid. The sudden frown that came to his demeanour called for attention. Azu Ilochina stopped talking suddenly. He stared at him.

Outside the wind howled without mercy shaking the bare London trees from side to side. It was grey and the slight snow that had flickered in the air the night before was too light to settle. But it had turned slushy grey as well.

The frown on Winston's face got deeper.

'Did you listen to all I have been saying, Winston?'

'Yeah, yeah, me hear you. But who's going to look after all dem chillun? Who? Who? Lawd Almighty, e 'ard. E 'ard.'

Was that all? Was that all his friend was going to say? Where would he start explaining to Winston that he was a

Nigerian and from the old Ibo kingdom. That in his culture they believed 'Ubakanma and onye nwe madu ka onye nwe ego' – a person who is rich in relations is greater than he who is rich in material wealth. And the Olisa who created the children will always create the food with which to feed them and the clothes for their covering. And that he was an only son, whose mother would never hear of his not allowing his wives to bear all the babies they were physically capable of bearing. He'd never heard a black man worry about 'Who's going to look after all dem chillun?' He knew his friend was not usually stupid, but this time he *was* stupid.

'What do you mean, who's going to look after them? I have a mother and when I qualify as a barrister, I won't practise but will go into Nigerian politics or go into business. A Nigerian businessman could be a millionaire in a few years.'

Winston could say nothing for a while but started laughing with his shoulders ashake not unlike his little son Marcus. Azu Ilochina joined too.

'Wo . . . wo . . . men. You busy man. Lawd Almighty! You favour one better that de other?'

'Yeah, that was before. Now all I want is peace.'

Well, we . . . ll, send them both to work. Every one feed 'im own kids. That'll show them.'

'But they are my children,' Ilochina exclaimed, warming up to this brand new idea which he had never thought of before.

'Yeah, yeah, me know. You . . . you somebody's child too. Dem wan' be baby machine, let dem carry on. But dem feed their kids.'

Both men laughed so loudly that their colleagues, who were warming themselves over another drum of fire, thought they were drunk. Unfortunately Ilochina felt that they would never understand the black man's joke in a billion years. He waved to them and said, 'Don't mind us.'

His gaze turned again to Winston, this time with respect.

This silent stammerer knew a thing or two. Though Ilochina came from Africa yet he was born in the city and schooled there. Winston on the other hand came from the hillside of Jamaica and he nurtured some home-grown strategies of survival which his friend might not have come across in all the law books he often lugged about.

Yes, that was what he would do, Ilochina decided. After all, both women collected family benefits from the state. The money was not enough, he knew. They had to go out and work to supplement it. He came to England to study law, not to slave his life out for children. Yes, they were his, but, as Winston said, they were theirs too.

He slapped his hand on Winston's back and cried, 'Winston, my good friend and brother from Jamaica, you have saved my life. Baby machine. Wait until I call them that. That will really hurt, because they were both trained teachers. Good. Thank you.'

The broad-faced guv'nor with folding chin stamped in, rubbing his hands in glee. The dejected workers sitting around the drums of coal fire could detect a glint of hope in his grey eyes.

'Got it then?' asked Bob.

'Yeah,' the guv'nor replied. 'Not much. But could be worse, an office block. Should take the rest of this winter. Work for everybody.'

The sigh of relief that went around was perceptible. Building workers were well paid in summer when the weather was mild enough to work outside. But to get an indoor job in a winter like this one, when the wind howled among the naked trees, was a bonus.

8

The Church

Gwendolen thought that the longer she stayed at school the more removed she was going to become from everybody. All her mother wanted from her was to be a good girl. And good girls for Sonia Brillianton were hard workers at home, looking good with pressed hair for church.

A new church started with Brother Simon who originally came from South Africa. Brother Simon was a pale-skinned half-caste, wiry and with a tiny mouth. If he had been a woman, he would have been undeniably pretty. He was tall and had a small balding head. Brother Simon met Sonia and Gwendolen one day when they were shopping at Queen's Crescent Market.

Gwendolen was momentarily distracted by an enthusiastic vendor who was shouting for attention from passers-by. The man was selling some huge slabs of fruit cake with thick layers of marzipan and icing which gave them the look of dark wood houses at Christmas. Her attention was drawn and focused on them, her mouth involuntarily watery. She jumped, swerving jerkily awake when she heard her mother call:

'June-June, come on, gal. Me no have all day.'

She walked up very fast, as fast as it was possible on a Saturday at the Crescent Market. Saturdays were busy days at the Crescent. Here was the teacher free from school looking for bargains, there was the unemployed builder in search of cheap tools, and at the other place was the young mother looking for inexpensive knitting wool for a winter matinee coat for her two-month-old baby. All kinds of people visited the Crescent. Sonia and her daughter were no exception.

On reaching her mother, Gwendolen realized that Sonia's call for her was more for security and assurance than for anything else. Her mother wanted the man who was chatting her up to know that she had a daughter and that the daughter was right there behind her. She would like him to go away and leave her to do her shopping. But Brother Simon was not to be put off. He flashed his smile on Gwendolen, a feat that required a great deal of effort because of the tiny size of his mouth. His teeth were yellowish, but otherwise perfect.

'Hi, little girl,' he enthused. 'Aren't she preddy?' Brother Simon for a reason best known to himself always fancied he spoke like the Americans. 'How you doin'?'

To all his well-meaning questions Gwendolen could only smile in reply.

By the time they'd finished shopping, however, Brother Simon had got their address and promised to call. He did call only a few days later to talk about his church.

Sonia and Granny Naomi used to go to church in Granville every Sunday and of course they took Gwendolen with them. But for some reason since she came to England, things looked and felt so different. The inside of the church buildings she'd seen looked so remote that she dared not ask why they did not go to church often here in London. She remembered one day shortly after she came to England when she was going to the launderette and she looked inside another church, very near to their house. She had known it was a church because the bell was pealing. The people were not particularly well dressed unlike the church-goers in Granville. Because they were all in dark blues, dark browns and grey overcoats, colours which looked ordinary and dull to her, she decided that they probably would remove those outer garments to reveal bright Sunday colours. She could not imagine people going to church looking so dull and unhappy.

She was so curious that after putting their washing into the machine, she crossed the pavement and went into the churchyard. She shuddered at what she saw. There was no joy here, she thought. It even looked as if it was colder in there than outside. She stepped back quickly but not before a lady with a stiff kindly smile asked, 'Have you lost something, dear?'

Gwendolen shook her head and walked away very quickly, her Wellington boots crushing the icy patches on the pavements. Her thoughts quickly swerved to the frosty air. All churches here must be for the very cold, remote whites, and it must be very cold in there as well. There was no single black face there. Hence she'd thought that black people went to church in the West Indies only. The people here must be worshipping a white, cold God. No wonder her family attended on special days only.

There was that spiritual vacuum in her family which Christianity, in the cold and remote way it was preached in England, could not fill. They needed a livelier God.

Convincing the Brillianton family was easy. They needed a place to go every Sunday, they needed to pray to God, they needed the Christian sermon preached to them in the warm humane way they were used to. Like the Africans, the West Indians loved to dress and look good. What other place was better to dress and look good than a church in which one was expected to praise and thank one's creator for all the bounties of life.

It did not bother the Brilliantons that the church was only a tenants' hall in a block of flats near Mornington Crescent. For as Brother Simon said, 'Wherever two or three are gathered in my name, there I shall be also.' In no time at all, Sonia made new Christian friends and so did Winston. Brother Simon, who had been ordained in South Africa, became the Leader. The women prettied the church hall so it looked warm and colourful. They sang the old missionary hymns of their childhood days. Hymns like 'Onward Christian Soldiers' and 'What a friend we have in Jesus' were favourites of Brother Simon. In no time at all the children, Marcus, Ronald and little Cheryl, could be heard humming some of the tunes.

The hall had a stage and on this a table was placed. In the middle of the table stood a fairly big golden cross, which Brother Simon said he was given by a monk who lived on the hills outside Jerusalem. Gwendolen and Ronald joined the choir, and the church soon became the very centre of their life.

It met their social needs because members did talk to each other even on weekdays; it met their musical and entertainment needs because members could sing and clap and dance to the Lord. It also met their spiritual needs because prayers were not read from a book but said loudly and personally. People could come forward to testify to what the Lord had done for them.

Winston became Brother Brillianton and despite the stammer that left hesitance in his speech, he was good at preaching the sermon. And because of Sonia's hard work, the Brilliantons became one of the leading families of that church near Mornington Crescent. Even though she was expecting another baby in the autumn, and her stomach was tumbling big, Sonia saw to it that her family always looked smart for church.

Gwendolen soon began to look forward to Sundays. They became busier on Saturdays, but it was busyness with a purpose. The church clothes were to be aired or washed, shoes to be polished, and in the evening Gwendolen and Ronald would rush to choir practice. Practising Christianity became a way of life. Each time a pair of new shoes were to be bought, the question was usually asked, 'Can you wear them to church?' And as for taking the buses to Finsbury Park and then to Mornington Crescent, it was like being on cloud nine. Gwendolen started taking a real interest in the way she looked in her church clothes on Sundays.

For school every day, she wore her wine-coloured gaberdine raincoat. But for Sundays, her mother bought a green coat with white fur round the neck, a white hat and gloves, white shoes, and white knee socks. She really did look smart. But when they got home, they had to change back into ordinary house clothes. To them church clothes were just that, clothes for going to church. You were not even allowed to wear them for Sunday dinners.

Word went round the black community living in Kentish Town, Hornsey and Camden Town about the new church and people began to leave the impersonal established Church of England where the Good Lord seemed so distant, for this one where somehow people felt that God would understand their language the more.

Gwendolen and her brothers made friends with people of their ages. That church and the reunion with her family became the two most important events she felt she'd gained since her arrival in England.

By the time Gwendolen became fourteen, the school had become a place of humiliation, a place of shame. A place where her parents were regarded as black illiterates who could not come to parents' meetings or come on open days. The thoughts of going there every day were not dissimilar to the thoughts she sometimes experienced when she recalled the fact that an older man had invaded the privacy of her body when she was still not nine.

She could explain this neither to her parents nor her teacher. And yet it was illegal for her to simply stop going to school. That would put her parents into more trouble. That much, Amanda had told her. There was no escape for her but to force herself to go to school every day, pay little attention to the teachers, refusing to let them come closer to her, in case they discovered her shame and ignorance, and

111

feign a kind of aloofness bordering on insolence, whilst waiting impatiently for another Sunday. Another day to sing to
the Lord.

9

Sonia Away

The church service on this Sunday was particularly long but spiritually uplifting. During the course of it, Mr Brillianton preached in his stammering voice about the evils of adultery. He said that the world was in chaos because of adultery. Adultery ruined and brought bad blood into otherwise good families. That it broke men's hearts to see their wives prattling on about eyeing other people's husbands or young girls dreaming of married men. The Lord was against it. The men in his audience nodded and said, 'Yeah, brother, yeah, man . . . Amen.' The women smiled worriedly and looked at each other.

Gwendolen looked at her father and worried. She worried because when the words became difficult, they jumbled together and only the members of his family could understand him. He was in such a state once or twice that he resorted to floundering his arms like a drowning man. Gwendolen held herself to her seat by sheer force. She loved her father dearly and since he'd started preaching in the church, her respect for him was beyond bounds. No one knew why the easy-going Winston, whose tiny wife Sonia could bully him into silence at home, talked so brutally about women whenever he took the pulpit. As usual though, he survived and, to Gwendolen's relief, he even had enough breath to say a long-winded prayer to God.

After the service, they had a women's prayer meeting, the kids' Angelic League and the men's prayer meeting. As Mr Brillianton never liked very much the members of his family going home separately after such a spiritually uplifting day, they all had to wait for each other. By 2.30 they made their way to the bus stop at Mornington Crescent. Marcus and Ronald, with their new haircuts and dark suits with matching bow ties, were the miniature of their father Winston. Sonia still favoured wide near-circular skirts but Gwendolen was now opting out, for the slimmer look. The only thing was that she had to make it rather long for modesty, as befitted a girl from a Christian home. She thought this unusual length ruined the whole dress, but she did not realize how stunningly beautiful she looked in it. She did not mind though, for, after all, was going to church not the highlight of the week for her?

They were so hungry by the time they got home. Marcus could hardly be made to change his clothes before tucking into his plate of boiled rice and tripe stew. They were in the middle of this when the sound of a scooter stopping noisily in front of their house reached them. As they were not expecting anyone, none of them saw the need to disturb their meal. They were too hungry. Who could blame them? They'd had nothing since their eight o'clock breakfast of porridge oats and hot milk.

None the less, they could hear the front door open and their Nigerian landlord talking to someone.

'Must be the la'lord's people,' Sonia observed redundantly.

Her husband nodded. 'Me know.' His mouth was full of tender tripe which had been allowed to cook slowly in its own juice.

But when they heard the landlord's steps coming thoughtfully up the stairs, they all stopped. He waited by their door and then knocked. Mr Brillianton looked from one member of his family to the other, adjusted his braces over his vest, wiped his wet mouth with the back of his hand and answered, 'Yeah, me coming.' When he got up, Sonia dusted the rice grains off his Sunday black trousers which he had not bothered to change out of, because he was so famished.

114

Cheryl, now rising four and a London child, got up. She wanted to see what it was all about.

The Brilliantons were no trouble-makers. Winston worked hard at his building site and his wife did all kinds of jobs to make ends meet. She could sew, at least for the family, she minded other people's children and the strain of this had once made her seriously ill. She recovered quickly though because Sonia's mind worked like quicksand. And despite all this, they never owed Mr Aliyu, their landlord. Winston Brillianton's wife made sure that the money for their shelter was the first thing she took out of her husband's pay packet every Friday evening. So Mr Aliyu seldom saw any reason for him to complain about this or that. And as for cleanliness, Sonia was obsessed with it. She or Gwendolen washed down their windows every Saturday, and when there was the slightest sign of part of their window net going grey, she would trek down to Queen's Crescent, buy a couple of yards of net more gaudy than the last one and sew it up. They were friendly with Mr Aliyu, but though they all spoke English, yet they found it difficult to understand each other.

Mr Aliyu was always impatient and thought that because he was studying engineering at a local polytechnic he could not be bothered with 'West Indians' who spoke funny. And the Brilliantons thought, Well, he may speak good, but he an uncivilized Africa man, man.' So his coming up the stairs slowly and knocking at their door, this Sunday afternoon in September, meant something very important.

It was a telegram. Mr Aliyu who had signed for it downstairs had had a peep at it. Granny Naomi had died in Granville.

'I have some news for you,' he announced importantly. Being originally from one of those African kingdoms to whose people understatement was equivalent to good manners, he referred to the fact that Granny Naomi had died as 'some news'. As Mr Brillianton 'could not find his glasses' Mr Aliyu's position was intricate. Should he be like an Englishman and tell this family what had actually happened? But he could remember quite vividly stories from his early moonlight nights in his village in Ijebu land; stories in which bearers of bad news could be killed. In his own culture it was quite correct to say that Granny Naomi had not died, but was very ill. If Mr Brillianton had been a Nigerian, he would have guessed straight away that his mother-in-law had died. But the man had had that part of his cultural heritage taken away from him by slavery. Mr Aliyu wished Winston could read and not pretend he had just lost his glasses. Funnily enough both men knew he could not read and it had been Mr Aliyu who had first, indirectly, suggested the lie to Winston years ago when he had caught him trying to spell out words on a piece of advertising that had come through their letter box. He had hated himself for catching Mr Brillianton like this and he had said hastily, 'I see you've lost your glasses.' And Mr Brillianton had replied, 'Yeah, man, me lost me glasses.'

None the less he apologized for disturbing their Sunday dinner, but called Mr Brillianton out. They went out into the small passageway which served as Sonia's kitchen. As he was about to open his mouth to speak again, Cheryl asked, 'Wha' is it, Mr Landlord?'

'Ge . . . get . . . back inside,' Mr Brillianton said.

Out of earshot, Mr Aliyu said, 'Your mother-in-law is very sick. Your wife must go home and see her.'

For the next few days, the Brilliantons' home buzzed with talks of injections, passport, medicine for toothache, medicine for rheumatism. No one knew why Sonia, who always double-checked letters from her husband when she was in Granville, did not bother to show this telegram to others. Maybe because inside herself she believed, like many others like her, that nothing that happened in England would be imperfect. If they met Mr Aliyu in England even though he came from Africa, and he told them that her mother was ill, then it must be so.

Guilt fuelled Sonia's behaviour. Something was telling her that she was probably too late. Her poor mother. She had not been writing home as frequently as she should have. For while it was understandable not to write at home in Granville, it was not so here in London. Mrs Odowis used to write for her, but when Sonia got closer to her, she felt she was better than Mrs Odowis in many things. At least she'd kept her husband. Winston might not be a book man like Mr Odowis, yet he was faithful to his family. She had her husband and Mrs Odowis did not. She also kept her flat spotless but Mrs Odowis said she'd rather keep her huge apartment comfortable. Why, sometimes that woman would buy second-hand clothes, wash and mend them and put them on her kids. Sonia would never do anything like that. True, Mrs Odowis paid her with cheques when Sonia minded her children for her, and each time they went to the local Barclays Bank, to cash them, Winston would go with her in his church clothes. And they used to get so worried when the cashier went behind the counter to check something before paying them. She'd asked Mrs Odowis once, 'Why dey go behind the counter?'

'Because they wish to check if I have enough money.'

'And you have?'

'Of course, why else would I give you a cheque?'

'Some people have more money than sense,' Winston had remarked.

That was why she stopped getting Mrs Odowis to write her mother. Sonia felt she lacked some real common sense even though she was studying in the evening. And if someone had asked, 'How does somebody with basic native common sense look?' she would have shrugged her narrow shoulders, wrinkled her eyes in laughter and replied, 'Me no know, man; but me know sensible 'oman when Ah see one.'

Now her poor mother was dying, dying without hearing from her for years. All because of her pride. Then her thoughts would switch to the present. 'June-June, don't forget to clean Cheryl's teeth every night. And Marcus, if you don't comb your hair the teacher will . . .'

'He . . . he . . . him no get hair. Rest yourself, 'oman.'

'Rest yourself, rest yourself. You say because she not your moder.'

Sonia burst into tears. Winston got frightened thinking she might slip into a mental hysteria. He comforted her clumsily. He was not used to handling her with care but when forced to do so he did it with deep concentration.

By the time Sonia left for Jamaica – the Jamaica she'd left over seven years previously – she had not only exhausted herself but everyone around her. They all breathed huge sighs of relief when they eventually took the train back to their flat.

Gwendolen was now the little mother, a duty she did not resent. She was used to doing most of the housework. Fourteen, going on fifteen, she was a real little madam. One happy thought that struck her as her mother left, was that at least she could skip school as often as she liked. Her father was always out, working on the site. Ronald and Marcus would not notice as long as she took Cheryl to her little school down the road. She could cook and eat what she wanted and clean the house when she felt like it. Somehow instead of dreading the responsibilities placed on her, she felt a kind of freedom which she could give no name. Her mother would be all right in Granville among her old friends, and they would help her with the new baby when it was born.

Gwendolen was stirring a pot of Quaker oats for her younger brothers and sister when she again heard Mr Aliyu coming up the stairs. Her heart almost stopped beating. What was it this time!

'Your father in, Gwendolen?'

'Yes, Mr Landlord, he is in the front room.'

Winston came out again. His stance was questioning. He

118

too was resting from the mental demands of the last week. Mr Aliyu felt he had to say what was on his mind quickly without any preamble.

'I have to tell you that your mother-in-law is dead.'

'A . . . aw . . . when . . . how . . .?' Winston went completely incoherent.

'Well, it was in the telegram. You see, among my people when we say that somebody is very ill, the men in the house should know what we mean. But I'm glad your wife is gone, which I think is a good thing.'

Myriads of thoughts ran through Winston's mind. Sonia had carried home enough medicine to equip a mini-hospital. He had gone to an Indian chemist nearby and told the man that his mother-in-law was fairly old, had bad teeth, maybe bad feet, and aching stomach. The good chemist had made him buy so many capsules, bottles, ointments and tablets just in case Naomi was suffering from one thing or the other. And all that money. They had collected their 'padner' money, Winston had borrowed a little from Mr Ilochina, his friend and colleague at work. They had not even had enough money to buy a return ticket. He simply promised to send Sonia some money when the time of her return came. Their church had prayed and fasted for God to spare Naomi's life, all because this stupid uncivilized African decided that telling him the truth was not according to his stupid culture.

Mr Brillianton's eyes went red, just like the colour of a ripe kernel. Talking would take too much time. Before anyone could stop him, he shot out one arm and it landed on Mr Aliyu's chest. The man fell crashing on to the banister railings of his old rickety house. Winston made as if to follow him, but for the cries of Cheryl and Gwendolen. 'Daddy, Daddy, don't kill the landlord man.'

He would have had a good job following him, because Mr Aliyu, with his bleeding head and twisted ankle, picked himself up quickly and ran as fast as his legs would allow him

119

into his own room downstairs. He knew what an angry African Caribbean man could be. He did not wish to take chances with a tribe which he told himself were kitchen knife carriers.

Half the trouble in this world is caused by people who mean well. Mr Aliyu thought he was doing the right thing. He was shocked by Winston's behaviour, but, Lord, the man could have killed him. When he collected himself and came to the foot of the stairs, he stared at the Brilliantons' flat, not quite believing what he had just experienced. If he had been this considerate to a countryman of his, he would have been applauded for being so tactful and for not wanting to gloat over other people's misfortune. He broke the news to Mr Brillianton, man to man, when he knew his wife was out of the way, and see what he received. How could he tell a pregnant woman that her mother had died? He shook his head. He could never understand these Caribbeans.

But Mr Aliyu knew and had read from many books that the gulf which was made by slavery that separated brother from brother was still too wide and too deep to be crossed by a single narrow bridge made of the wooden plank of the English language. His feelings were not dissimilar to those early Bible people who were building the Tower of Babel. Lack of communication brought confusion. Mr Aliyu did not know where to begin. He could still see the red in Mr Brillianton's eyes. He could also see the picture of his children holding him, pleading with him not to kill the landlord man. Basic instinct advised caution. Aliyu avoided the Brilliantons like one avoided the plague.

10

Winston's Roots

It was on a morning in late September that the letter from Mr Aliyu's solicitor was delivered. Winston had left for work and the letter arrived after he'd gone. Even if the letter had arrived whilst he was still there, he would not have picked it up. The family never wrote to people and since one mostly reaped where one sowed the Brilliantons did not blame the world for not writing them. They missed nothing. The jobs of going out to work, cooking, cleaning and for relaxation rearing children, were enough to fill their days. Consequently, whenever there was that odd occasion when a letter did arrive, it was Mr Aliyu who invariably picked it up, took it up and read it to them on the landing.

The Brilliantons were law-abiding people until Winston felt that Mr Aliyu was robbing him of his dignity as a family man.

Aliyu, who knew what that particular letter contained, did not bother to open it as he used to, but kept it on the front room table. Soon Ronald, who not unlike most boys of his age always ran through the tiny hallway and up the stairs, came scampering by.

'Ronald, Ronald,' Aliyu growled.

Ronald opened his mouth in wonder. No one could blame him, for Mr Aliyu had not spoken a word to any member of his family since their father's show of anger. When he stopped suddenly in his tracks and turned himself slowly and mechanically, Aliyu could see that, though Ronald had his mother's face, fairly bony legs and a gait with a bias, leaning to one side even when he ran, nearly all his movements were his father's. That man must have strong blood in his veins for all his children to be so much like him. Ronald walked down the stairs stiffly like a soldier, with doubt written all over his face, wondering what Mr Aliyu was calling him for. He was not frightened of the man after seeing the way his Daddy dealt with him only a few days previously. His normally brown eyes now turned black. On seeing those eyes, Aliyu left the letter at the bottom of the stairs and went back to his room. He did not need to say anything.

Ronald snatched the letter and for no reason at all ran up the stairs two at a time. He read the back of the envelope when he got to their sitting-room and knew that it was for his father. The orange and white antimacassar that Sonia had made for the television carried several baby photos of the children. Carefully, Ronald looked for a place in between his baby photo and a glass horse and wedged the letter there until his father returned.

It did not occur to Winston to ask Ronald to read it. He felt his son was too young and, like Gwendolen, he carried the fear that probably little Ronald could do what the adults could not tackle. So he took it to his friend Mr Ilochina.

'What have you been doing to your landlord? Did you really batter him? He wants you and your family out of his house in four weeks.'

'Me know. 'Tupid man. He lied to me, you know. Lied to me just because me no fit . . . well, 'tupid African.'

When one's dignity had been bruised, relating it to others could be another hurt. Double hurt. Winston looked at his friend as he sat outside on a wooden bench that had been abandoned by whoever had lived in the dilapidated house they were renovating, and sighed. To tell this man, another African, that his landlord had lied to him because he could not read his own telegram would be exactly that, another humiliation. Mr Ilochina knew this, and he was not going to allow Winston to suffer it. Having worked with him for four years, he knew he might be uneducated, but that did not mean he was unintelligent. He had never seen a more hard-working and fearless man. Winston would climb any ladder, however high, as long as there was a job to be done. He had watched Winston handle the road-digging machine with his bare hands as if it was an animal to be tamed. Education and native intelligence are not always synonymous.

A long silence fell between the two men. Ilochina hated the landlord who had the audacity to turn his friend out of his house and who he suspected behaved in an arrogant way. Could he not at least have talked to them first, instead of rushing to a solicitor? After all, the Brilliantons paid their rent on time and did not owe him a penny.

He unwrapped his sandwich and started to chew it mechanically as if he was chewing his morning chewing stick. With every munch, he was allowing his anger to fester.

'Arrogant Yoruba fool,' Ilochina spat.

'Wharr . . . wharr . . . you say?' Winston asked.

'I swear by my dead ancestors that that man is a Yoruba man, and I'm telling you that he is arrogant and a fool.'

'Hmm, just because he a Yoruba man?'

Both men relaxed into easy laughter.

'You deserve a new council flat, you know. Those rooms are too small for you, and as for those narrow and badly decorated stairs, they are the pits. Our women put up with anything. I mean, your pregnant wife going up those narrow stairs.'

The image of the house loomed in Ilochina's mind. It was one of those Victorian houses with several steps leading up to the ground floor. Maybe it was because it had a basement flat. Then inside the house had that tired-looking yellow wallpaper, peeling off the wall here, patched with another there. It was clean, Sonia saw to that, but too choky with the heavy smell of rich African-Caribbean food. The house always smelt of beans as well. Yes, his friend needed a new council flat.

'Why have you not applied for a council flat before?'

'Me no know how ... bu ... but we happy there. The landlord be in trouble too, with the council, if me apply.'

'Who told you that? Aliyu? Then he has given you the rope with which to hang himself. I wonder why he did that. I know, I know. The arrogant fool. He thought you would not know how to go about it. He did not know you have another Nigerian as a friend. I'll show him, leave it to me, I'll show him. Tomorrow we'll go to the Tribunal.'

'Where dat?'

'I'm reading to be a lawyer, you know. So leave it to me.

'First, don't pay him any rent from today. He'll be too scared to ask you. When we get to the Tribunal, we'll show them this letter and you just move when they give you a flat, even if it takes a year.'

'The lan'lar's rent, what then?'

'Save it, don't give it to him. He is too proud. It takes a Nigerian to know another Nigerian, you know.'

'You no like Yoruba people, dey from Nigeria too?'

'I'm Ibo, you know. Not the same tribe, not the same language. We don't behave like that. We are nicer people,' Ilochina said without realizing how vain and arrogant he was sounding.

Mr Brillianton, who could see all that, tactfully said nothing but just laughed at human nature in general.

'We have it, you know. People from Grenada say we Jamaicans eat monkeys.'

Ilochina laughed too. 'We eat monkeys. We call it *ewen*. We say monkeys have ugly faces but delicious meat.'

In the streets, an early autumn wind howled, scattering yellowing leaves about. Some of these brown and yellow leaves were blown inside the glassless house they were

124

redecorating. The house without its glass panes looked like a skull without eyes.

Then suddenly Winston asked, 'Is Yoruba from the Ashanti then?'

Ilochina looked at his friend, pulled his cap an inch downward as a protection against the wind and smiled. 'Who told you about the Yorubas and the Ashantis?'

'Well, Ah know. Me gran'father, him never a slave, you know. Ah . . . ah . . . ah think he Ashanti, but followed his sweetheart Adaora to slavery. Them went to Brazil, you know, then ca . . . ca . . . came to Jamaica. Them going back to Africa, then them start having chillun.'

Ilochina's eyes opened. 'You mean he volunteered to go into slavery because of his woman! This beats the band. This makes Romeo and Juliet sound like a child's moonlight play. I can't believe it!'

'Dat's right, man. Me tell you. Bloody African.'

For no reason at all the two men started to laugh. They could imagine a woman doing a thing like that. But an African man of over a hundred years ago, that was something else.

Where had he read that black men of those days were bestial and heartless? Ilochina mused. 'You sure?' he asked again.

'Yeah, the story dey in me family ever since. Me see dem graves, you know. Me happy dem did not reach Africa though.'

'What did you say your grandmother's name was?'

'Adaora,' replied Winston.

'Well, that's neither Yoruba nor Ashanti name. It is an Ibo name. And your grandfather, the great lover, what was his name?'

'Me no fit say it well, you know. 'T's Keke Kwekwu Tijani.'

'You know, Tijani could be Hausa, Fulani, or even an Arab from Timbuctoo. He must have been a great lover. Those early Muslims stuck to the Koran. Fancy going into slavery

125

because of a dame. Obviously, he had no money to buy her freedom. I've never heard a story like this before. Some men!'

Whenever Ilochina read the story of Mrs Simpson and the then Prince of Wales, he used to think how soft in the head some men allow themselves to be simply because of one woman. But look at his friend Winston, the offspring of people capable of making the same sacrifice. Aloud he said simply, 'Stupid African.'

'Ah know. 'Tupid.'

And they both laughed again.

'Don't you think you've had enough break?' their overseer reminded them not too unkindly. An indolent laughter followed this remark from the other workers as well. They knew their guv'nor. An easy man who had a clever way of really getting things done.

Ilochina was dying to share the jokes with them, but the difficulty of race restricted him. How would they take it? They might even use it against them. What a shame, he thought. Stories like that would have brought them together, stressing their commonalities and the vagaries of human emotion.

Towards the end of the day, Ilochina asked Winston, 'Can you do it for your Missus? Go into slavery for her?'

'Don't be 'tupid, man. Me a Christian nuh. Dem days people not Christians. Dem be uncivilized African Muslims. Nuh Ah know better. Me a Christian nuh, man.' Winston winked at Ilochina as he made this statement. He was not completely devoid of humour.

'I know what you mean. Christianity has made us all softer and maybe more individualistic and wiser. Now, Tijani would have spent all his life praying for his sweetheart and not actually going into slavery with her. But I am sure my wives can do it for me, not because they love me, but because none of them would give me up for the other.'

'Then, dem must lo . . . lo . . . lo . . . love you, man.'

'Love, shio! None of them would give me up for the other. You know, just to spite the other woman.'

Winston corrugated his brow, in a vain attempt to follow his friend's drift. He could not see any sense in marrying two women in a place like London, anyhow. And as for one woman not giving up one man for another . . . it was too confusing. The argument was too circular for Winston. Then rather unexpectedly, he announced, 'Me hungry, man.'

'Adaora married Tijani and they ended up in Jamaica. What a world,' Ilochina murmured to himself as if singing a litany.

11

Sonia in Jamaica

About a year ago, if someone had stopped Sonia in Holloway
or Stroud Green during one of her rushes to buy sweet potatoes
and tripe to make supper and said to her, 'Look, Sonia, I think
you need a rest,' she would have given the person one of her
loud happy laughs, displaying her badly fitted teeth. She
would have said, 'Me tired? Me all right as rain, man.' And
she would plunge the listener into an anecdote of her day's
activities, starting from what she intended giving Winston for
dinner, to what material she was going to use in making
Cheryl's latest church dress. There was always something for
her not only to do but to worry about, talk about and even
hurry about. And however much she hurried, she was always
late for finishing the project. She would invariably finish the
dress just minutes before the family left for church.

She had enough money though, for Winston was not a
stingy man. If anything he was not too keen in finding out
what his wife did with the housekeeping money. 'He not
dem ambitious ones talking bout 'ouses and cars, but 'im
pleased with the pace of we life,' Sonia had told her friend
Gladys Odowis several times, and she knew that she fitted
perfectly well into this tempo.

The sudden announcement of her mother's illness rocked
the very bottom of her life. She was neither so young nor a big
enough fool to think that anything would last for ever. The fear
was always at the back of her mind. And this sudden announcement brought it home to Sonia. Throughout the preparation
and the flight to Jamaica, her thoughts were going up and
down like a see-saw. One thing she fought very hard not to

allow her mind to wander to, was death. When her mind came near to the edge of such thoughts as 'Maybe me Mammy don die long since', she would jerk it back with such a force that she would feel it affecting the child she was carrying.

Where would this baby be born? she wondered. If her mother was not too bad, she would return to London in a few weeks to have the child. But if Naomi was too ill, she would stay longer to look after her. After all, she usually had normal pregnancies and there were friends in Granville like Uncle Johnny, Roza, her mother's church friends. She had seen many babies 'birthed perfect' in Granville. Anyhow Kingston was never too far away since she had all their padner money.

Sonia felt a little guilty about that money. She had paid in their contributions for the past ten months. They had planned to collect theirs last so that they could put it away in a bank for the rainy day. Now she had collected the whole money. And Winston would have to pay the last two instalments all by himself. He was a good man, Winston, and maybe this was a rainy day. She had enough money tied around her waist to last her Mammy two good years. Her Mammy would be really happy about that. Sonia allowed herself a smile as the picture of her happy mother conjured itself up in her imagination.

Her mother deserved all their savings. Her mind switched back to her childhood days, where they had lived on the hill on a knife's edge, gathering honey, selling it at the harbour and using the money to buy food, mainly corn for cornbread, cornmeal and cornflour. Her Mammy grew plenty of vegetables in the yard. They had their own chickens, because chickens were easy to rear. Chickens ate anything from their own droppings to the family's leftovers. Being an only child, she had an egg for breakfast every other day. In a good honey year, she had a new dress at Christmas, but in a bad year, her father would go down to the harbour and do any odd jobs including fishing and she would have to make do with an old dress. That used to make her father whom she called 'Fa' really cross. She called him 'Fa' because he had called his father that, 'during dem slave times'. People made fun of her sometimes, but she and her Mammy Naomi 'paid no mind to dem gossiping neighbours, who know no better'. As far as her mother was concerned, nothing was too good for her only daughter Sonia. Because of this, neighbours gave her the nickname 'Little Marm'.

All those days were gone now. Her father had died when he went to the coast to fish and was caught in the heaviest rain of the year. The rain was not quite up to hurricane level, but it caused a big havoc. Rickety shacks were blown away, some trailers along the hills collapsed and those selling fish and honey from their boats tied up at anchor did not have enough protection against the wind that roared with the voice of the devil non-stop for five terrible days.

As Sonia had not told anybody of her arrival, she took a taxi from the airport to Granville. She was impressed at some of the changes. But as she neared her old home, she could see that poverty still existed in plenty by the hills. The tracks to the shacks looked narrower and dirtier. There were children everywhere. On the other side of the track were not only poor trailers, but people living in carcasses of old cars. The smell of rubbish filled the air.

Uncle Johnny was sitting quietly in front of his shack thinking about old times and all the friends and neighbours he had lost. Pity that Naomi never trusted him fully after that nasty episode with her grandchild. He had now changed, he had become a born-again Christian and he knew that God had forgiven him. But the nasty women in the neighbourhood never forget. Anyhow, Naomi was now gone. Her shack would soon be sold and new people would have to move in . . .

His thought was cut short by a Kingston taxi that was slowing down. Uncle Johnny was thinner, but still jaunty.

He saw Sonia, and could not restrain himself. 'Ah, London lady, welcome, Sonia. Welcome. You don look splendid. Welcome.'

Roza heard his voice and looked out of her window. She ran out, pushed Uncle Johnny aside roughly and embraced Sonia. 'Ah no fit know you again, Sonia. London don suit you. Welcome, Sonia.'

Shivorn, now a big girl, started taking Sonia's things inside Naomi's shack.

Sonia noticed that Roza gave the keys to the shack to her daughter to open the door. Whilst everybody was smothering her with greetings she managed to say, 'Me Mammy sick. Whey she?'

There was an instant silence. But Uncle Johnny jumped and came forward. 'Yeah, Naomi sick in 'ospital. Come in, come fust, rest a while, then we take you to see.'

Sonia was so suspicious that her voice went panicky. 'Me wan' go straightaway. Ah wan' see me Mammy.'

Uncle Johnny's hand was gentle but firm. 'Come in first, Sonia, come in, daater.'

Sonia took one look at the room, at the bamboo bed that was now turned against the wall, at the unearthly tidiness of the room. She looked Uncle Johnny straight in the eye and said piteously, 'My Mammy don die, not so?'

Her friends had no answer to give her. They just shook their heads and cried. They allowed her to cry, but Roza shooed Uncle Johnny away. 'What you doing here anyhow? Go out of this 'ouse,' a woman whom Sonia did not know said to Uncle Johnny in a loud whisper.

'Shush, shush,' said Roza.

'No, me no wan' see dat dirty man fe here. Me no care if he become born-again Christian. A dirty man is a dirty man to me.'

The woman's voice was hushed as the house filled with sympathizers.

Shock and sorrow snapped the taut string that had held Sonia's sanity together. She cried and raved for weeks, and people did not know what to do. She was not completely mad, but she was not herself. Her mother's neighbours, her friends all helped. They made her local potions, they talked to her, but all the time not reaching her at all. It was a miracle that she survived the birth of her stillborn baby as she did nothing to help the poor child's progress. By the time people knew she was in labour, it was too late to do anything for the child.

With the help of the Pastor of the church howling prayers by the door of Naomi's shack, and the local midwife rubbing Sonia's stomach with a mixture of herbs and lemon grass, the child came out. If Sonia was aware of what was going on, she did not show it. She simply looked blank. But the midwife, Mama Jackson, gave her more of the mixture to drink, and that mercifully sent her to sleep for over twelve hours. When she woke, she had that glazed look of the mentally ill. Since people did not know what else to do and because their Pastor was getting tired of praying, it was decided that as Sister Naomi had been a good Christian woman, Sonia should be taken into church shelter.

Uncle Johnny, who would not let neighbours shame him into silence and who was now a very good Christian and respected in the church, suggested that maybe they should write and tell Winston Brillianton of his wife's illness. But Shivorn's mother Roza, who in church circles was now known as Mrs Sister Blackson, said, 'You wan' mess up people's life again, Johnny? Ah no care how many good deeds you don done these days. A bad man always a bad man. Keep your dirty fingers off Naomi's pie. Now which of oonu man wan' hear say 'im missus don go crazy? Give her time, man, she soon recover from the shock in no time at all, Winston none the wiser.'

Since Uncle Johnny had repented his sins in the front of the Apostolic congregation, he had learned to be angry silently.

133

Raising his voice would make people say, 'Leopards neber lose dem spots, you know.' But he gave Roza an awfully ·dark and unchristian look. And with his shoulders slouched, sulked away, his not so white robe sweeping the dust.

'Some dem Christians don sin more than the very Satan,' Roza continued in a loud voice for a good measure. This raised a gentle laughter from the knot of loungers standing by.

They did give Sonia time. She started to recover. Being in an atmosphere that was not unlike a relaxed holiday camp did help a good deal. The only thing that disturbed the calmness was the prayer sung in the early morning, in the afternoon, and in the evening. She did not have to worry about her meals, her family's meals, their washing, their bed-making and the children's bed-wetting. She did not even have to worry about the weather. To pay for her keep she had to sell most of the medicines she had bought for her mother. Roza packed them all off to the Jewish man Mr Lasky who had a chemist's shop by the alleyway off Jones Town in Kingston. He paid her handsomely and requested more. The chemist then sold the medicine to tourists and sailors who wandered around the harbour. The Apostolic church forbade white man's medicine. Some people who belonged to the Rasta group said the medicine was from Babylon and that it would do Sonia more harm than good. But Sonia rallied none the less, and praised the Lord with the other sick people living in the church haven.

When she went back to Naomi's shack, the pace of life was still slow. She was not one of those people to put on airs simply because she had lived in London for over seven years, but the temptation to show off her good-quality clothes was too much to resist. As she got better and stronger, she wore her new clothes, put on her nice shoes, and carried her beautiful handbags. All these made her stand out in the congregation. And the Pastor was always inspired to say thanksgiving prayers whenever Sonia was in church, which was often.

Suddenly Sonia started to see the possibility of a new life away from Winston. She truly loved her children and as she got better she longed for them. But the thought of living by herself as a person, with no mother to look after, no children to feed and no man to cook for was at first disconcerting. She felt frightened. She felt like a person without a purpose in life. Like a person without roots. She knew that good women were not supposed to live and exist for themselves. They were expected to remain alive for others. They were created to look after members of their families, to boost the ego of the man in their lives, be the man a father, a husband, or even a son. And they were to nurture and act as agony aunts to their offspring. But to live for themselves was not to be. There must be something awfully wrong with her to discover such happiness in the selfish habit of doing exactly what she wanted to do. 'Lawd, forgive me, a terrible sinner,' she prayed.

Yeah, she must be a terrible sinner to find out the joy of taking her bath slowly, cherishing the warm water, the satisfaction of massaging her own body herself with pure coconut oil, and the joy of trying on several dresses before choosing the one she would eventually wear. Roza, Shivorn's mother, helped her with her cooking most of the time. And she felt like a real Marm.

Previously, she used to pity single women, but now she was not so sure. She had thought that they must be missing sex and men terribly, until she started sleeping peaceably on clean sheets without disturbance all night. She could even sleep in her own blood on her bleeding days without the added worries of how Winston must be feeling. What she sometimes missed was his presence, just his solid self, since he was neither a great talker nor a conscientious listener. But was Winston missing her? she allowed herself to wonder at times.

The children? Yeah, they would be missing their Mammy. But Gwendolen was there. She, a little Mammy herself.

So, Sonia Brillianton got about rediscovering the Jamaica of her youth. She made many trips to the harbour, not knowing exactly what she was looking for. She saw the bright lights of the tourist hotels. She recoiled at the number of young girls who had to live by selling their bodies. Somehow she was an outsider. She watched people going in and out, people swimming, people drinking fizzy drinks and sparkling wines. She could not go in. She could not join in any of these activities. The thought of being unfaithful to Winston did not appeal to her. There was no need, because the temptation never arose. She was a little saddened by this, but to herself she said, 'There be two Jamaicas, man, two Jamaicas. One for the rich whites and browns with education and sophistication, anoder for the black race.'

That heavy thought did not weigh on Sonia too long. She shrugged her shoulders and allowed the sunshine to wash over her. 'Was me not near death's door? Me Mammy done go, me Fa too long gone. So what to do? Make me enjoy the sunshine.'

Then suddenly the sense of guilt started to become heavier and heavier. Had she mourned her mother long enough? Why was she not missing her family? She would write to them, she would. But writing was not so easy either. Before she went to England, she could ask the Indian letter-writer, now, with her new sophistication, she could not bring herself to ask him again. They all knew she'd been to London. And what a laugh to know that somebody who'd been to England, the country in which the queen lived, the very 'Moder Kontry', and stayed there years, could only recognize the numbers and was not able to write to her husband.

Uncle Johnny used to help with such matters before. But now, he was so distant. At one time she thought he was trying to avoid her. She had asked Roza only the other day, and her answer was so vague. 'You don' need men like him no more, Sonia. Uncle Johnny done change. Him not so nice a man any more. Just leave him be. What you want from him anyhow?'

'But he a good Christian man nuh. Him and me Mammy quarrel before she die?'

'Look, Sonia, you just de recover from serious illness. No trouble yourself no more 'bout him. Him come visit you?'

'No, I think him run away from me.'

'Well, leave him then.' Roza's voice was very harsh.

Though Sonia was determined to talk to Uncle Johnny, she never had the chance. He avoided her throughout the rest of her stay.

Sonia thought of asking the church Pastor to help her but as he was new in Granville he too did not know that she could not write. To cover her shame, she went to church carrying her mother's hymn book and Bible. She knew the numbers of the hymns but sometimes it took too long a time to find them. So she invariably gave up. Many members of the church sang from memory. Most of the songs were childhood favourites with rousing repetitive choruses. Oh, serving God in Jamaica could be a soul-lifting experience. No wonder, the early Africans fell for it and threw away their gods. The gods that demanded inaudible incantations and grunts.

On Sunday, on their leaving the church, Sonia mentally calculated that she was not so bad off. The shack where her mother had been living would make a small sum, when sold. But suppose she was returning to Jamaica at a future date. Suppose the government should say 'All blacks go home', what then would she and her family do? Where then would they stay?

'Me love it here, you know. Church clothes on Sundays, the sunshine. Me love it, man.'

Roza stopped in her tracks. She was a beautiful plump

woman. Her skin which used to be as tight and shiny as that of yellow apples was beginning to get dry in places. She had a beautiful shape too, for her dresses were always pushed back with her high African behind and the top of her was ramrod straight. She was wearing a light yellow dress with white spots. The short sleeves and neckline were edged with white bias binding. Though the dress looked tired and over-washed, yet one could see that it had been carefully starched so that its crispness glowed. She had on a white beret and was carrying the matching white handbag that Sonia had brought her from England. She stepped back, her hands on her hips with her plump shapely legs planted wide apart as if to have a good look at Sonia.

Roza looked her up and down, as if she had just seen her for the first time. She took in her straw hat with net, her white lacy gloves, her stiff taffeta dress, and stared at her matching shoes with a fashionable buckle, and said, 'You say wharr, Sonia? What you say, 'oman? You gone ma – '

Then she suddenly stopped, remembering her friend's recent illness.

Sonia did not miss Roza's dramatic stop. She did not under-stand why she could not say anything without its being interpreted as a sign of madness, simply because she had a mild attack of hysteria on reaching Jamaica, when she real-ized her mother had actually died. But why did Mr Aliyu and Winston play her such a bad trick, hiding the truth from her? Why did they let her buy all those medicines? She had had to pay extra in order to bring the cartons into Jamaica. Making her buy medicine for someone who had actually died. Nasty, wicked joke. But she was well now. That mental illness is one of those mishaps many people wrongly think the sufferers never recover from, was new to Sonia.

But that was not what Roza meant. She was saying 'You gone mad, woman,' as she would have said to anybody. What stopped her was the fact that Sonia to her had actually been mad, and that her question did not make sense. Roza opened her mouth to explain, but she could not make it that easy. She allowed a long silence to follow during which the sounds of the grating of their shoes on the pebbles sounded so loud, almost like a mini-earthquake. Then she plucked up courage and said what she had wanted to say at the beginning. 'Nothing dey here for you to love. Only wuk, wuk, and wait your reward in heaven as the Pastor done just say.'

'Not bad here, Roza,' Sonia repeated, more to assure herself than Roza.

'Specially now you get money to spend. When your man stops sending you money, you come hate this place. Nutting happens here, nutting.'

'He no send me money, you know. Ah still have some of we padner money, na one whole year padner, you know. So him no send money yet. Ah fit sell the honey farm though.'

Roza reached her shack first. She then said to Sonia all of a sudden, 'You hear from Winston? You write to him. You going back, you know. Must go back. Your pikneys dem, what of dem? Must go back.'

Roza knew she could not write much. They grew up together. Sonia felt betrayed somehow. Anyhow, how was she to write Winston? Some friend!

Sonia felt sad. The song 'Count your blessings one by one', which they had sung as the offertory hymn and which she had thought of humming when alone, died in her chest. Roza suddenly made her feel as if she had no blessings to count one by one. Well, maybe she must go back. Back to London with its rain. London with its grey skies. London with its green trees and concrete pavements. London where she could make money looking after other people's children, where she could sew endless clothes for her family. For relaxation, she and Winston made love when the children were asleep. London where her family and their friends were. How long had she been away? How long had she been ill? A year or two? 'God died for the truth, time done fly like crazy bats with wings.' But why Winston no write?

But Winston too could not write, for the same reason that she could not communicate with her family. They were both isolated in their illiteracy. A problem that never bothered her before loomed so large. Her children must learn to read and write. She must go back home. Home? Where – London? Home is where the people she loved lived. Her Mammy's gone, and her Fa too. But Ronald, Marcus, Cheryl baby, Gwendolen and Winston were all there in London. So what she doing here for so long? Yeah, Roza right, think me crazy.

If she could write, she would have written her friend Mrs Odowis to find out how her family were. She could have communicated her doubts to her. Suddenly she realized that though Mrs Odowis came from Africa, and she from Jamaica, they had more in common. She could no longer relate to Roza the way she used to before she left for London all those years ago. Roza could only talk of the London of her dreams, but she knew the reality that was her London. She would go back, of that there was no doubt. This had been a long holiday of self-discovery. She had changed. The sunshine and easy-goingness were no longer her priorities. Those were across the sea.

The money she would get from selling her mother's shack. The shack in which she was 'birthed', in which her Fa gone out to his death, in which Gwendolen was born and her mother Naomi had died, would have to be sold. The money from the sale would pay her fares back to London. She remembered the prayers her mother had said for her when she was leaving for England. 'Go to England dem, and make money and return quick.'

Sonia's ghostly laughter disturbed a rat under the bamboo bed on which she was lying. Suddenly, the night became endless.

12

Emmanuel

People say that 'Every day is not Christmas.' Even happy people have their moody days. Dogs and mentally ill people are said to be affected by the moon. Mr Ilochina had long noticed these changes in his friend, Winston. The two men got on very well. They both worked hard to feed their families, but sometimes Ilochina noticed that his taciturn friend became even more quiet. He would go about his work slowly and methodically without acknowledging anyone's presence. If Ilochina tried to probe him with his usual banter, Winston Brillianton would turn those deep, black, set eyes on him and he would shrink into deeper silence. And if Ilochina had disregarded the dismissive behaviour and probed further none the less, Winston would have said, 'Loo . . . loo . . . look, eberyday not Christmas, you know.'

But of recent, the silence was becoming too long and the sighs of his friend too deep. Ilochina was getting tired of waiting for Winston to get over whatever it was that was bothering him and be his usual self again.

One day, they sat astride a pile of foam, discarded from a derelict house, for their lunch break. Winston started to roll and unroll a cigarette paper.

'I don't know you've started smoking,' Ilochina said tentatively.

'Ah s . . . moke at 'ome in Jamaica, you know. 'Cause Ah work in a cemetery, Ca . . . Calvary Cemetery, and to walk home . . . Ah go thru White Road. You . . . you get White Road in Africa? You have cemetery dere? You know wharr Ah mean, cemetery wharr dem tro way dead bodies?'

Winston was ready to talk. Ilochina's legal mind was re-awakening. Something terrible, almost too terrible to give name, was worrying his friend of many years. He hoped he would be of help. He had pulled all the strings in the book to make the council give him a four-bedroom flat. The authorities wanted to put the Brillianton family in a hotel, but thank goodness, they claimed they could not understand Winston's English. Ilochina's persistence and Winston's bulky presence did intimidate the bureaucrats. They hurriedly put them in an 'emergency flat' in another part of Camden, but Winston was delighted. The boys had a room, Cheryl one, one for Winston and Sonia, and there was one extra which Gwendolen quickly claimed. Winston was so happy about their fortune that many a time he was tempted to ask his friend to help him write a letter to Sonia to tell her of the family's good luck. But not after the humiliation from Mr Aliyu. Yet all that was over months ago.

'You know in Africa, men have several wives,' Winston began.

'I have two wives, remember, and I live in Britain.'

'Yeah, yeah, me know. But do you marry your daughters?'

Ilochina was a bulky man too. He used his bulk to slow down his work, whenever he wanted to. But Winston's question shot him up like a bolt. He tried to talk but his mouth went dry. Winston was the one who collected himself quickly enough to ask, 'You all right?'

'Yes, I'm fine. What did you ask again?'

'Oh, Ah forget,' Mr Brillianton said quickly.

Ilochina was offended. What have those culture killers done to a nice brother like this? First he had asked him several embarrassing questions, whether they lived in houses or trees, now he wanted to know whether they had cemeteries or ate their dead relatives. But all that he could ignore. But to ask if a father could marry his own daughter! That really beat the band. A daughter belonged to the father, her bride

142

price was his. If the daughter was chaste, it would enhance her father's position and make him richer. So why should a father wish to ruin his own wealth?

Then he remembered a moonlight story which his mother told him when he was a boy. The man in the story had committed an incest with his daughter and, according to the culture of the land, the women of the village executed the man. And if the man had not been caught, he would have been killed by thunder. And when the women took hold of his penis and were about to chop it off, he burst into a song of agony: 'Na me born am, na me fuc am, na me giam belleoooo. Please forgive me, na me ting did it ooo.' But the women were merciless, because it was a sin against the Earth. They pounded him into a pulp with their cooking utensils. Every woman in the village was expected to give at least seven blows with her odo handle. It was so terrible that such stories remained what they were, stories and legends. But to hear a full-grown man actually saying it, made his whole body shiver. What had slavery done to a nice brother like this? His heart cried again.

He intensified his gaze on Winston. And Winston shifted uneasily. Ilochina's gaze started to ask many questions. And he could see that Winston was not going to say a word. So he told his friend the story. He explained to him that through the moonlight stories, he learned of the sins that were against the 'Earth'. He told him the meaning of the 'Earth'. That the land is the soul and life-blood of a community. That the land never belonged to an individual. That from the land we are nourished. That when we die we go back to the land to manure it, in order to feed the next generation. That so our 'Chi' or souls go in circles. That to offend the land or Earth was to offend something greater than one's soul. And a father who had any sexual urge towards his daughter had offended the Earth. Ilochina thought he saw Winston shrink into a smaller size.

And surprisingly without a stammer, Winston asked, 'And

if dem no catch the fader and the fader pay no mind about the bride price?'

'He would be discovered because the daughter would talk to the women. Daughters are very close to their mothers in our land. If he is not discovered, he will surely be killed by an Earth force like thunder, you know, natural electricity, drowning, just an Earth force. Natural disaster or what we say, in legal terms, the "acts of God".'

'Aw,' Winston said in a distant voice.

Gwendolen was so playful. She would walk about the house with her flimsy gymslip on and when amused she would lift her leg up and laugh out loud, like a woman teasing a lover. And she was sixteen. Her young bosom taunted him. What could he do? He was not drunk. He just went in to her, hoping she would fight him off like any other woman. Because she was like any other woman to him. She was almost grown before she came back into his life. He tried to equate this young and vibrant person with the baby he kissed goodbye years back in Jamaica, but could not. Cheryl was his biological and social daughter. But somehow, Gwendolen was only a biological one and he never really felt socially responsible for her. She looked so much like her mother, the bow legs, the bias gait, leaning to one side of her. She was like another person, yet the type of woman he favoured, small, vulnerable, just like his Sonia. And like this other woman he expected her to fight him off. After all women were expected to do that – ward men off. He was not prepared for the look of resignation on Gwendolen's face. He remembered vaguely that when he was overcome by desire he had begged her to give him herself, because he was her Daddy, and if she loved him she would not deny him the little favour. He did not expect Gwendolen to believe him. Men say all kinds of nonsense when roused. No woman with her head rightly screwed on believed such rubbish. But Gwendolen did. The girl was stupid.

But Gwendolen remembered Uncle Johnny. He had said to her, 'Every gal done done it. Dat's why they're girls.' She remembered too that you got into trouble with the old women, if you should tell them. But she wished her father would not ask her to do this. She could not scream, because though he begged, he covered her mouth with that strong hand of his. It was soon over. What she did not expect was her father's reaction. Yes, she fought timidly, but she was not a novice. She had been taught what to do. In this project she was already adept, much much older than her age.

'You allow men to do this to you before, June-June?' the enraged father cried. He thought he was going to be the first. What a disappointment.

'Yes, Daddy, many times in Granville. Many, many times. Almost every night for years.' Gwendolen was growing very fast. She too was learning to shock. She was not going to allow the world to blame her for the second time. No need to tell a lie now. Her Daddy might as well know all. After all, he was her Daddy.

'Shut up, shut up, me say. You bitch. Why you no say so before? You for stay in Jamaica. B . . . bitch. You allow men to trouble you and you no tell me or your Mammy. You wicked gal. Devil gal. Wicked.'

And he allowed his anger to overcome him. And he started shouting at her. Gwendolen became frightened. Cries of fear escaped from her mouth, and Ronald woke, and Cheryl started to howl, and Winston blindly rushed into his room. He shouted to the other children to go to sleep because June-June was having a nightmare.

The following day was a Sunday. It took her a long time to get ready for church. When her father Winston started to preach about the sins of the world, she wondered if her father did not know that what he did to her last night was a grave sin. She looked at him as if in a daze. Something was telling her that this man, though her father whom she loved dearly,

145

was not going to get away with it. The pain was too deep to surface. Uncle Johnny was a stupid old man. But what of her lovely Daddy? To her, he was dead now. This one preaching was his shell, not the real one any more. Where would she find the friend to talk to? To Jesus? He was so far away. Gwendolen went back to the shell she had built around herself against the adults in Granville. She had been out of it the day her Daddy came to pick her up at the airport and she had given him her hand to lead her to the future. Now she had to go back into it.

On Monday, she missed school. What was the point? Her father was normally not violent. He stammered a lot, but his solid silence was intimidating as well as protective. Now he seemed to be creeping about in his house. She saw, too, that he had lost the right to tell her what to do. She noted the helplessness of this walking shell, but was not quite sure how she was going to deal with it. The damage had been done. No going back. So whenever this shell padded into her room at night, when the boys were asleep, she would not make a sound. She would just lie there very still, suffering his anger and guilt.

She was a wicked girl, he had said so himself. Uncle Johnny had messed her up: a fact she thought she was going to keep from her parents for ever, since it would cause them pain. Now that her father had known and had condemned her, he had become somebody else too. And for this somebody else, she had to lie very still, because she had no solid and protective Daddy to shield her any more. Also, no one was going to know about it. Oh, what was her mother doing in Jamaica all this time anyhow?

Yeah, the school did write a half-hearted letter asking where she was, but she ignored them. They never did understand her anyhow. She was not learning anything, only wasting time putting on a ridiculous purple uniform and going there and sitting around doing nothing. Anyway, there

146

was so much to do at home, clothes to wash, dinner to get, chores that would be waiting for her, school or no school. She might as well stay at home. But she made sure her brothers and Cheryl never missed school. And strange enough, they obeyed her. She felt like their little Mammy.

Gwendolen had heard enough about pregnancy and childbirth – the only lesson that made sense to her at school – to know that she was pregnant. She did not tell Winston. He was so distant and silent these days that one could have mistaken him for a man who had lost the use of his tongue. And his silence made Gwendolen more and more guilty. She felt like a child who kept on stealing money from her mother's purse, but knew that one day, just one day, she would be caught. Even the loud laughter and thigh-lifting he used to do when happy disappeared. Sometimes she felt like going to him in broad daylight and assuring him that all would be right. But would it be all right in the end? She did not know. So her feelings see-sawed. One minute she would be in deep despair, her heart pounding, especially when she looked out of their window and saw girls from her school walking down the road. Other times she would be so happy and became almost obsessional about the way she looked. She saved enough money from the housekeeping allowance to buy loads of cheap make-up.

And those old women started to look at her in a curious way. Sister Esmee did not stop at looking, she went further. She started to ask questions.

'Gwendolen, you go to school so?'

'Yeah, Sister, I go to school.'

'Gwendolen, you get a boy-friend?'

What type of silly question for a sister in Christ to ask anyone. Gwen jutted her chin forward, her nose in the air, and did not bother to answer Sister Esmee. That sister was too much of a Nosy Parker anyhow. Then Gwen heard her say with a kind of roughness in her voice, 'Brother Winston, we wan' taak to you.'

Gwendolen's heart sank. She swallowed hard. Her feet wobbled. With the corner of her eyes, she could see the two adults talking. Her Daddy was looking furtively at her. Normally they waited for their father after church to say all his hallos and how-do-you-dos to all their friends. But today, one look at Esmee and her Daddy told her that they suspected what she had known for almost three months, but had refused to give name. She decided to go home alone. Their new flat was within walking distance anyway. Her heart started to pound again. What would happen now? She had pushed the thought of it all to the back of her mind, hoping that something would happen to solve the problem for her. She'd never heard of any girl who was made pregnant by her father before. The teachers did talk to them about sex at school, and many a time she and her friends made jokes about it. But the subject of what to do if your father made you pregnant was never discussed.

When Winston returned from the church, he looked drained. Now she knew. If those ladies, Esmee and the rest of them, were not sure of her pregnancy, they must have asked her father some close and embarrassing questions. He said nothing to her, and she said nothing either. But he stopped padding into her room at night. Many a time, she caught him watching her with the corner of his eyes. As there was nothing she could do about it, she just lived from day to day.

She stopped going to church and would hide every time Mrs Odowis came to see how they were. Mrs Odowis did not come often, because she was busy with her family. But even though she was close to the Brilliantons, Gwendolen did not have enough courage to tell her. She had this fear that not only would they all blame her, but that her father could be jailed. This country was strange.

She had the whole day to shop for their bread, potatoes and tripe which she would later make into a stew. Their new garden had a sun-porch and she liked to stand there enjoying the mild spring sunshine after doing the house chores, waiting for her brothers and sister. Without knowing it, she was beginning to feel like and innocently to enjoy the role of a housewife.

Suddenly, she noticed that this boy from the other side of the estate started saying hallo to her. She said hallo back. Then one morning, he asked abruptly, 'What's your name anyway?'

Gwendolen felt that that was not a nice way to ask people their name and said so. But she did not ask him his. So instead of saying that he was sorry, he said, 'My name is Emmanuel.' He did not even stop there. For like Sister Esmee, he went on to enquire, 'Aren't you supposed to be at school, anyway?'

'I don't like school,' Gwendolen said without any hesitation. She had heard that statement made often enough by many of her class-mates. 'I don't like school', a statement that would not have made sense in Jamaica. For what was there to like about school anyway? You just went there to learn a lot of meaningless jumble, which you would spend the rest of your life putting in meaningful order again. She was enjoying her freedom, she implied to Emmanuel.

'What do your parents say?'

'Mum is in Jamaica, and Daddy does not care one way or the other.'

'I bet your Daddy does not know you are bunking off school.'

'So what are you then, a police officer? You're not too old for school as well.'

Emmanuel laughed, displaying the braces in his teeth. 'I went to school faithfully, never bunked off. My father wanted me to be a doctor. He told all his friends that I was going

149

to be a clever doctor, but though I went to school and did everything the teachers said, I never became a doctor. So Dad is mad at me all the time. So I stopped school and he became madder. What is your Mum doing in Jamaica then?'

Gwendolen could not answer because for the first time in her life, she'd found somebody who could put into words some of the things she was feeling. She was laughing so much that tears came into her eyes.

'So what do you do apart from avoiding your Daddy?'

'Oh, I go to Youth Opportunity.'

'Youth Opportunity, what's that?'

Emmanuel laughed now. 'Don't you know what Youth Opportunity means? Coo . . . they ram it down your throat in our school. Everybody knows what it means. Even my mother, well, stepmother, knows all about it. She can't wait to get me out of the house. Since I left school, it's been nag, nag, nag . . .'

'What do you do there? Will they take me or is it for boys only? Oh, yeah, I forgot, I won't be able to go, I'm too busy cooking and washing.'

Emmanuel had thick brown brows. He knitted them together, and at the same time clasped his palms as if in prayer. He looked really silly like that, but what he was doing, was thinking. He did not think that what Gwendolen had just said was right somehow. But then Gwendolen was of West Indian parents and maybe that made it right. He cleared his knitted brow, unclasped his hands and tried very much to be polite and not too inquisitive. 'Do you want to know my name?'

'Unless you have other name besides Emmanuel. You told me before, remember.'

'Oh I forgot.'

'You forget so easily. You're mad.'

They both started to laugh again.

'Look', Emmanuel said, with a little hesitation. He knew

150

how strict West Indian dads could be, but he would try anyway. 'Would your Dad mind if we go out one night?'

Gwendolen started to laugh afresh. 'Go out to do what?'

'Hmmm, for a drink.'

'Aw, I'll ask. If he says yes, I'll tell you tomorrow. Must dash in now. Otherwise I'll stand here laughing all morning and not clean the house.'

Gwendolen was taken aback by her father's jubilation. He started to stammer so rapidly that she could not make out what he was saying for a while. His happiness was so infectious that she laughed with him too. Something that had not happened in months. He kept saying, 'June-June, you got yourself a man nuh, you big 'oman nuh.' He repeated this so many times that even Ronald started calling Emmanuel Gwendolen's sweetheart even though they had not been out together.

Amanda and the other girls had told her how strict their parents were. That much she knew. But she was lucky, she thought. Her nice Daddy did not mind.

Emmanuel was surprised too. But he was not complaining. He had thought taking a young black girl out would be extremely difficult. This was a change for him. Life was becoming really impossible, so much so that many a time he felt suicidal. He was learning carpentry at the Youth Opportunity. He liked it very much. He enjoyed creating things, not just with wood but with other materials like paint and paper, but carpentry was near enough for the time being. He knew he had disappointed his father. But then the more he tried to be academic, the more he slipped lower down.

Before his stepmother returned from her office cleaning job, Emmanuel had washed himself and put on his new jacket, which he bought from a woman at the Youth Opportunity place. The woman had a catalogue, and she was learning how to start a business. So her persuading most of the students to buy from her was a good practical exercise.

151

Gwendolen was waiting for him in her church dress and coat.

'You going nuh?' Winston asked.

'Uh-huh,' Gwendolen replied proudly.

Winston smiled. 'Ha . . . have a goo' time, gal,' he stammered. Those church women would soon learn that Gwendolen had got herself a boy-friend. This, please God, would cover his shame. And Gwendolen was not the type of girl to speak up against her Daddy.

Emmanuel, for no reason at all, kept asking her what her mother was doing in Jamaica. When Gwendolen told him that she went because of her sick mother, who had now died, he then remarked, 'I bet if your mother was here, she would refuse me taking you out.'

'Why would she do that?'

'Well, I have not known you long and I'm white.'

'Yeah, but she might not, because you're only Greek.'

'Yeah, but I'm white and you're black, and your parents may not like it.'

'My Daddy did.'

'I notice that. Strange though, but I like it. Don't you?'

Gwendolen beamed. She'd never been out with anyone before, white, blue or pink. Colour was not her problem. She was out to enjoy herself in her best dress and with a nice friendly boy.

They took a bus and went to the other side of Camden near Regent's Park. They walked half the park in the darkening evening, and Emmanuel showed Gwendolen where the zoo was. 'Only it's too late now, we can't go in. One day, we'll come during the daytime.' Then when they were tired of walking they went into a pub.

'How old are you?' the man behind the counter wanted to know. Emmanuel did not like being asked his age in the presence of all these people drinking and in such a loud voice.

'All right, all right, I'm not deaf. I'm twenty,' he lied.

152

'And that bit with you?'

'She's not a bit, she's my girl and she's em . . . em . . . eighteen.'

Gwendolen was overdressed with ribbons and bows and schoolgirl's shoes. Emmanuel knew he felt like calling her Cindy doll when he first saw her in all her finery, but refrained from saying anything. The landlord said he was not sure, so he refused to serve them.

Emmanuel really decided to impress Gwendolen. 'This is racial prejudice, just because my girl is black,' he cried in righteous anger. 'What of her individual rights?'

'It has nothing to do with her colour. I don't care what colour she is and you for that matter. You're not from the House of Windsor with all your whiteness. I'm just not serving you both alcohol. So get out!'

Gwendolen, who had never had time to enjoy the excitement of annoying adults this way, found the whole thing hilarious. She could not stop laughing. She did not care whether they had beer or orange juice, making all this palaver over nothing was fun.

'If you don't do as you're told, I'll get the police,' the landlord threatened.

Emmanuel froze, but his watchful eye followed the man as he picked up the telephone. Then he said disappointedly, 'Let's go, Gwen.'

Outside, he beamed and said, 'That was nice, wasn't it?'

'Yeah, and you know so many big words. Prejudice and individual – what's individual rights? Hmm, you must have learned a lot from your school, white Greek boy.'

'No I never!' Emmanuel almost exploded. 'That school never taught me nothing. I learned those words from reading the newspapers.'

'Yeah? You read the papers? I don't believe you.' Though Gwendolen's voice was teasing, she was proud to be going out with a boy who read the papers and who could recall the big words he'd read as well. Curiosity palpitated her heart, but she suppressed it. Maybe one day, she too would learn to read the papers. If only she had had a teacher to teach her privately how to read, and not be sent down in disgrace almost, to that horrible 'remedial class', telling everybody how dumb you were. She would learn, one day. She would.

'I read them from front to back.' Emmanuel's voice proudly cut into her thoughts. He was now boasting. 'I don't buy them. People leave them in buses and trains, and I pick them up, the clean ones mind you. Then I read them over and over until I get another one. One day, I am going to know how to use so many big words and that would make me into a politician.'

'What is a politician? What do politicians do? Are they like the police? Hmmmm, po-li-ti-cian. Sounds like policeman. Are they the same word?'

Emmanuel laughed so heartily that Gwendolen joined too, though she did not know what he was laughing at. But looking at his face go red with amusement, and those funny braces on his teeth, was enough to set Gwendolen off.

'Gwendolen, you're crazy.'

'I know, and so are you.'

'I know that too. My mother, well, stepmother, says that to me every day.'

Off Parkway, Emmanuel told Gwendolen to wait outside, whilst he went into an off-licence to buy a bottle of cider for Gwendolen and two pints of lager for himself. He did not know which of the two had more alcohol. All he knew was that a girl should drink from a bottle and a man from a can. Gwendolen did not know the difference; she simply enjoyed the sweetness of the cider.

They sheltered at the tube station in Camden Town and went drinking and making rude remarks about anybody who happened to stare at them. A police car roared past and Emmanuel hiccoughed and said, 'I don't like police cars.'

154

'Me neither. I don't like any policeman. I hope you don't become one when you learn all those big words.'

'You're daft. Politician is different from policeman.' He hiccoughed again. 'Let's go to your place. Will your father mind?'

'He's asleep maybe.' She laughed.

Gwendolen had no idea how Winston would behave. She did not know how this lovely evening would end. But there was nothing bad in trying.

Her guess was right. Her Daddy was asleep on his favourite fireside chair with the television on. She and Emmanuel walked on tiptoes into her own room.

When there, they at first simply started to giggle. They felt triumphant, in having cheated the adult world all evening.

Gwendolen had seen sex scenes on television. She used to wonder why people seemed to like it. From her limited experience, sex was a humiliation in which women had to give in to their men just to make them happy. Her stay in England had taught her she could refuse. With her Daddy she was too stunned to say a word. Emmanuel was different. With him it was a play. It was an escape from reality. She pushed to the very back of her mind the knowledge of her pregnancy. They played, they fondled. And the fact that they were mildly drunk made things easier still, but Gwendolen knew what she was doing. Emmanuel was not that drunk either. They both knew what they were doing.

Soon her condition would be obvious. She might as well have a little pleasure – the type she'd seen actresses enjoy on television in bedroom scenes. Emmanuel was light, he was young. Emmanuel was fun.

'I've really never done this before . . . well, not to this extent,' he said hoarsely, searching for her face in the dark night.

'My head is cold. I must cover my hair, otherwise it will be ruined and it takes ages to curl,' Gwendolen murmured to prevent him from asking her intimate questions. She might be tempted to speak the truth.

'Oh sorry,' Emmanuel said, jumping up. 'What do you cover it with, a hat? Where is it?'

Gwendolen pointed to it and Emmanuel brought the woollen hat Granny Naomi gave her years ago. It had now expanded to double its original size, but Gwendolen had kept it fluffy and clean and used it as a comforter every night. It kept her ears warm.

'Do you think I'm good?'

'Wharr . . . oh my Lawd, white boy. You very good. You perfect. You're loving.' Gwendolen was almost sobbing now.

She would have liked them to go on like this, just living like this. And to send to hell all worries about education, about race, you brown, you white and me black; and to say 'so what' about her pregnancy. Why should life not be this simple!

She jolted herself back to reality when she saw Emmanuel peering at her. Tears were running from her eyes now.

'Please don't cry, Gwendolen. I didn't mean to . . . well, next time I'll buy a condom. I didn't know the evening would end like this. Honest, Gwen, I didn't mean to . . .'

She put her fingers over his lips.

'So many tings you no understand, white boy.'

'Stop calling me white boy! How would you like it if I call you black girl?'

Gwendolen giggled through her tears, and they clung to each other once more. Just like two kids drowning and who had to cling to each other to keep themselves afloat. Once more, now without any regret, they allowed themselves to float into the realms of fantasy.

At length, Emmanuel could see the early light of a new day peeping through the thin curtain. He got dressed quietly and slipped out of the house. So quietly, that when Gwendolen woke up, she thought at first that she had dreamed it all. But the chocolate bar which they had intended eating later was still there and so were the tissue papers Emmanuel scattered on the floor in his excitement.

So it was real, this type of life. So it was possible. So, one could really care for another person.

Winston was not unaware of what was going on. He heard them when they came in. He did pray for God's forgiveness and thanked him for sending a deliverance in the person of Emmanuel. He consoled himself that Emmanuel looked like a nice boy, who could be a good playmate for his daughter. Fate, he knew, had played him a bad joke in not making Emmanuel a black boy, but a white boy-friend was better for Gwendolen than no boy-friend at all. For all that he was very grateful.

13

Sonia's Return

Reality hit Sonia frontally at London Airport. The immigration officers wanted to know why she was coming back to England after nearly a two-year stay in Jamaica. They were impatient with her fast patois voice. And if they were impatient, Sonia was the soul of patience. She learned this very early from her Mammy! 'No need to vex with the authority dem.' And her personal experience reminded her that anything that had the slightest hint of white authority would be slow but steady. She knew they would eventually let her into England, because she'd lived and worked there for years and her family were there. But she also knew that with her being black and alone, the immigration people would like to have their fun. She 'paid them no mind', after all did she not have all day? She had not told anybody that she was returning. The place was warm and she was not hungry. The officers, noticing her vulnerability, asked her to wait. Sonia waited till all the other passengers from her plane had been seen to.

Wicked snide jokes were made of her. Unfortunately for them, though she was alone, she was completely impervious to their jibes. A female officer pointed out to her that she would catch cold if she kept wearing her stockings without suspenders.

'You should not tie them with a string at the top of your knee. Your skirt is too short and it shows. You see, if you don't mind my saying so, I can't help seeing the string.' Her voice had that condescending candy tone used by the vulgar to address the afflicted.

It never occurred to Sonia to tell her to go to hell and to stay there, or to remind her that her false hairpiece was askew and that it did not match her natural hair. Or that her denture made her look like a grinning skeleton. Such confident observations were left to the likes of her children who were not going to be satisfied with half-measures from the society in which they were born and in whose reshaping they were playing their parts.

Sonia simply said, 'Aw', and they laughed and let her go. She laughed too but it was that uncertain laughter in which one was aware of being the object of fun and yet helpless to do anything about it. One thing such treatment did to Sonia was to make her feel small and stupid; to make her retreat into a greater sense of insecurity.

The officers loved the likes of her, the lower working-class blacks. Life would have been easier if they were all kept that way, in picturesque ignorance from which they could be called upon to display their physical agility in sports or to wail their fate in low haunting melodies, for the amusement of all.

At length their faces relaxed and they smiled at her, sweetly waving exaggeratedly as if to a child of four. Sonia saw it all with the corner of her eyes and she heard their voices sink into a confidential whisper. But she just let it all pass over her like spring water over a duck and went her way. But not before she said in an undertone, 'Stinking Pinky.' She was by then out of earshot and about to board the bus that would take her to Central London.

June in London is a month of roses. Their various shapes, sizes and colours gave Sonia's part of London the look that carnival floats would give to roadways. Their sweet smell filled the air, making it heavy and gaudy. Modest council houses, privately owned three-ups-and-two-downs, and huge five-to-eight-bedroomed houses all had a rose-bush or two in front of their gardens.

160

As Sonia tumbled out of the bus that took her to the front of her house off Stroud Green, the gaudy scent filled her lungs. Even in June the sunshine was pale, the air watery. It was nothing compared to the direct sunshine of Granville where the hibiscus was full-blown and fire-coloured but inadvertently covered with dust.

She dragged her case along the grey pavement noticing the square cement slabs as if for the first time, the trees now full of leaves, the shut windows, the quiet and indifferent streets. Her arms were going limp and she was forced to put her case down. Putting her hands akimbo she remarked under her breath, 'So much done dey change huh?' If she had been a poet, if she could write all her feelings down, she would have at least written Roza about it. But like millions of black women to whom education – the means of communicating their thoughts to another – was denied, her confused and yet exhilarating feelings died in her head. For however glorious an admiration, however noble an idea, if it is not written or communicated and shared with another, it might as well not have been experienced at all. Sonia picked up her heavy case, walked the few paces to her house and lifting the knocker gave a big bang on the door. She had not taken her key with her when she left because the hurry was that much. However, she was home now, and someone was sure to be in.

There was no response to her several knocks. Gradually she was becoming aware of the chilly air in her light white cardigan and white hat. She knocked again and, getting no answer, peeped into the letter box like a child. Yes, she was at the right door. The straight brown stairs were still there and so was the yellow wallpaper with green leaves. The naked light bulb still dangled in utter loneliness in the hallway. She could not see their part of the house, because the stairs curved to the right before opening on to their own landing. Unwittingly, she went down the doorsteps on to the pavement and looked at their window. She smiled. 'June-June change the curtain, and maybe them dey school. Lawd, wish me take me key wid me.'

She saw a silver-haired woman coming up the street and waited to find out the time. 'Three o'clock,' the woman snapped without looking at Sonia. People get so offended here, she thought. Me only asked for de time! Lawd ha' mussy. June-June soon come back. She sat by the steps and waited.

She saw schoolchildren passing. But no Gwendolen, no Ronald and Marcus or even Cheryl. She thought of her Cheryl baby and smiled. She be big girl nuh, a big 'oman at school nuh. Sonia was getting chillier and chillier and knew that she needed a shelter. She could not just go to the next-door neighbour and say, 'Please could I sit until my children return from school?' No, this is Englan' she's arrived. She not in Granville nuh. This is Englan', where eberybody mind dem business.

She must go somewhere though. Her feet ached badly now. But an inexplicable sense of unease was enveloping her. For no reason whatsoever, she started to worry. Where were her family? Reluctantly she dragged her heavy suitcase to Mrs Odowis's flat.

It was one thing pulling a heavy suitcase along the pavement, but when one had to carry it up several flights of stairs to get to a third-floor flat, it was killing. Sonia almost collapsed at Gladys Odowis's door.

Mrs Odowis's little girl Ijeoma opened the door. And instead of inviting her in, she ran back inside excitedly and shouted, 'Mum, Mum, Ronald's Mum is back. She's here. She is standing outside by the door and she has a suitcase with her.'

Gladys Odowis ran out welcoming. 'Ah, Sonia, woman from Jamaica, welcome back. We thought you have forgotten all about us in that sunshine. Welcome. Come in.'

'Lawd Almighty, Mrs Odowis, me tired, man. Me so tired.'

Sonia groaned, feeling the weight of all her thirty-eight years.

'I am not surprised. When did you arrive? Welcome.'

'Since eleben o'clock dis mawning me reach airport.'

No sooner was she seated than Gladys cried, 'Well, have a cup of tea.'

Sonia smiled. The corners of her eyes made little wrinkles. Yeah, back to the cup of tea routine, she thought. And aloud she said, 'Me wait fe me door, but nobody don return from school yet.'

Gladys got out her proper teapot and put two tea-bags in it. She set out the cups and saucers, milk jug and sugar bowl, all on a posh Marks & Spencer's tray. She was trying to impress Sonia. One look at Sonia told Gladys that she had slipped back a little. Her white straw hat was too beautiful and quite unnecessary for that slightly tight dress she was wearing. As as for those stockings . . . Gladys always hated tights and stockings, and she never acquired the habit of wearing them all the time. She found them sticky and uncomfortable. But the few occasions circumstances forced her to wear them she made sure they were worn properly and without any ladders. But Sonia's were badly worn and had laddered in places due to the long journey.

'Sugar?' she asked solicitously.

'Yeah, me take three, you know.'

'I remember, Sonia, and you didn't put on an ounce of weight. I don't know how you do it. You're even slimmer now. I think it is the sunshine at home. It burns all the fat.'

'The food too. Not much frying, not much meat. A lotta boiling.'

The tea was refreshing and so were the Woolworths biscuits.

When Gladys saw that her friend was getting her breath back, she said gently, 'Sonia, I'm sorry about your mother's death. Winston told me. It must have been very upsetting and in the condition in which you were. What happened to the ba – '

The eyes Sonia focused on her were sad eyes. ' 'Im die too, die quick, quick, just like that.' And she flipped her thumb and her middle finger.

'Sorry, Sonia.'

They munched the biscuits in silence for a while, Sonia wondering whether something terrible had happened to her family.

'Winston and the kids, dem all right?'

'Oh yeah, they are fine. I saw them only a week ago. They've all grown. But my husband, the children's father, he's gone back to Nigeria. He's married another woman. They had a white wedding. I saw it in a Nigerian paper.'

'No, Mrs Odowis! But you no divorce him, how 'im marry again?'

'Hmm, our men they don't care. But I am happier now. Free to do anything I like.' Her eyes went to the suitcase Sonia dragged in with her and she remarked, 'Your case is very heavy. We black women, we never travel light. Did you see any African women at the airport? We are like tortoises, we carry all our worldly goods on our backs.'

They both laughed. Again Sonia felt closer to Gladys than she was to Roza. They were like lost children. They had stayed away from their countries of birth too long. It would have been nice if they could feel their beating heart each time the British national anthem was sung. But no, they could not do that either. Because even if they had stayed all their lives here, they would be perpetually marginalized and that would always make them suffer a kind of religious, social and political paralysis.

'You know,' Gladys volunteered, 'you'll have to go home and ask Gwendolen to come and pick up this case. It is too heavy.'

'But dem still dey school.'

Gladys laughed again. 'I have good news for you. Your family have moved into a beautiful council flat, in St Pancras Way, not too far from here. That's why there was no answer to your knocks.'

'When dem move?' Sonia asked aghast. 'Where to? Me no know, you know.' All these questions tumbled out from Sonia's lips. She was almost childlike in her curiosity. 'The house big? Lawd ha' mussy! Nice, eh?'

Gladys wanted to ask if she and her husband never wrote each other. But remembering her position as a husbandless and one-parent family, she kept her mouth shut. That was the trouble of being a one-parent family. You never felt confident enough when confronted with women with husbands even though you knew they were having a rotten time. And when one of them came to visit, you tended to over-entertain, to show that you did not lack much, despite the fact that the family had only one adult instead of two. What would she have done if her husband Tunde had treated her that way? Moved from their address without writing her about it? She would have raised hell. But it would have come to nothing. But Sonia was more excited and surprised than angry. She'd seen her own council flat and knew that the accommodation would be much better than they had when they were living with Mr Aliyu.

'You mean to say Winston gotta council house fe we? De man no 'tupid, you know. 'Im no 'tupid at all,' Sonia cried, shaking her head.

Gladys wanted to ask, 'Aren't you angry with him?' But she restrained herself from doing so. Maybe that is why Sonia is having a perfect marriage. Maybe I am too sensitive. I should have learned to turn a blind eye to such things. If Gladys suspected that the lost contact was due to the couple's inability to write each other, she did not think that was enough reason. But look at what Tunde had done – going home without any provision for her and the kids and

165

marrying another wife. She and Sonia had their crosses to bear. The crosses might be of a different colour of wood, but they were crosses all the same.

Marcus answered the door-bell as Gladys Odowis pressed it on that wet June evening. He let out a scream of joy on seeing his mother. The kids dragged Sonia in. They were hugging and shouting and as for Ronald, he was trying to say so many things at once, that neither Gladys nor Sonia could make him out.

Gwendolen stood by the kitchen door, a wooden ladle in her hand, smiling nervously. Behind her stood a white boy of about eighteen or nineteen, with black hair and a red face, who was abstractedly biting his lips.

'Who dat?' Sonia barked.

'Gwen's sweetheart,' Marcus said laughing.

Sonia's face clouded immediately. The white boy was visibly shrinking.

'Whey your Daddy?'

'Gone to work, Mum,' Gwendolen said weakly.

'Dis time of night? Hmm, that man Winston, 'im done go crazy,' Sonia remarked.

Gladys Odowis said something about her not being too keen on leaving her children alone. So she had to dash. She refused tea and told Gwendolen to come and collect her mother's things in the morning.

'I'll go in the morning,' Ronald announced enthusiastically.

Gladys looked at him and smiled. How fast kids grow, she noted mentally.

When she said, 'Good night all,' and closed the door, it sounded as if she was cutting through a thick and suffocating air. Presently, she was in the streets with her thoughts.

Gosh, that girl Gwendolen! Her skin looked so fair and her bosom so full. How our girls grow so fast in this chilly country. But could the tightness of that skin be all due to growth? God have pity on us. I hope rainclouds are not gathering in Sonia's

166

family. What a trick of Providence! Sonia did not deserve this. Was that why Gwendolen was always in the bath whenever she called? And where did Winston go this time of night, leaving that white boy there? Some fathers! Gladys allowed her imagination to have its full sway.

A car hooted past her. A huge tree in the middle of the sidewalk had its roots joining its trunk like legs twisted in agony. It was June, yet a biting wind told her she could expect no mercy from the darkening summer evening.

Providence was unfair and had dealt Sonia a double blow. Could she have done anything to prevent it? No, nothing. This heavy blow was unjust and savage!

The clarity of the bell ringing from Christ Church on the hill told her she was near her home. Her thoughts were that abstracted. Poor, poor Sonia.

14

Institutionalized

The social worker was puzzled. She was a trained worker, one of those half-castes who used every available cosmetic to emphasize their whiteness. Her mother was from Trench Town and her father white. She did not say white from where. Having established her whiteness, she went into a beautiful studied Jamaican accent. This was the part that was called for in this case. She spoke the patois so well, because she had been 'home' so many times, she told the gaping Brilliantons.

Gwendolen was somehow not deceived. She had mixed through school into this society more than her parents and had learned from Amanda and the other 'Yellow Niggers' what it was like to fake black when the occasion called. What was bad in their just being themselves instead of being white one day and black the other? Anyway she would not trust this one, not one bit. She was too beautiful and too artificial.

The social worker wanted to know how come Winston allowed a white boy to sleep with his daughter inside their house. But nobody was giving her any sensible answer.

'Na lie, me tell you. A lie,' Sonia screamed. 'Dat gal, roll 'im waist so, see me nuh, see me nuh.' She went on to demonstrate. 'Na man 'im want. Me go back home for me mudder, two minutes, she hitch up with a dirty white.'

Sonia's actions were fierce. One could easily have confused her anger with hatred. Could a mother hate her daughter? Impossible. She carried her for nine whole months, after all. Had a mother any right to suspect her daughter? Unimaginable. Not even when the daughter had become a separate person for over fifteen years. Good mothers were not permitted to think that way. So, since it was not morally right to voice what she feared, Sonia sheltered behind bad language, exaggerated actions and uncontrollable anger.

The young social worker, who could not see beyond the facts presented her, asked, 'But wait, Mrs Brillianton, does Gwendolen roll her waist inside or outside the house?'

'She done roll it in 'ere, me tell you. Me no know for who. But she did it 'ere. So imagine what she done do outside to bring that poor white boy in 'ere. Me no wan' she in dis 'ouse. Tink of the church huh? We good Christians, you know. Me 'usband a preacher too.'

The social worker looked at Winston Brillianton, who sat, with feet wide apart, in his deep grey trousers. His dark brown eyes sank deeper into his head, his skin shining from good health, but his looks were neither here nor there. He opened his two hands and closed them again – a gesture he was wont to use when preaching. He was very uneasy and all could see that he would rather the earth open up and swallow him. 'What do you think of all this, Mr Brillianton?' the social worker asked.

For one split moment, he felt like jumping up and chanting the obscene song Ilochina told him the man in his African moonlight story sang when confronted with a similar situation. No, he would not do that. Gwendolen had not said anything against him. That closeness between African mother and daughter had been lost during the slave passage. So Gwendolen had said nothing to her mother. He could see that. ' 'Oman, me no know. Ah no fit say nutting.'

'The man go a work, me tell you. How he for know wharr happened, when he go a work?' Sonia screamed again.

Gwendolen refused to say a word. She just stood there by the door, whimpering from fear of what her mother would do to her in her present mood. What was she to say? From where was she to start? She peered closely at the social

170

worker and suspected that the woman would march her father to prison if she hinted to her what actually happened. Emmanuel was the only friend she'd made in recent months, now this would ruin everything. But she was determined to let him know the truth as soon as things quietened a little. This was not the right time.

Sonia had rushed to Emmanuel's house to tell his father that his son had made Gwendolen pregnant. The father simply called his son and told him to move out of his house. If he was old enough to sleep with a girl and make her pregnant, then he was old enough to maintain her. He was a good Greek and the less said about it the better. He was a busy man with other children to look after.

Emmanuel looked at Gwendolen and just wondered how he could have made her pregnant in such a short time. But then he remembered from the biology lessons at school that it could happen easily, even the very first time. Well, he had never made a girl pregnant before, so he could not say with authority. Astonishment spread over his face and he kept saying inside himself, 'Me a father, me a father?'

Gwendolen kept telling herself that it was not right. She was pregnant before Emmanuel came into her life. She breathed in, and just as she was about to shout and say, 'Me Daddy gave me the baby,' her eyes caught her father's, deep-set inside his head as if they were about to disappear inside his very skull. But though those eyes were sunk into his black face surround, there was a pleading glint that stood out reminding Gwendolen of the eyes of black cats at night. That glint seemed strong and capable of knowing what she was thinking. She knew that if she spoke out now, her Daddy would suffer more. Emmanuel somehow became stronger and was shouting back at his father. He was free to do what he liked. He made that perfectly clear to his father. But the adults were busy squabbling and had not given them time to sit and talk.

171

Gwendolen looked at her mother. Sonia was blacker with anger against her and, she suspected, against her Daddy for not condemning her in the presence of all these people. Gwendolen knew her mother by now and knew that she was one of those women who would do anything to have a man by their side. And she would not have enough courage to accuse her husband in public. The social worker should be able to guess when her mother was saying that she was shaking her waist whenever she walked, even in her own home. All these adults probably were suspecting in the corner of their hearts what they thought could have happened, but were too scared to even ask her. But then Emmanuel was using this opportunity to hurt his father more. He did not make it to medical school and he had now added salt to the injury by making a girl from a council estate pregnant, and a black girl for that matter, him being such a good Greek. And her mother saying that she was the daughter of such a good preacher.

Then Gwendolen's mind went back to Granville. To that time when she was a child and had told the truth to Granny Naomi. People had blamed Uncle Johnny but she would never forget the hatred that followed. Granny Naomi first hated her for not telling at the time, and then for driving an old and very helpful friend away. If she had shouted in time, she would have scared Uncle Johnny away. There was no need taking him to court, he was an old family friend. But he stopped coming to their shack and no longer helped Granny Naomi on her bee farm. They became poorer as a result and Granny never allowed her to forget that. And to cap it all, people started to stare at her whenever they saw her pass. Some good mothers always called their daughters in whenever they saw her playing with them. Only Shivorn was faithful because her Mammy and Sonia grew up together in the same road. Could she go through all that again here in England, and here where they say they could put a man away for doing it to his own daughter? No, I won't let them put my Daddy away.

Unable to stand the argument any longer, Gwendolen ran into her room and banged the door shut.

'You see what Ah mean,' Sonia cried. 'She no care, no care at aal. Na man she wan'.' Glaring at Emmanuel she said flatly, 'You have to take 'er away. You have to marry 'er. Me fed up.'

'Eh, nobody is talking of marriage here. She's your daughter after all. Why do you want to send her away so soon?' Emmanuel's father protested half-heartedly. He might not have approved of his son's behaviour, but he could not imagine a black girl like Gwendolen as a daughter-in-law.

'Den you teach your son not to go about bloating innocent schoolgirls,' Sonia spat in her perfect London English.

Gwendolen blocked her ears and cried with her mouth shut. What was she to do? She did not need an outsider to tell her that the woman standing there meant law and authority. She was not that dim not to know from her experiences at school that black people were not particularly sought after. Marriage? She'd never given that a thought but it would be nice to have a home of her own away from her Mammy and Daddy. Good Lord, what was she to do?

Dry-eyed, she listened intently to the voices of the adults talking in the room down the corridor. She heard Emmanuel's father's voice still raised, then she heard her Daddy's voice swearing by the Bible to his daughter's innocence. She smiled wryly. Daddy can talk when I am not there. Outside a bus swooshed past and then a white laundry van. It was a damp evening and the leaves on the trees were green and hung low, letting water drip down.

She must have slept. She woke and the streets were quieter. Her parents were still talking. Then they stopped. Her mother was murmuring now. Her parents were making love. Her

173

Daddy was grunting on her mother as he used to on her in this very room and on this very bed. Her mind reeled. Too much to carry – too much, too much. She stuffed her ears and felt betrayed. Another car swooshed past. Gwendolen slipped her feet into her brown, still wearable school shoes and went out. It was a humid summer night with rainclouds. The air was almost pure, fresh and wet. The gentle wind fanned her from all sides. But she kept walking. She did not know where she was going. All she knew was that she left home around two in the early morning, and she had to keep on walking in her school raincoat. She was walking against the traffic, and thinking of everything and of nothing. Just walking to the end of nowhere.

The sun came out and she knew it was morning. She did not know where she was and did not care. She could not tell whether she wanted to die or not. One thing was sure, she was not going to let that woman take her Daddy away. Then she remembered her Daddy's grunt in the other room with her mother, and her mind became confused again. Which god would tell her if her Daddy was right in doing what he was doing and if she had to keep quiet and behave as if he did not do it to her? Another confusion, and she felt like tearing her soul away from her body. She wished her mind could run away from her body so that they would not see her again. But her body refused to let her mind go. They were together, body and mind. She knew because she was feeling the ache of walking. Another night came and another day. Was there no end to London, to England? The walk was endless, and she had not reached the end of the world yet. The end of the world, where there would be no Uncle Johnny, where there would be a nice and loving and loyal Daddy like those on television and where a mother could talk to her daughter gently, and believe her daughter when she told her things. Her body was weighing the mind down now. She saw a small park, and the temptation to lie on the bench was too much. The body won. She lay on the bench and she slept. And it was a dreamless sleep.

Gwendolen was in one of those tiny parks on the fringes of Hertfordshire which still had keepers who shut the gates in the evenings. The keeper woke Gwendolen and told her it was time to go home. She opened her mouth to speak, but it was jammed. She tried to stand straight and firm, but her feet wobbled. She stared at the man for a while, again not trusting what she might say. This man did not even look dangerous, he was white, not coloured or yellow, and he was looking at her with concern. Was the concern real, or was it as faked as Uncle Johnny's concern? She decided to ignore him and lay down on the bench again.

The park-keeper noticed her muddy shoes, her dirty school raincoat, and decided that this was not a case he could cope with. He did not wish to be accused of anything, especially as she was a black girl, and he decided to call the police.

Gwendolen was taken to a cell in a local police station. They could not charge her with anything because she did not speak. After a face wash and toast and tea in the morning, she was asked to go. She stood there looking round vacantly.

'What is your name, girl?' asked a rather unexpectedly sympathetic policeman. Gwendolen was really lucky. She fell into the hands of a rare breed of police officers: those who were trying to police the community, rather than make names for themselves.

'You have to tell us who you are, love. You know, why you left home.'

Gwendolen simply stood and stared. She was not frightened. It was just that she did not feel anything. Her brain and mind were blank. Her look was glazed and vacant.

'We'll have to ask you to go then and warn you not to sleep in open places again. It can be very dangerous. You

175

were lucky Mr Close found you. It is not a good place for a young girl to lie alone late in the evening.'

'It is not even a safe place in the daytime these days.' A woman police officer, who stood behind the desk with arms folded, joined in. 'So you have to go home.'

Home? Gwendolen thought. She would never feel at home in the flat any more. Not with her Daddy nervously watching her, not with her mother so angry and Ronald and Marcus making insinuating remarks. She was not going back there, not any more.

The policewoman left her place behind the counter. Gwendolen watched her approach with the corner of her eye. A method she knew her observers failed to notice. She did not know what to do and she did not know the right thing to say. But she was not going back there, and she was not going to tell them where her home was.

The policewoman touched her shoulder and showed her the way out.

Gwendolen screamed. Something that had been bottled inside her for so long seemed to escape, and her mouth gave vent to a jumble of Jamaican patois and London school cockney. Her voice was raised and she talked and kept talking and kept saying in different pitches, 'Me no wan' go 'ome.' She talked of Granny Naomi, who sounded to her listeners like a kind of witch who lived somewhere in North London, in Granville Road or somewhere. Then she said her home was Granville Road in Jamaica, then she changed her mind, it was not in Jamaica but off Mornington Crescent. They allowed her to talk. She stopped shouting because she was exhausted, and her voice went so low that they could not hear what she was saying. Then with no warning at all, she became violently sick. It was too late to run to the toilet she knew was behind the counter just there in the cell where she spent the night. Her mind became clear enough to feel shame. It could not control her body. Her humiliation was total. She dragged herself outside and sat exhausted by the steps outside the police station. And she was still talking to the wind. But the wind had no answer.

She heard the telephone ringing. It was ringing all the time at that place. She watched with the corner of her eyes the policewoman watching her. Eventually the policewoman came out and gentled her inside. A cleaner was mopping up her sick. She looked away, not wanting to see her shame. The sight of it made her feel sick again inside.

When a police car came to take her away, she followed without seeing, without saying a single word, and without resistance. She did not know where they were taking her and she was too tired to want to know. Her mind told her that she must have been stinking, because though the policewoman who was to sit next to her managed a professional smile, she sat well away from her. Good thing, because her body was too tired to do anything about it, and she needed space to lay her head.

Open roads edged by neat houses sped by. Then came factories outside London and the rain. Bored with watching the rain, Gwendolen slept. She did not know for how long. But the policewoman woke her in front of this huge house that at first looked as if it was standing in a cemetery. But there were no gravestones. Maybe it was a courthouse. But Gwendolen followed the woman officer.

They went through a long corridor with rooms only on one side. The other side had windows high above their heads. Those windows opened into the huge garden. The garden had very high walls and beyond the walls she could hear the sounds of a bus passing.

A young man in a navy-blue suit and white shirt with a Tommy Cooper hat came by. He bowed low and said, 'Good morning.' He said 'Good morning' to everybody as he walked lightly like a dancer. He must be mad, thought Gwendolen. How can you bow and say 'Good morning' to everybody? It was all right in Jamaica but if you behave like that here people will think you're mad. The policewoman answered the young man with a pitying smile. Gwendolen did not bother. You don't say 'Good morning' to people like her.

They then got into a small office and two black women in nurses' uniform took her particulars from the policewoman. How did they know who she was, that her name was Gwendolen Brillianton? She had never said things like that to them. Then she saw a middle-aged woman with one breast hanging out feeding a big doll like a real baby. Then it dawned on her. This must be a hospital for the mentally sick. She was not going to stay though. She was not mad, she only needed a place to stay.

The black nurse called her. And she was asked to take off her clothes and have a bath. Then Gwendolen panicked. 'Why am I staying here?'

'Just for a little while until things are sorted out,' the nurse said in a reassuring voice.

'I don't want to stay, not here. Look, this is a nut-house, I don't want to stay. I'm not mad, just pregnant. I don't want to stay.'

There was a little struggle, but she was overcome expertly with a gentle force rendered by another nurse and an injection from a man in a white coat.

Gwendolen was put in a clean but out-of-fashion crimplene dress, the type worn by the likes of Granny Naomi. She was by then past caring and again drifted into sleep. She was aware that she was shouting intermittently, she was saying, 'Leave my Daddy alone, I don't want him to be locked away, no, no . . .'

The faces of the nurses swam around her. So did the face of the doctor. Again she went to sleep, in a bed with bars like the ones her parents had for Cheryl when she was very little.

In between sleep, she wondered if the outside world was

going on without her. What would Emmanuel be thinking? What would her mother be thinking? What would people say in the church? Were they praying for her? Did they remember who she was?

A woman was singing not too far from her. Her bed was screened off from the other patients. And the woman with the doll was padding about in bedroom slippers cooing to her 'baby'. Gwendolen touched her belly. She was having a baby too. She'd missed four or five periods now and her mother had found out. Older women had a way of knowing. Look at those in the church. They knew. Something started to tickle her stomach. What was it? The baby? No, not only the baby but also her future and her reason for being alive? The only thing she could call her own. She saw again the woman with the hanging breast. Her own baby would be a real one just like her sister Cheryl had been when she first arrived in England. The baby would look like Cheryl. Then they would all know that Emmanuel was not the father, because her baby was going to be a real black baby and not a yellow one.

Because of the baby she decided not to make any more trouble. Her thoughts started to clear. The nurse had told her not to fight, because if she did they would go on giving her the injection that could harm the baby. So if she wanted to keep the baby, she would have to obey.

'I don't want to go back to my Mum, that's what. I don't hate my parents, it's just that I want to go away from them, to be on my own, in my own room.'

Probably if Gwendolen had guessed that the nurse who looked so small and unsophisticated was at least ten years her senior, and that befriending her was part of her treatment, she would have clamped her mouth shut. But maybe not. Childbirth is a great leveller for women. Even women prime ministers had babies! She started to think herself lucky to meet a down-to-earth African nurse who had pitied her and started to tell her things her mother would have told her if she had not gone to Granville when she did.

The nurse was a bit of an actress too, or maybe working in a hospital like this was making her behave like an actress. She looked this way and that, adjusted her cap and said, 'I love having babies. It can be the most beautiful experience a woman can ever have. At home in Ghana, my mother went through it six times. But me I have three, three only and no more. You know why? In this society you look after your child yourself, right from the day you return from the hospital. So you may not have many. My advice is, enjoy it just as if this is the only one you'll ever have. If you don't give them any trouble here, they may arrange for you to have a flat soon. You see, none of the other patients here is pregnant and you're so young.'

'But, nurse, what's your name?'

The nurse smiled. Gwendolen is getting better. She should be completely cured. She is so young. The doctors would be pleased. Aloud she said, 'Ama.'

'Nice short name, Ama. It means something, don't it? What does it mean? A princess?'

The nurse laughed out. 'Something like that.' And immediately Gwendolen detected the professionalism in her voice. 'Who is your baby's father, Gwen?'

For the first time, the gravity of all that had happened to her weighed down on her shoulders. If she said that she was being locked up in a ward for the mentally sick so that her Daddy would not be put away in a jailhouse, this woman might not understand. She would tell someone one day. She must talk to Emmanuel about it first. She could not bottle it up in herself though, otherwise it would kill her. She knew she had been shouting and saying nonsense, the woman who kept singing next to her bed had told her so. Had she told them about her Daddy then? But why wouldn't her Daddy stand up and tell the world that he did it? Why wouldn't he

180

stand by her? Instead he went to that room and to her mother. She wanted to hate the two of them. But if she did, then she'd have nobody to love. She had to love people around her. She had been brought up that way. To disperse love, although very thinly, to all your aunties and uncles. She sighed. She suddenly felt so old. Her childhood had been stolen from her.

'I am not mad, you know. I just wanted to leave home and I was so tired.'

Nurse Ama nodded in sympathy, but went on talking. 'Things are different here. If my mother had been in this society, they would have locked her up. She used to shout at us to wake up, eat our food, wash our clothes, and she beat us if we refused. Good thing she was in Ghana. Here they have these "civilized" rules. And if you don't obey them, they'll either put you in jail or if you're lucky they'll put you here.'

'But I've done nothing wrong!' Gwendolen cried.

'Well, that policewoman asked you to move from their office, didn't she? And you did not move. Well, if you'd been a black boy, it's jail for you, my girl. They probably would have sent you to jail for resisting arrest, but thought better about it.'

'How did you know who I am? I never said nothing.'

'Your parents reported you missing, I should think.'

Her parents, her parents, could they do such a thing – go to a police station to report her missing? No, it must be Mrs Odowis or her Daddy's friend, that African man Mr What's-his-name. Her Daddy would be too scared to report it.

'They can come and see you, you know. Whenever you want. You know, when you're nice and ready for them. You kept saying you did not wish to go back home, so they – I mean us, well, the doctors, don't want to push things. And one thing, you can still abort the child. If you don't want it.'

'Abort? What is abort? Of course I want the child. I've

181

never had anything of my own. Can they take the baby from me by force?'

'No, they won't. But, Gwen, babies are not dolls, you know. They grow and cry and demand much of your time. If you don't want it, you can either abort, you know, flush it down the toilet, or if it's too late for that, you can send it away for adoption.'

Gwendolen looked at Ama closely. These last few months had really matured her.

'Did they send you to tell me all this? I thought we were just having a good chat. Well, tell them that I want my baby. It is not going for any adoption to no white family with money. I want to take care of my baby. What did my Mum say? What did my Daddy say to all that? I'd like to talk to my Mum.'

'Yes, they can come any time. Your mother is very worried.'

Gwendolen's heart melted. Her mother, her Mammy worried about her. She would like her to know that she was keen on keeping the baby, that she and the baby would not be a burden to her. She would educate herself and get a good job. She could work in nurseries, since she was good at looking after babies. She could even work as a dinner lady or, like Ama, work as a nurse for mentally sick people. Because after living with them for several weeks, she knew that most of them were harmless. 'I suppose everybody's peculiarity is madness to the next person.' The woman with the breast hanging out had lost two babies in a fire at the same time. The young black man walking up and down had failed his exams and disappointed his parents. And she herself would not tell them the whole truth, so that they would not jail her Daddy. Maybe she would talk to her mother one day, woman to woman. She thought: my Mammy coming to see me? I must tell her all. Especially, if she comes alone. I must tell her. But suppose she hates me like Granny Naomi?

For the first time in many months, Gwendolen actually

smiled. Life might not be that bad after all. Nurse Ama had said, 'I should enjoy my baby.' There, in Africa where she came from, babies are a woman's greatest achievement. She was not going to be a woman baby machine though. One or two would do. It would be nice if she could have a man to help her. But that would be asking God too much. 'Count your blessings one by one' she quoted mentally. She had a mother who showed signs of standing by her, a baby of her own and maybe if her Daddy could face her, a Daddy as well, and Marcus and Ronald and Cheryl. Oh, she was rich in people.

But what of Emmanuel? That young man had given her so much happiness the last few months. Would she lose him if she told him that the baby was not his? He was so stunned at being called a father that he had not bothered to ask her how advanced the pregnancy was. He would have to know anyway, because she was sure her baby was going to be a very black child, like herself, like her Daddy and like Cheryl used to be when she first saw her years ago. Would that drive Emmanuel away? At the moment, I have his friendship and that is all that matters. The future will take care of itself.

Gwendolen smiled, as the thing inside her tickled her again in agreement to her thoughts.

15

Sonia's Intuition

For three consecutive Sundays, Sonia noticed that her husband, Brother Winston Brillianton, had neither preached nor given out any announcements as he used to before she went home to Jamaica. She tried to find out from Sister Esmee, but her answer was so evasive that she realized it was not accidental. They must have decided that Winston was no longer good enough to preach.

Did Winston allow himself to go to church dirty, when she was away? Did he go to church late? Did he preach a sermon to upset anybody? What could he have done? She was becoming restlessly uneasy. Her intuition was telling her that something was wrong. Even Brother Simon somehow became distant. When she asked Winston, he said that it was due to his stammer.

'But you stammer before, yet you managed to preach the Word of the Lord?'

'Me, me, no fit read. You know dat, Ah preach from me 'ead.'

'Den, your head dry up nuh?'

'Sonia, look, look, me tire, me pay no mind, anyhow.'

She had to hold herself tight not to go into hysteria. Roza had told her not to worry too much, otherwise her illness would start all over again. And that was the part of her Winston did not know fully. They all knew she had lost the baby she was carrying and everybody was sorry. But they did not know how deeply the shock had affected her mentally. Not that it would have bothered Winston. It was only that as things stood in her family, revealing the fact would help no one.

Least of all her daughter who they said was now in a mental home. Good job she did not tell people all that happened at home. They would have said that madness was hereditary. No, she was not mad. But was Gwendolen mad? Were all her Christian friends avoiding her because she looked mad? Sonia looked furtively around herself, first pulling her skirt into place, then adjusting her hat and then holding her handbag a little away from her body, the way she thought proper ladies did. Then she looked up and saw Marcus running in circles with the tail of his shirt showing under his Sunday jacket.

'Marcus, Marrrcus, your shirt-tail showing. Tuck it into your pants!'

Marcus ignored her. He went on running with another boy. They had been cooped inside the church for so long that the end of the service was like being let out of prison. They were enjoying themselves and sweating profusely into the bargain.

Sonia looked around her, turning her head as she did so, very unlike her daughter who could watch people without moving her head. A trick Gwendolen learned in Granville. A trick that enabled her to watch unnoticed what Granny Naomi and Uncle Johnny were up to.

Sonia wondered how come rainclouds gathered around her so heavily? Why was she now determined to go and see June-June, and make it up with the child of her youth? And after the disgrace she had brought to the family by allowing herself to be made pregnant by a rootless boy who did not know what the inside of a place of worship looked like! She was angry with her. Angry with her carelessness, angry at her youth, angry at the way she could now speak English better than her own mother did, angry at her confidence. Yet somehow she was dreaming of something better for June-June. She did not have the faintest idea how her children were going to make good. But she wanted them to. She

186

had dreamed that maybe June-June would marry well, a good hard-working black man from Jamaica. She had prayed hard for this secretly. Prayers could move mountains.

Why was that social worker asking if June-June rolled her bottom inside or outside the house? Who would she roll her bottom inside for? Marcus, Ronald, or Winston? Those people did ask silly questions. They would not even let her see her daughter when she wanted because they said June-June might not want to see her yet. That did annoy and surprise her not a little. But the greatest astonishment she had was that her husband was taking all these nonsense laws calmly. He kept telling her that here you did not fool with officials. And that they knew what they were doing. She must go and see Gwendolen though. After all, she was carrying her grandchild. The child would be half-caste – 'Yellow Nigger'. That would be fun. She did not care which colour her grand-child was as long as the baby and June-June were all right.

Sister Esmee invited her for tea in the church hall. But there was something in her voice which chilled Sonia's soul and she declined the invitation. Why were the sisters being so strange to the members of her family and herself too? They could keep their tea. She was not going to drink it for sure. She told them that Gwendolen was ill in hospital, but did not say which hospital. Sister Esmee and Sister Dorcas asked perfunctorily what the illness was. Sister Esmee's pencilled-in brow arched like a fisherman's hook and her mouth twisted to one side like that of a dying fish. But before Sonia could answer, Winston materialized from behind her and asked, 'How she know? She a doctor?'

'No, of course not. How can she possibly know? These children, they pick up all manner of diseases these days, don't they, Sister Esmee?' Sister Dorcas, who had been in England most of her life and who had served in the Women's Auxiliary as a cook in the Second World War added in her uppish English voice.

So, they knew of June-June's pregnancy, Sonia thought. That was it. Her whole family was to be stigmatized because June-June fooled around with her boy-friend when she was away in Jamaica. So that was it. She was a bit tempted to tell them exactly where June-June was. But something inside her told her that these women were too 'Christian', too perfect and maybe too close to understand her plight. She herself did not know the dimension of her plight, but she was not even going to try to describe it or give it a name. She smacked her lips together and made for the bus stop in front of Mornington Crescent station. It was only two stops to their new flat in St Pancras Way but her shoes were not made for walking. They were probably dancing shoes, yet Sonia could not resist the bright silver colour, the thin heels and double buckle. The shoes were very lovely to look at, because they were not cheap. But they were not practical.

Winston was late in returning from work the following day. Sonia had waited with bated breath, thanking God that at least the social workers now said they could go and see June-June. She bought a packet of chocolate and some flowers, and then decided against the flowers. She bought a bottle of orange juice instead.

By the time they found out where the hospital was in Friern Barnet, it was getting dark. The street lamps were yellow and that made the streets ghostlier still. They did not talk at all. Winston was breathing heavily and she panting behind him. After jumping in and out of several buses, they got to the huge gate. A man who looked like a gardener told them where to go. They went along this one-sided corridor to some dark, narrow, cemented stairs and knocked at a yellow door that had Ward 12 written on it. It was locked.

A nurse soon opened the door, the inside of which was painted red like the door of a room in a children's nursery school. They were led through another corridor, this time a shorter one, and along which they could see some patients lying on beds. A young black man of about eighteen or nineteen was shuffling up and down with saliva dripping down his mouth. A bib was tied around his neck like a baby's.

Sonia's heart was pounding. She wanted to hold her husband and cry out, but one look at his face told her that not only was he shaken, but that he was not going to give her any sympathy.

Then abruptly they entered into a large sunny living-room, in which chairs were arranged militarily against the walls. At one end was a huge television. It was showing a chat show which none of the people sitting was watching.

Gwendolen saw them and looked away.

'Gwendolen, you Mum and Dad are here,' shouted the Ghanaian nurse unnecessarily.

One patient politely gave up her seat and asked them to sit down, next to Gwendolen. Sonia, still shaken, accepted the seat. She was surprised at the politeness. But she noticed that all the others were sitting down and staring vacantly. Apart from the young man who kept walking up and down, with saliva dripping from his mouth, and dragging his feet noisily, they all looked at first like people waiting for death. Sonia took her eyes off them and asked Gwendolen in a low voice, 'Are you all right?'

Gwendolen nodded.

'Look, me bring orange juice and chocolate.'

Gwendolen took the packet of chocolate, opened it and started to hand it to all those sitting around. As everybody took a piece, their individuality which heretofore had been asleep wakened. One woman who had a green half-knitted piece on her lap picked it up and started to knit furiously and asked again and again, 'Gwendolen, is that your father and mother? Is it your birthday?' The repetition of these questions made her look like a talking parrot. Others just ignored her.

Gwendolen sat down again and left the remaining chocolate on her lap. Her eyes did not stare into vacancy like those of the others, but they were staring at the hands she folded on top of the chocolate box.

How was she going to tell her mother who the father of her baby was? It was wrong, she had been naive, and did not bargain for pregnancy. She had thought that it would just be like her experience with Uncle Johnny. She did not realize that it would be different now that she had grown into a young healthy woman. Her mother would understand. Her mother would not tell anyone. Her mother would not allow them to put her Daddy away. If they did put him away, who would pay their rent and bring the food money? Yes, her mother would understand.

She looked up once and saw her father standing as solid as an oak by the window. His standing there radiated dependability and solidity all rolled into one. A father any girl should be proud of. But he did not even come near to her. She did not look into his eyes for fear of what she would see.

'Medicine, medicine!' shouted a nurse, wheeling in the medicine trolley. Everybody's name was called and they were given different pills to swallow. Gwendolen had only one type, thank God. The others had to swallow so many different colours that they looked as if they were popping Smarties into their mouths.

'What medicine be dat?' Sonia asked in an attempt to make conversation.

'Sleeping tablets,' Gwendolen replied, knowingly.

It was a good thing the nurse told her what it was. She thought that that was really grand of them, explaining each tablet to the patients. But she noticed that most of the other patients were told their pills were just 'to make them better'. What exactly the pills were, no one knew. Anyway, she was not going to stay there long. She would like to leave the place.

She looked at her mother again. Was she crying? Her mother crying for her? If only people like her mother and

Granny Naomi had taken the trouble to tell her how much she was valued, she would have estimated herself a little higher. She would have been able to stand up to her Daddy and say, 'Don't, Daddy, me tell me Mum when she comes back.' But how was she to know that her being in a mental hospital would affect her parents this way? She gave in to her father because she did not wish to cause trouble for anybody. And if she could bear it with that stupid Uncle Johnny who forced himself on her, what of the Daddy she loved? It was a lot to give, but then could your own father hurt you? All was so complicated.

Her father saw Sonia's tearful eyes and boomed, 'Come on, Sonia, come on.' Gwen stood up abruptly, wanting to say, 'But look, Dad, I am carrying your baby.' Though the words were formed in her mouth, yet she could not voice them out. Would her mother believe her? Would all these people believe her? She sat down again dejectedly. Maybe Emmanuel would believe her.

'Mammy, tell Emmanuel to come and see me.' It was akin to the voice of a child whose mother was going to the market and who did not want her to go. Sonia noted the tone of the voice. The voice of that June-June of not so long ago, who used to trot along with her to the post office to collect the money Winston had sent from England. Now her daughter was in a mad-house. But she was not mad. She was all right. Why did they have to put her here? Because she was a black girl?

Sonia nodded. 'Me tell him.'

Winston led his wife away. All that Gwendolen planned to say melted in her throat and formed a big lump of hatred against her father, against all men. It was like magic. One minute she was innocent, the next she was full of vindictive hatred. What game was her Daddy playing? The same game as Uncle Johnny played? She got up and wanted to scream, but pulled herself down again. She had to be very careful.

This was not a place where you were allowed to give in to emotion. But she was not going to say anything. So it was her fault now. So she had brought disgrace to her family. Her father had taken his wife away and they had left her in a loony-bin. All right, she would have the baby, she would not tell on her Daddy unless it was absolutely necessary and she was going out of here into a place of her own. If they had no place for her, she would rather stay there because if she stayed under the same roof only God knew what she could do to him.

And her mother crying all those stupid tears? Could she not guess that she wanted to talk to her? How could she be so blind? So busy playing the little wife, when even the social worker who did not live with them had almost guessed the truth. Maybe her mother knew, but did not want to accept it. Well good luck to them.

With her head up, she smiled at her friends and marched to her bed. She lay down and fell asleep.

Outside, Sonia wanted to know why Winston did not say a word to his daughter.

'What you wan' me to say in dat loony place?' he cried in righteous anger.

Yeah, it was eerie, those vacant eyes, those pouchy faces and those shuffling feet. Yeah, it was unnerving. But they were leaving their daughter there. Did that not worry him?

Winston did not answer. He was deep in his own thoughts.

Sonia sniffed all the way home. It was late and very dark by the time they got to St Pancras Way.

But the thought kept nagging at Sonia: why Winston na taak to June-June?

At night, Winston came towards her in his usual clumsy way, but a kind of inspired energy came into her and she pushed him neatly out of their bed and he landed on the floor. She got herself ready for a fight. She protected her face just in case he decided to box her ears.

192

But Winston did neither. Instead he picked himself up, took one of the blankets and went to the front room.

Something was very wrong. She did not know where. She had treated Winston the way she had never done before in all their married life and he had slunk away like those white men do on the telly. Those men who have no courage to face their wives because they have a guilt to hide.

But Winston was not going to keep quiet any more. She was going to make him talk. No, the man must talk and talk himself dry. Why did he allow a white boy to stay in their house with their unmarried daughter anyhow? Gwendolen was supposed to be at school. Winston would have to explain all that to her, to the church where he preached every Sunday and to their friends; why he allowed such a horrible thing to happen to their daughter June-June.

Tomorrow evening Sonia would call the church elders to hear what Winston had to say for himself.

16

Winston's Death

It was not necessary for Sonia to get up too early this morning because the kids were on holidays. She noticed too that they had acquired a kind of independence which was not there before she left her family for Granville. They had now learned to get their breakfast without bothering her. None the less, she still got up, because she feared the mess left in the kitchen and the sight of her little daughter holding the frying pan in the air was wont to make her stomach go into a tangled twist. Yeah, she would get up early this very morning because she had to tell Winston to return straight home after work, in order to have a word or two with Sister Esmee and Brother Simon. She was not going to tell Winston what they were going to ask him, she would keep that till the evening. She knew that it was not a good thing to start the morning with an argument, especially for a man that did the type of job Winston said he was doing these days. To climb ladders to the fifteenth floor of a half-finished building to decorate it was enough to send anyone dizzy. No, she was not going to let him go to work with a family argument on his mind.

A crash came from the kitchen and Marcus's raised voice reverberated all over the flat. That decided her. She jumped out of bed, calling Winston to stop his children from yelling the place down. Oh yeah, Winston had not slept in their bed. He must be in the living-room. So many rooms in this flat. They needed getting used to.

'Naw, what's de trouble, eh, Marcus? Whey your Daddy?'

'He's gone to work,' Cheryl whined. 'Marcus struck me on the head and . . .'

Sonia was not listening. Absent-mindedly, she took the milk pan from Marcus and started making breakfast. So Winston had rushed off to work before she had time to talk to him. That man must be trying to avoid early morning arguments.

She pacified her children and peace descended as they ate their breakfast.

Sonia went to the room where Winston had slept and she saw her pink blanket nicely folded on the settee. He had been into their bedroom and taken his work-clothes whilst she slept.

Suddenly her body felt so heavy, as if she had been carrying the whole world on her shoulders. This was not the home-coming she had dreamed of in Granville. Since her return, everybody had become so strange and tactful. Even Mrs Odowis, that bubbling African friend of hers, started thinking before she opened her mouth to say a word to her. As for the church people, she had felt let down because they now seemed to talk in riddles. Well, not to worry, maybe they were all blaming her for going away in the first place. And maybe she shouldn't have stayed away this long. She would make it up with everybody this evening. She would invite them to talk it all over; bring it all into the open. She hoped Winston would not choose this day to go and drink with that African friend of his, Mr Mechima or whatever his name was. Those African people, they have so many long names.

Gwendolen, Lawd ha' mussy. The poor gal in dat damn crazy place! No, her daughter must return home. Why was it Winston did not press those nurses to release June-June? After all, she was not mad. Only sick. The type of sickness Sonia herself had had. In Granville, she was taken to a church haven where everybody prayed for her and where all the church prophets laid hands on her head and fasted over her. Here, they put a lill chile in a crazy-house just because she ran away from home. Good Lawd.

She must hurry and fix the house before going to invite
Sister Esmee. And on her way back, she must get them a little
something to eat. Would it be right to ask Mrs Odowis? Yeah,
if she's free, she could come too.

She picked up a rug and went to the small balcony and
started to beat the dust from it. A black man and a police
officer came into the estate, peering at the numbers of houses.
Poor man, fancy being arrested on such a fine morning. They
passed the front of the flat again: it looked as if they were
looking for a flat on their part of the estate. She watched
their movements with the corner of her eyes, looking like
her daughter Gwendolen. She folded the rug she was beating
and went in. Now why was she keen on getting rid of the
dust in that rug? After all it was for Cheryl's room. And her
visitors that evening were not going to come into the little
girl's room. She was at sixes and sevens this morning.

The door-bell rang. The black man and the police officer
were there. She could see their outline through the net
curtain. Now why were they knocking at her door? She
looked closely now. That man, she'd seen him before. Winston's African friend.

'Yeah, come in, come in. Wharr happen?' she cried, her
heart fluttering like the feathers of a bird in the wind. Her
mouth was dry. The eel of fear that was wriggling in
her stomach was growing bigger and bigger every second. It
felt as if any minute now, it would grow so big and explode
inside her. Winston was in trouble. She knew it. Or maybe it
was Gwendolen. It never rained with her, it always poured.

No, they did not want tea. No, they did not want juice.
Yeah, they had seen Winston at work that morning.

Mr Ilochina, the African man, started to talk in his posh
African voice. Sonia wondered why they had come in mid-
morning just to talk about what life was about. She knew all
about that. What was the man trying to say? She understood
only part of what he was talking about anyhow.

197

The policeman did not know what to do with his hat. Then he decided to remove it. Then he stood at attention; then he put his hand on his heart and announced, while Mr What's-his-name was still talking, 'Your husband passed away, Marm.'

'What? Wait a minute, wharr you two talking about?' was all Sonia could say.

The policeman nodded. 'Your husband, Marm, Mr Winston Brillianton . . . there was an accident at work. There was a gas explosion and he fell into a drum of tar . . . he stood no chance . . .'

Sonia stood up, walked to the policeman: 'Who you talking about, me ask you?'

'He suffered no pain,' the poor policeman went on, determined to do his duty down to the last letter.

'No! No! No!' Sonia crumpled into a chair. Everything went into a daze. She had brought ill luck into her family. Three weeks ago, they were happy until she returned from Jamaica with her bad luck. Her mind had killed Winston. She'd refused him sex last night. The last night of his life. And she who was supposed to be his missus, she'd done that to him. And all because of June-June. No, that daughter of hers was evil. Since they brought her from Jamaica, she'd been evil. And she, Sonia, was defending her only to kill her husband and bread-winner. That child had worried her father sick. Winston did not know what he was doing. His colleague said they had told him to wait until the gas had been tested, but he said he would go and test it himself. 'Just as if he wanted to die,' Mr Ilochina the African friend had said. Good Lord, what was she to do now? With three young children and Gwendolen and her baby! Where would she go?

Days passed. Mrs Odowis kept coming and going. Emmanuel's father forgot his anger and visited frequently. His wife took a liking to Sonia's spontaneity.

When Brother Simon and the Sisters of the church came the following evening, they started to pray about hell and brimstone. They insinuated that it was better to die than wallow in the mire of sin. Sonia felt again that they were talking in riddles and swore at them. They were not grateful for all the good preaching Winston had done in that church and all the other contributions he had made. Was there any human being who had no sin? So what great sin had Winston committed that warranted their referring to his death as God's vengeance? They should leave her house. She never wanted to see them again. Brother Simon was sure she was over-wrought and prayed God to calm her. They left. They had promised to come to the funeral.

'Mrs Odowis, you see what people are? You see how these church people talk 'bout Winston. The man go a work and him daughter get pregnant. So why send him go to hell for that? It was not his fault. Children raised here different, you know.'

'Me wan' church funeral for Winston, but our church people funny to him. Me no know why,' Sonia sobbed to Mr Ilochina.

'Don't worry, Mrs Brillianton. You buy everything here, even beautiful funerals. This is not like African people. In my town, our people will not bury your husband, I'm sorry to say. But here in England, money buys honour.' This was the nearest Mr Ilochina could trust himself to go in hinting to Sonia what he suspected happened between Winston and his daughter. He knew that Sonia might not speak the English language well, but then who did? Yet she was a shrewd woman.

Sonia kept quiet for a very, very long time. She absent-mindedly twisted the ring on her finger, looking down on her lap and not straight at Winston's friend. The big wall clock in the room boomed the hour.

'You see, we are an extremely superstitious race, we

Africans. But those superstitions are arrived at after generations of watching the forces of nature. Gas and electricity are Earth forces we call Ani. They have their way of meting out vengeance.'

Funnily enough, Sonia laughed. The corners of her eyes crinkled in amusement. Her dentures which she rarely showed in public, were visible. This woman is not stupid, Ilochina thought.

'What of people who die knocked down by lorry and them who die in the air?'

Mr Ilochina sighed. He had done his duty. This woman and her daughter should now get together and plan their lives anew. If she could forgive her husband, to the extent of not wanting to talk about it, then she must have already forgiven her daughter.

Gladys Odowis came in and Sonia plunged into the funeral arrangements.

'Will there be a vicar?' Mrs Odowis wanted to know.

Mr Ilochina nodded.

'You mean a vicar will be present even if the dead person did not belong to his church?'

'Easy. In fact there are churches inside the cemetery.'

Winston rode home like an emperor in a huge American-designed coffin decked with flowers. Mrs Odowis, Mr Ilochina, some of Winston's distant relatives in London, Mr Papaloizou and his wife, Emmanuel, Marcus, Ronald and Cheryl and most of their neighbours in St Pancras Way went to the cemetery with Sonia.

They sang a beautiful song Sonia did not understand. They read prayers from a book and she poured sand on Winston's coffin. The world seemed empty. What was she to do now?

The social worker brought a lawyer and they told her she was entitled to a huge sum of money because her husband died at work. The building firm begged the solicitor to settle it out of court, but the barrister refused. Mrs Brillianton had her family to raise. They should have made sure the machines were safe, the man maintained.

The guv'nor was very sorry about this, but gave Sonia a couple of thousand pounds to help her through the immediate expenses.

The excitement of the promised money and the money she had in hand almost drove Sonia crazy. She made so many wild schemes. She bought new sets of net curtains for her flat. She never liked the idea of using the nets from their old flat for this new one.

Then another thought struck her. She called on her friend Mrs Odowis and said, 'Mrs Odowis, Ah go back to Jamaica on holidays, you know. Take Cheryl with me.'

'But, Sonia, you've only just returned. Who will look after the boys?'

'Gwendolen will. She so good with them, you know.'

'But she's expecting a child of her own. And you said only yesterday that you did not want to speak to her again. You have not even been to see her. I noticed she was not at the funeral.'

'Ah know. Me know. Me no tell her yet. She no well enough, you know.'

'Then how can she look after Marcus and Ronald? Sonia, you have to calm down. It looks a lot of money now, but when you start spending it at random, you'll find it won't go very far.'

'They say more to come, when the solicitor man finish the case. No bad, eh?'

Sonia almost made Gladys Odowis jealous. My friend is going to get all this money. Ilochina said it could be anything from £30,000 to £60,000 because the insurance was going to pay it. Gosh, that would be enough to buy a house, she thought. But the woman was so excited and near hysteria. Well, she would work at her own education and that would compensate for the fact that her husband left her and went back to Nigeria after battering her and leaving her with two children.

'You know, I think we should make a date to go and see Gwendolen soon. She's entitled to some of the money, you know.'

'No, God died for the truth. I want the money in me hand,' Sonia declared flatly.

17

Gwendolen Alone

It was when Gwendolen was in a sheltered home, High Cross, in Tottenham, that Emmanuel told her of her father's death. 'Death, but how?' Gwendolen asked unbelievingly. She had never seen a dead person. She could understand the death of a relative who lived far away. Like Granny Naomi. But her father? He was very much alive in her mind. She had been planning how she would stage the showdown with him. And after that, how she was going to forgive him because she would keep her child and try to find a job, build a career. Death meant all these plans would not come to fruition. She felt cheated. Death meant finality. She looked up at Emmanuel to give her a further explanation, as if he had caused the death.

Emmanuel shrugged. 'An accidental death at work. Gwen, look I am sorry. He's been buried, we all went, but the doctors say not to trouble you in your condition. That was why he could not come to see you again.'

'I know that, a dead father can't come to see his daughter, even I know that.' Gwendolen was silent. She wanted to cry, but tears would not come. What would Emmanuel think? What would people say when they learned that she did not shed tears for her father? She started to sweat though.

'You like a cup of tea?' Leslie, one of the patients, asked solicitously.

Gwendolen nodded.

He went to get her the tea. The kitchen was open-plan; it opened into their sitting-area. They were allowed to make their own breakfasts and lunches, but the cook came in the evening and prepared hot suppers. Everybody had to clean out his or her own room – an institutionalized way of readying them for the outside world.

Did she kill her father? Did she will him dead? 'What of my Mum, how is she taking it?'

'Oh, she's OK, I guess. When she feels better, she'll come and see you.'

'You can cry if you like,' put in Leslie, who, though sitting a little away from Gwen and Emmanuel, was listening to what they were saying.

Gwendolen faced him squarely and challenged, 'Why should I cry? Because little girls are supposed to cry when their fathers die. Well, I am not a little girl any more, I am a woman carrying a child.'

Leslie shrugged his shoulders, collected the tea-things and shuffled to the kitchen. Though he had fully recovered from his brief mental exhaustion, he was still taking some medication which slowed him down. He normally was a strong-willed young man who could master his physical weakness with sheer determination. He'd told Gwendolen a few days ago that he used to work in the City before his illness. Gwendolen had wanted to know what people did in the City. And Leslie did not bother to explain. Now he was butting his nose into her affairs. Shuffle, shuffle, shuffle, Leslie the shuffler. Why could he not wear proper shoes instead of those ragged slippers?

Gwendolen decided to change the conversation. 'My flat is almost ready. It is in a block, but it is a nice quiet area. I've been to see it. Can you imagine, me a flat of my own.'

Emmanuel grinned, relieved to know that she, too, did not like to dwell on death in a clean but depressing place like this. 'Do you want me to come and help you furnish it?'

'Yeah, if you like.'

The Social Security gave Gwendolen money to put a modest carpet on her floor. Emmanuel found a broken table on a skip and put it into shape. With the carpet and table and an old bed which the social worker brought from somewhere, she felt well off. But for her window curtain, she had to undo the seams of an old flowered dress which no longer fitted her.

Gwendolen enjoyed her new freedom. There was not enough money and she had to budget carefully all the time, but she was not going to be dependent. She wanted to see her mother, though, but the social worker and Emmanuel kept telling her to wait. She very much hoped her mother had not died too. Things were changing so rapidly. One minute she was a schoolgirl, the next she was a young woman expecting her first child. A young woman who had lost her father into the bargain. Losing a parent aged her. She thought she must look like those old people who sounded funny any time they mentioned that they too had parents once. Old people like Granny Naomi seemed to be born old, like they'd dropped from the sky. While your parents were alive, you always felt young. What she felt now was protectiveness towards her brothers, her sister and her new baby. Her mother? Well, she was now a widow, who probably, like most widows Gwendolen knew, had developed strange vague ways of moving and talking. To her, widows always looked into the distance when talking to you, as if their eyes were searching the world for the husbands they had buried. And some of them ceased to care about the way they looked. She would like to see her mother. She would like to help her.

She had been told to call the woman upstairs if she felt any pain. How bad did the pain have to be before she asked for help? Running for help at the slightest pain made you look stupid. She had been having some niggling pains and heaviness at the top of her legs, as if she had lingering indigestion, but they soon went away. Imagine what would have happened if she had kept running upstairs for help every time she had felt uncomfortable. She knew that you could only afford to say things like that to the father of the child or to your parents. Well, at the moment she had neither. And she must look for a good opportunity to tell Emmanuel that he was not the father of the child. Or should she keep quiet? Any person over twelve years of age knew that it took at least nine months for a baby to be born. But Emmanuel had never asked her when the child was due. She could say it was premature. But to what purpose? So that she and Emmanuel would live like husband and wife, pretending to love one another, when all they would be doing was trying to live cheaply and to give the child a home. Her mother and father lived happily ever after. But was that what they called love? No, she did not want any of that. She would tell him the truth. If he still wanted to be her friend after that, it was up to him. If not, it was up to him too. Meanwhile, she needed his occasional visits, his humour, and she felt he needed her too. So what harm was in that?

A few days later, something seemed to open inside her as if she was having a huge period. But this time, instead of blood it was water. And with each spout of water that ran down her legs, she felt lighter. The pain became prolonged and intensified. She was scared. Why wouldn't they let her see her mother?

It was four o'clock in the late afternoon and luckily Moya Duffy, another one-parent woman living upstairs, was just getting tea for her children. She quickly telephoned the hospital and came down to Gwendolen's flat.

'Have you got your suitcase packed?'

'No, I was meaning to do it sometime.'

'Well, you haven't got much time now. Where is it?'

Gwendolen held her tummy and started to laugh. 'I have no suitcase, but I have plenty of carrier bags. What's the suitcase for? To bring the baby in?'

Moya and Gwendolen laughed through the next rather minor contractions.

'When you return from hospital, you must ask them for a special allowance. You need a case to put your clothes in.' She ran upstairs and brought a battered one which they had to hold together with string. Into it they flung Gwendolen's new nightdress and housecoat. Her school shoes and a headscarf.

'You crazy, you know that,' Moya said.

'I know, I bet I became crazier after they sent me to that loony-bin. Haw, haw, haw. Lawd ha' mussy. That was a hot one.'

'I told you, it's not a bloody holiday, you know. But you'll be fine. Just keep your chin up.'

Then Moya asked, 'Is what's-his-name coming to see yer? He comes almost every week, don't he?'

'When he comes, tell him I'm in hospital.'

Moya nodded. 'Good luck.' She gave Gwendolen a peck on her cheek.

The ambulance took Gwendolen away. Fear had made her grow up. Why wouldn't her mother see her anyhow? The nurses at the admission desk asked her for particulars and she gave her mother's name and address as that of her next of kin, and then was admitted.

A new kind of awareness was coming into her life. In Granville, one had to love all the uncles, cousins and aunties, because they were all related. She had tried to continue that kind of loving here. But for the past five months, she had been making new kinds of friends. Friends who were not related to her at all. Friends she could like or even love, without her wanting to live their lives for them and them wanting to do the same to her. It was a kind of relationship that did not choke. Was that a good thing? She did not know. But one thing she knew, in Granville no way was a single girl going to find herself alone in hospital having her first baby by herself, especially when she had a mother living.

Emmanuel was as rootless as she was. Moya, the Irish girl

upstairs, had talked to her often and Gwendolen baby-sat for her a couple of nights. Ama from the hospital popped in once in a while on her way from work and so did her new social worker. Maybe her Mum suspected what happened between her and her Daddy. Well, she did not mind her Mum rejecting her, but Sonia must hear her side of the story. Was that why she did not go to see her Mum herself, when it became clear that she was not coming to see her? But she felt so guilty. She was not proud of what had happened, and her Daddy dying so soon after. Did he kill himself? Was her Mum blaming her for that too? Her mother had no right to condemn her!

For the first time in many months hot tears clouded Gwendolen's eyes. The contractions were getting fiercer too. 'It's not a bloody holiday,' Moya had said a while ago.

At eight o'clock, they told her she had a visitor. It was Emmanuel. She had never seen anyone looking so lost and confused. She had to smile and said, 'After all, when you came to see me in that sheltered place, you did not look so frightened.'

'This is different,' he said hoarsely, looking this way and that, as if he was going to take off, and make a run for it at any minute. He studiously lowered his eyes, not knowing how to look at the bloated women dragging their feet up and down the corridors. There were nurses dashing in and out like souls possessed. Emmanuel wanted to know when she was going to have the baby. He wanted to know if she was in any pain. She said no, she was not in any pain. And that was a cue for Emmanuel to start his banter about what he did that day, and how his woodwork was progressing.

Suddenly Gwendolen let out one scream, and Emmanuel was by the door. The scream was more a heart-rending howl like that made by a hound about to be strangled. Emmanuel took just one look from the doorway and fled down the corridor screaming for the nurse and doctors.

Gwendolen was wheeled into the labour room and was then asked if she would like Emmanuel to be present at the birth.

'Can't I have the baby without him?'

'Of course, it's up to you,' came the muffled reply from the obstetrician.

'The baby's father then?'

'He's dead.' Gwendolen's voice was flat and final.

The little girl was very small, just a little over five pounds, but she was perfect.

Like magic, Gwendolen experienced what millions of women had felt for years and years before she was born and what they will always go on experiencing. She could no longer recall the pain and the sleepless nights she had been having the last weeks. The bundle in her arms could grow to be another disappointment; she could grow to be a princess or just another ordinary woman; but in that moment when a baby first appears in the world, the heart of any new mother warms to the new flesh of her flesh and blood of her blood.

In the morning Ama came. 'She's cute, just like a black Cindy doll. She's beautiful and tiny. She won't have a weight problem,' Ama declared, with her African woman know-all certainty.

'Really? If my child looks like my Daddy, what should I call her in Ghanaian language?'

'Why Ghana? You're not a Ghanaian. And you can't give a girl the name of your father. You can give her the name of his mother, if she looks like her.'

Gwendolen could not see much likeness between this baby and Granny Elinor, but yes, she could call her 'Father's mother's come back,' or something like that.

But more than anything she wanted a special name that could portray what this child meant to her. How could she explain her feelings to Ama? One thing she was sure of, her daughter was not going to be given a foreign name which she could not pronounce. The image of her mother Sonia still struggling to get 'Gwendolen' right loomed in her mind's eye, and she giggled. When she told Ama what was amusing her, both of them laughed. Then Ama stopped and was serious. 'Look, you're too young to give your child a name. What of Emmanuel's people. What of your people?'

Gwendolen smiled like an old lady. 'Does she look like Emmanuel? She's a little black princess and not a half-caste. She's a pure Mandingo lady. Look, my friend, I have no people. I have a few friends; you are one of them. But I want a name that will show that this baby is my friend, my mother, my sister, my hope, all in one.'

'I know the Yorubas of Nigeria and the Ibos use the word "Mother" to mean best woman friend, a woman's saviour. Of course, a mother and even a husband can call a woman "Mother", but never "Baby" like they do in the West. If a man called me "Baby" I'd kill him.'

'So, I'll say "my mother, my friend, my sister is here". How do you say that? Or is it not possible?'

'Of course it is. I think the name is not a Ghanaian one. It is a Yoruba one. It is "Iyamide". My mother, my female friend, my female saviour, my anything-nice-you-can-think-of-in-a-woman's-form, is here. Iyamide.'

'Iyamide. I like that. Thank you very much. When I become rich, I'll visit Ghana and Nigeria and take Iyamide with me. "Iyamide." You see, I can pronounce it. It has music too. You play with the "m", don't you? "Iyamide".'

'But your mother is still alive though. I don't understand you.'

'I know she is. But this is my pet mother. Please write it out for me.'

Emmanuel came in the evening with a bottle of orange juice. He was laughing.

'You scared the living daylights out of me last night. All that screaming.'

210

'Yeah, I was going to have a baby, that was why.'

'Corrr, she's so tiny. What are you going to do with her? I mean, can you take care of her? Babies are dependent, you know. Heh, is she going to look like me later? Does she look like me now?'

Gwendolen chuckled, so much so that her sore stomach ached. 'You're crazy, you know that, Emmanuel. How can you be a father of a full-term baby in five months! You're just a baby yourself, Emmanuel.'

'What? I wondered about that, but I thought maybe it was early. You mean . . .?'

Gwendolen nodded. 'That's right, Iyamide is not your daughter. She's mine, you see.'

Emmanuel's face went a shade darker. Gwendolen momentarily blamed herself for speaking the truth, but she knew that she could not live with such a lie hanging over Iyamide, who was an innocent. No, it was better so.

'Who is her father then?' Emmanuel asked, looking suddenly older. He was very angry, and was trying very hard not to show it in this open ward, where relatives and new mothers were aahing and cooing over their new arrivals.

'He's dead!' replied Gwendolen looking away.

'Cor, you surely could do better than that. Where did he die, in Vietnam?' Cynicism was written all over his face.

'Yeah, in World War One.'

'You're really mad, you know that, Gwendolen. I don't get it . . .'

'Shush. Don't raise your voice. But listen, this may not make sense to you, but just listen. At least of all the people I know, you used to listen to me. Please don't go away, at least not yet. I didn't mean to deceive you or anything like that. I tried to speak out several times, when that row was going on, but was never allowed to speak. And since I've left home, you're the only one I've got. I didn't want to chase you away.'

Gwendolen was tempted to add that if she had spoken the

truth then, she would have ruined her father. And now that he was dead, she would tell no one. Let them keep guessing. She looked sideways away from the hands she was twisting as if she was wringing water out of a dishcloth, and noticed that Emmanuel was watching her, waiting for her to continue.

'Does that make sense to you?' Gwendolen's voice was full of despair. In her recent fast growth, she had learned how hurtful it could be when you suddenly realized that you were being used. But she wanted his company and affection and someone to laugh with. Her parents became remote. Emmanuel was the only one available. Surely there should be something good about it somewhere.

'Yeah, and if that baby had been light-skinned, you would have pinned her on me, wouldn't you?'

'No, Emmanuel, I would not have. And don't turn nasty. I can't say that I wouldn't have been tempted to do that when I was living with my parents. But now I have learned that I can work for my salvation by myself. This place is not like Jamaica. If I was tempted, it's not that I wanted you to support us, it would have been because of your company. We only met four and half months ago. Even I know that no baby could be made in such a short time. Please know that I was not scared of my parents, but I was scared you'd stop caring.'

Emmanuel started to stare at his sneakers. 'Sorry, Gwen.'

Gwendolen sat up straighter, determined to say all that was in her mind. 'But, Emmanuel, thank you for being such a friend. You've taught me how to read the evening paper, you've even made each of our trips to the fish and chip shops an adventure. Now I have read a whole book written by a black woman. And I will read a lot more.' She giggled because Emmanuel was smiling. 'You know, you deserve to go to heaven for all that. You are a saint. Saint Emmanuel.'

The smile evaporated from his face as he said, 'Maybe if I

had known you were carrying another person's child, I would not have done it. Who is the father anyway?'

Gwendolen ignored his question and smiled. 'I don't know if you would not have cared. You were nice. You were my friend when I needed one. This baby allowed you to show the goodness in you. You have to thank Iyamide for that. She's so good.'

'How come you become so wise all of a sudden?'

'I am a mother now, and I have read a book from cover to cover. This woman told all her life's story in her book. It was like seeing a whole life's span rolling out before you, you follow her going to places she's been, experiencing the agony she went through in a bad marriage, and her coming out of it, to raise her children and open a new life for herself. Oh, Emmanuel, I'm so glad I can now read. I am like that person that was blind who became suddenly sighted when Jesus touched his eyes. I can now share the thoughts of other men and women who lived outside Granville. You now make me see.'

Emmanuel was confused. He could not cope with adulation. Moreover, he was not aware he was doing something particularly nice. In fact he had no idea what they were going to do after the birth of the child. He had heard his father mention adoption once or twice. But he enjoyed visiting Gwendolen and laughing with her, teaching her how to read the *Sun*. He had given her the book *A Black Person's Story* because he knew it was written by a black woman. And with Gwendolen, he did not need to be anybody but himself. So telling him now that he was an angel for doing things that gave him a purpose in life, was confusing. How was he going to cope? How would he tell his parents that after all the bally-hoo the child was somebody else's? And that Gwendolen had kept quiet because she valued his friendship? He could understand her, but his father would not. How could he? He did not see the joy that was radiating through Gwendolen simply because she could read and finish a book. Had his father ever been so needed and appreciated? A good thing Mr Brillianton had died. Because he did not know what his father would have done. But Gwendolen had made him stick to his new trade. He had to, because that was the first thing she always asked when they met. 'Now what happened at work?' Even his stepmother had observed this some months ago, and had said, 'Black girls are sometimes so ambitious, they can be a great steadying force to the men in their life.' Yes, Gwendolen had steadied him. But for the moment, he was still confused.

Emmanuel walked out of the room like someone in a daze. Who was the baby's father? When did he die? Why were there suddenly so many deaths? Her father and the father of her child? He stopped and looked back at Gwendolen who was still watching him. No, they could not be one and the same person. Never! Fancy his thinking such terrible thoughts. Was it biologically possible? He was not sure. Then he realized that he was still clutching the flowers he'd bought. He returned to the bedside, gave Gwendolen a kiss on her forehead, left the bunch by the side table and left really slowly.

Gwendolen stretched into the sheets. She cried, but not too much. Like an old woman she said to herself, 'I don't think he'll blame himself in the future, when he learns, as I have now done, that nothing is meaningless that is given for the love of another person.'

18

The Settlement

Marcus, who was fast becoming more like his father every day, ran to the door on hearing the knock one early Sunday evening in February. It was now over six months since Winston's death. Sonia and her friend Gladys were in the living-room arguing as usual over what was to be done about Gwendolen.

A well-built man in his fifties, with a rather big head, came in. He said 'Good evening' to Gladys and to Sonia. Gladys thought she heard the man call Sonia 'Baby' but was not quite sure. She was engrossed in Gwendolen's affairs. She normally was a woman who minded her own business and one of those Africans who did not wish to get involved in the happenings immediately around them in England, because they would be going home someday. Winston's death changed that. They all remembered too clearly him talking about his retirement and how he was going to live in peace and luxury in his birthplace in Jamaica. He did not even make it to a pensionable age to say nothing of retiring home and living in peace and luxury. The death of someone so close, made them all the wiser.

Gladys waited for Sonia to introduce the new visitor, but she did not. She simply carried on as if the man wasn't there.

Ronald politely left the centre of the settee, which was directly opposite the new television set, for the man. He smiled at Ronald and sat down. He took off his grey hat and placed it on the side table, with a practised air, which betrayed his familiarity with his surroundings. Gladys did not know much about men's clothes since her former husband did not believe in buying many. But if this man's clothes were not of the very best, then they were well cared for. He exuded class without being stuffy. He knew Sonia and Gladys were talking about Gwendolen, but he simply focused his attention on *EastEnders*, playing on the box. Before he came in, the soap had been going on as background to the conversation. But now he made Gladys aware of it. Sonia continued to ignore it anyway.

'That child disgraced 'er Daddy, you know. Him a preacher too. My back turn only two minutes, she get sheself hitch up by a poor whitey. Dem not white, you know. Dem just Greek.'

'What does that matter anyway? It's done now. She's your daughter. You know something, why don't the two of us go and visit her? I would have done so, but I don't know where she lives. The social worker wouldn't give me her address because I am not the next of kin. And who told you that Greeks are poor people? They're not poor, you know.'

'You know we church, the black one, Brother Simon's church, dem forbid me give 'usband big, big funeral; dem blame 'im for letting June-June get a sweet'eart. But that gal too like men. Just men. Ah tell you, 'snot Winston's fault,' replied Sonia, completely ignoring Gladys's comment about the Greeks.

'A church that can condemn a father just for that is not a good church, I'm sorry to say. But you gave him a big Christian burial. The only difference was that a white man said the prayers instead of Brother Simon. Winston's gone to heaven. God is not going to ask him the colour of his funeral prayers, is he? Oh, what a muddle.'

Sonia laughed. And Gladys glanced at the solid person who sat watching *EastEnders* to see whether he would laugh too. But he did not. What an arrogant big-headed Mr So and So, thought Gladys.

'Oh, dat gal vex me so. And Winston's money, dem never pay it, you know.'

'Ah, so why did you buy all this new furniture and that music-centre, must have cost you a fortune.'

'Ah pay deposit, you know. Ah show dem the solicitor's letter and dem let me take the goods. Come, come and see my new bedroom.'

Gladys Odowis could hardly believe what she was seeing. It looked as if a whole floor of a furniture shop had been lifted and placed in Sonia's bedroom. The four-poster bed had a lacy canopy, the type seen in glossy films and television dramas. The bedside tables which matched the new wardrobes were out of this world. How did her friend Sonia come to know about this high-quality furniture? It was not the type seen along their local broadway. This was all upmarket. She did not know that Sonia had such high taste. And that was not all. The children's rooms now had new beds, wardrobes and even matching curtains.

Surprisingly enough, what annoyed Gladys Odowis most were the curtains. Because she knew that Sonia made beautiful curtains, she knew that Sonia enjoyed making things like curtains for herself. Something told Gladys that there was a new person working on Sonia, and she did not like it.

Gladys managed to control her voice when she said: 'Sonia, this must have cost a bomb.'

'Ah know. But me get £60,000, you know. The solicitor man tole me. Look, look.' Sonia dashed to her new writing-desk and brought out the claims letter.

Gladys opened her mouth and closed it. Then she said, 'If I ever get this kind of money, I would put down on a house.'

Sonia laughed. 'Ah thought so too. But my man said rates high. Rates high, man.'

Gladys narrowed her eyes. 'What man, Sonia? So soon after Winston died.'

'It's past six months now. Him say 'im wan' marry me, you know,' Sonia added, lowering her voice to a funny kind of whisper.

Gladys's first reaction was to feel cheated. She could not get any maintenance from her husband and look at Winston leaving all this money for his family. Yeah, her husband Tunde had a better education, but all he used the education for was to protect himself and be able to convince the authorities that he could not afford to maintain his family. And yeah, she had a better education than Sonia, but see how hard she'd had to work at her studies to make the education give her a subsistence salary. She could never get all this beautiful furniture even if she had pledged her next ten years' income. And look at Sonia. Why was it Sonia did not consult her? Because she sensed she would be envious as she was now? Or because she knew she would have stopped her? Now which of these two sentiments was true? The battle that was going on in her mind must have shown on her face.

Sonia saw it, and said, 'Me tink of you, you know. Two good chillun and your husband leave nutting for you. Mr Odowis's a bad man. Look at me nuh. And the security done give me the weekly book, more than Winston's pay. They pay me rent too.'

Gladys felt like crying and telling her to visit her daughter alone.

Gladys caught herself in time before she actually said what was in her mind. A voice inside her reminded her that she was now working as a leader in a mothers' and toddlers' place. It was a secure job in which her children could play whilst she worked. The pay was not bad, only she would never get the type of furniture Sonia got. But then what would she do with it? She knew she did not like heavy and expensive things around her. So what was she being jealous about?

'You know, me old blue sports radio, you can have it, Mrs Odowis. You can have some of the chairs too. Ah pack them in the store at the back.'

'No, thank you, Sonia. But they are new, the chairs and

218

the radio. Your husband bought them just a while ago. They are still perfect.'

'Ah know, but me no like them. Winston 'tupid. Dem too dark. Ah like these ones with glass tops.'

Sonia led Gladys back into the living-room. The solid man was still watching the television. Something told Gladys that they wanted her to leave.

As she picked up her coat and adjusted her knitted beret, she said in a rather loud voice, like someone who was aware of having wasted the time of another, 'We'll go and see Gwendolen next week. It would be nice to know how she's doing.'

Sonia saw Gladys out. She felt compelled to talk and talk about this new man called James. This James called Sonia 'Baby' and she thought that was nice. But Gladys Odowis, whose culture revered the older woman, felt like throwing up. Who wanted to be called 'Baby'? If a man should be mad enough to call her 'Baby' she knew what she would tell that person. In this she was like Ama, Gwendolen's friend.

This new man could drive a car but Winston could not have read the road signs to save his life. Winston was so much at a disadvantage in Sonia's mind that Gladys cried, 'You sound as if you hate the man. As if you are looking for reasons to erase his memory from your life. You sound as if Winston did something really terrible to you. Because if you are talking about the Winston I knew, then I'll say you're wrong. He was a good provider. He was the father to your children. Why do you denigrate him like this? You may want to be called "Baby", but I don't, because I am a full woman in my prime. I am proud to be so and I have my own babies. So why should I feel flattered for a man to reduce me to a state of dependency like a baby? I think some white women like it. But I've never yet met a black woman who would not box the ears of a man who called her "Baby". Baby indeed! Just grow up, will you, Sonia.'

219

With that she marched busily into the darkening night.

Sonia stood there in the cold February night looking into thin air. Winston was everything Gladys said he was, so why did she feel this eel of distrust coiled about the memory of the man she'd been married to for over ten years? Aloud she said, 'Ah still wonder why he died the day he did and the way 'im did. Ah just wonder sometimes.'

19

James

Sonia's new man, James Allen, was a higher-class Caribbean than Winston. He worked in the hospital morgue. One of his reasons for keeping quiet in polite company was that all his jokes were about dead bodies. He told Sonia's children about a man who kept opening his eyes and smiling at him each time he tried to put him on the slab for the doctor. And when he was with Sonia, he talked about how people look when dead. And Sonia, who was at first frightened, learned to laugh at his grim jokes. At least James could talk without stammering, at least James could crack jokes, albeit grim ones. She was fed up with Winston's silences.

When Sonia first met James, he was very sympathetic. It was the day they told Sonia to go and identify Winston. Winston did not look beautiful in death. His face was burned almost beyond recognition and his body was broken. The nails were square and cut neatly across. Sonia knew it was Winston because of those fingernails. They remained perfect, still pinkish white. Those signs were enough for her. That blackened face with its eternal lipless grin was not the face of the Winston she knew. She did not realize that she was howling until James came in, dressed in a white suit like a nurse or a doctor — Sonia did not know which — and offered to take her back to her address. The fact that she had been sitting next to a black man who knew the right thing to say and who was driving what looked like his own car intrigued Sonia. She invited him to take a mouthful of Jamaican rum, even though both of them did not drink that much. She learned later that James too was shaken. Winston looked terrible in death; that ghostly grin. His lips were gone and his ears too. Lawd ha' mussy.

James's job in the morgue was secure with a real pension, unlike Winston's seasonal work in the building trade. And he was a Yellow Nigger, big and handsome. He had a wife but 'me tired of her, you know,' he had assured Sonia. The wife had no children and as the marriage was almost twenty years old, there was no hope of their having any.

Sonia, with her scatterbrained attitude to life, and still suffering from shock, unwittingly encouraged James. She very much wanted someone to depend on, especially as the church in which she worshipped was failing her. She did not feel like reaching out to God on her own. She could not. She did not know how. Church-going and praying were things people did in groups. You spread your prayers for everybody present, and they prayed for you too. But the English Christianity in which people are taught to pray individually was alien to her. Sonia wouldn't know what to say to God. James filled an important vacuum in her life. He prevented that thin thread between sanity and insanity from snapping.

And James, whose wife had grown hard out of familiarity and disappointment with life and whose flat was always neat and quiet, welcomed the noisy domesticity of the Brilliantons' home. His ego was boosted when he found that he could still attract women with his car. Winston did not have enough education to go to a driving school, to say nothing of buying a car. And knowing a black man, even though he was a Yellow Nigger, who drove his own car, impressed Sonia not a little.

With a new man, she felt she needed a new bedroom. James did not push her into furnishing her flat, but he did not discourage her either. After all, she was not spending his money. He went with her to the big furniture shops to explain to them that Sonia's big money would soon be paid. He showed them the court's estimate, and the shops saw a good business. Sonia spent a little over £5,000 doing up her new bedroom.

Every evening, after work, James would come to St Pancras Way instead of going to his home in Grafton Road. Hearing some of his most favourite tunes played on the modern synchrome system was bliss. Sonia excelled in cooking. She'd stopped cooking tripe but could now afford good fish and steak. As James loved desserts, Sonia also reactivated her sweet tooth. So Sonia, that very skinny woman, was becoming quite tubby. The children were happy because their mother was happy. And their schoolwork, which nobody bothered to check, surprisingly improved. Ronald, by being sharp, outgoing and charming, found himself in the A-stream in his comprehensive school.

Ronald had no idea what he was going to do when he left school but he planned to study for 'O' levels because that was what everybody in his class wanted to do. He read all the letters written to the Brilliantons and sometimes told Marcus off for being slow.

James, the fifty-nine-year-old morgue worker, loved this full family atmosphere, though he could not be bothered with school reports. Ronald did not press them upon him either. His father had never asked for them, so why give them to this new man simply because he could read the newspaper? And James actually bought the *Sun* newspaper!

He was reading the *Sun* when Sonia returned with a frown on her face. Mrs Odowis had made her feel slightly guilty for having some fun.

'All right, Baby?' James sang out, without taking his eyes off the paper he was reading.

Sonia's face broke into little wrinkles around the corners of her eyes. To see her man really reading a newspaper! She was lucky. And outside was parked his ten-year-old car. Of course Sonia did not know it was ten years old, all she knew was that James could take her to the local pubs in his car, once or twice a week. And next to his job James Allen worshipped his car. It gleamed and was fully stocked with the latest tapes of different kinds of music. From gospel to the latest reggae, and even some old classics.

Sonia had noticed that for the past weeks, James did not bother to go home first. He came to her flat straight from work. Consequently she busied herself in the kitchen whilst her man read the newspaper. Ronald was writing in his school books, Marcus watching a taped repeat of an episode of *The 'A' Team* on their rather huge, 27-inch telly. Somehow that television seemed to have taken over the whole room. The children called it their cinema, because they rightly felt as if they were in a movie house given the size of this new TV. Cheryl was playing with a doll, combing and recombing its blonde hair. Bob Marley's plaintive voice wailed, 'No woman, no cry' from the music-centre.

Then Sonia's voice called above the noise, 'Cheryl, come to the kitchen and help Mummy. You big 'oman now.'

'Yes, Mum,' replied Cheryl as she slowly put away her doll and made for the kitchen.

To Sonia, life must go on. Winston was dead. Somehow it seemed as if he wanted to die. Sonia did not know why for sure and it was not right to suspect what she did not know.

She piled a plate high with potato chips, chips which she cut really fat and plump, man-size chips. She did not like to feed James on those skinny dry ones. By the side of the chips, she wedged in huge spoonfuls of minced meat fried with onions, and on another plate was a heap of green plantain cooked with black-eye beans. The aroma of the food wafted into the television room. James purred. He could hardly wait to be served properly on the new dining-table, before he started to tuck into the steaming well-cooked supper. After the meal, Sonia brought a bowl of cream which they all used to top the apple pie she bought from the local baker's shop.

Of course, life must go on.

When later in bed, James purred and called her 'Baby' she felt stupid. She could not answer. She blamed herself for being so weak, for allowing Mrs Odowis to influence her. After all, Mrs Odowis was an uncivilized African with all her taboos and superstition. Yet she did not answer when James called again, 'Baby, are you all right?'

James instantly ignored her and went to sleep. His stomach was too full of minced meat and cream anyhow.

20

Iyamide

When Gladys knocked at the door leading to the Brilliantons' flat in St Pancras Way that wintry evening, it took an unusually long time before it was opened. Even Marcus, who was well known for opening their door to any salesman or woman who happened to be hawking around that part of North London, had the slowness of an old man this evening.

Gladys and Sonia had decided to go and see Gwendolen that evening. It was to be a surprise visit. They had decided to choose an evening because Gladys worked during the day. Gladys did not have much time for herself, what with her family, her job and her studies. But she felt that Sonia was a friend, a friend who stood by her when she was having her own marital troubles. Also an instinct was telling her that Sonia needed a close friend. She could tell that she had not fully recovered from Winston's death. Winston, though a quiet person, was a man with a presence. Such people are not easily forgotten. Gladys could see beyond the veneer of Sonia's present forced cheerfulness. Her laughter was too hollow to be real. She had bought four pairs of shoes the other day, not paying her rent because she knew that Winston's money, the £60,000 she had not yet received, would pay all her debts. She told Gladys she needed some new shoes to go to court in. 'They wear suits to dem court places, you know.'

Gladys tried to tell her that £60,000 was a lot of money, but could she not wait and see whether she could invest it in something? Sonia even declared that she did not want the money in cheques or bank drafts. 'I wan' me money in me hand.' She was wont to emphasize this by pointing one finger into the palm of the other hand. This gesture never stopped provoking laughter. Mr Ilochina had said once that Sonia would need a bigger hand than the one she'd got to hold such a large sum. But Sonia was adamant. 'I wan' me money in me hand.'

All was quiet this evening. As Gladys stepped inside, James Allen called out, 'Ah, good evening, Mrs Odowis.' Gladys never trusted that man, not even when he was trying to be nice like now. He was trying too much to be real.

'Good evening, Mr Allen. How's the family?'

'This is the family,' he said lightly.

Gladys ignored him. She went straight into the sitting-room and James shut the door and went out. They all heard him start his car.

They've had a fight, Gladys thought.

Sonia's eyes were swollen, not from a beating, but from crying. The story quickly poured out of her: she had not wanted to bother Gladys about coming to the court with her that day. When her case was heard, she found the insurance company refused to pay all Winston's money. He had been warned not to go to the top of the construction site because it was too dangerous, the others were not ready and the job could be done later in the day. But he had insisted that dismantling the machine would not take him any time at all. Even his friend Mr Ilochina had tried to pull him back but he'd broken free. And when he was halfway up the ladder, his helmet had slipped and fallen off his head, because in his hurry he had not fastened it properly under his chin. So when the machine exploded and threw him burning like a torch down the fifteen-storey building, the impact of his fall broke his brain open. As a result they advised her to settle out of court.

'And what did your lawyer say?'

'The man 'tupid. He just agree with them. 'Im say many witnesses dey dere.'

They had led Sonia into another chamber and decided they would give her only £10,000. But half of it was to be put away in trust for the younger children. Of the remaining £5,000 half was for Gwendolen and the other half for herself. Sonia screamed, 'You understand dat? Injustice. You see me nuh. Dat gal. That me daatar! God died for the truth. Ah kill her, you know. Me go kill her. And the solicitor man, me have to pay him too!'

'Good Lord, what do they want you to live on?'

'Dat, dat book dem give me. Dat all.'

Gladys looked at the Widowed Mother's Allowance book and noticed that the amount allocated her was quite substantial, because Winston always worked. He had worked throughout his stay in the UK. But that was not the point at the moment. The thing was that Sonia's hopes had been raised too high. This was far from fair, thought Gladys.

Sonia started to cry again and Cheryl cried too.

Money was not everything, Gladys tried to imply in consolation. After all, she was managing on a smaller income when Winston was alive.

'Why did I bring dat debil, proper satan to me home? Winston jumped to die because church people blamed him for allowing June-June to stick up with a whitey. And nuh she more share of Winston's money than me. Me kill her, you know. She not my pikney. God died for the truth.'

'Mum, Mum, when I leave school I can get a job in the Civil Service. I'm going to study for "O" levels, Mrs Odowis.'

'Ronald, "O" levels! You're a good lad. Keep it up. You don't have to leave school if you don't want to. Your mother can manage all right. We all do eventually. If you're this good, then you must go to a university.'

'Where is a university? They pay them better dere?'

'No, Mum, it's a place for more education. After three or

four years, I'll get a degree. But I must get my "A" levels first.'

'You mean like dem Africans carrying briefcases about the place? Mrs Odowis, why you telling them all dat for? No money, there's no money. Me no like such talk.'

'I do paper round,' Marcus, who like his father would do anything for peace and quiet, added in his father's gentle voice. His deeply set eyes bored into the souls of both women. He was fast growing into a solid quiet man. Whilst Ronald was slight like Sonia, the two boys looked so different and yet so alike, especially as both carried their father's deep-set eyes.

Gladys had never seen so much distress in one human being as she saw in Sonia that evening. For some reason she could cope with her husband's sudden death, but not with this. This seemed to be taking from her all the hopes she had entertained for the future, and she rightly felt she could not cope with life without hope.

Gladys talked some more. She tried to tell Sonia that she had a brilliant son, who could get a good job even if he did not go to a university. She reminded her that her Widowed Mother's Allowances were more than what she herself got from her full-time work. She begged her to look at Cheryl who was crying her heart out, just because her mother was sad. At length, she left the family, praying that God would comfort them for the night. Because it felt as if Winston had just died.

But God works in a mysterious way. Fancy Sonia and Winston having such bright and promising boys like Ronald and Marcus. And they are both positive thinkers. Pity Sonia cannot see these qualities for what they are, she thought. She must remind her friend of them again some other time.

Sonia was still dazed from shock and disappointment when the following Saturday she walked into the London

Emporium in Stroud Green to buy meat. Stroud Green near Finsbury Park on Saturdays looked like an African market. One could buy anything from bitter leaf to cocoyam and negro yam, from kolanut to sugar cane; from guava to mango. Next to Brixton market in South London, Stroud Green was the Mecca for the Caribbean, the African and some Indians. The irony of it was that all the shops were owned by Indians. Apart from New Beacon's bookshop on the other side of the road, the shop owners were Indians. There were one or two white men's shops, but they looked out of place as if on alien ground. Sonia knew where to get her tripe, her offal, her salted fish and her negro yam. She was not in a mood for fancy foreign food of cakes and frozen vegetables. She wanted solid African-Caribbean food inside her. The way she was feeling after the crushing disappointment of the court, made her wish to spend as little time as possible in the kitchen frying endless chipped potatoes.

She was engrossed in her problems and looking pathetic when a woman came up from behind and hit her on both her cheeks. Her loosely fitted dentures flew out on top of the Indian butcher's glass case and would have gone straight into the meat if it hadn't been for the glass top. The Indian butcher man might then have found it difficult to decide whether the teeth came from the goats' or pigs' heads lined up inside the glass case. But neither Sonia nor the Indian man was given the time to think of them. Sonia was temporarily blinded. 'Wharr . . . ' she tried to say as she spun round. Her attacker, however, had not quite finished. She was about to hit her again, when the butcher's assistant caught her arms and parted the two women, saying, 'Not here, pleeze, not here.'

'You bitch,' spat the other woman. 'Taking my husband. She wan' James, you know. Look at she . . . hm . . . she has paws. Your husband not cold in his grave, you wan' another man. You can't wait for your man to be buried. If James late to come home tomorrow, I know where you live. So hands off my husband.' With that she kicked Sonia's shopping trolley and trampled on it. 'Bitch, bitch!'

She left with another woman who dragged her off. Sonia could fight if she knew the fight was coming. But this was so sudden, so unexpected, that Mrs Allen had turned off Stroud Green and was walking towards the bus station at Finsbury Park, before Sonia recovered. And then she looked at the people in the queue – some black, some white – and nearly all the blacks knew her! She was a frequent visitor at Stroud Green. She picked up her twisted trolley and made to walk away, to prevent herself from crying right there.

'Here, here, take your teeth,' cried the butcher's assistant.

This was the height of degradation. She knew that all eyes in the queue were following her, and she did not miss the burst of laughter that broke out spontaneously seconds afterwards. It was a terrible experience.

And all because of Gwendolen. If Gwendolen had not met Emmanuel, if Winston had not been too soft to drive the boy away, if the church people had been kinder to him, if this, if that . . .

Sonia went to Gladys's home and sat down even though Ozi, Mrs Odowis's little boy, told her that his Mum was away shopping and he did not know when she would be coming back. She smiled and told the boy to go and play. She would wait for his mother.

'Do you really want James?' Gladys asked later matter-of-factly. 'Because if you have to spend all this money just to impress him . . .'

Sonia denied with heat that that was what she was doing. She was spending the money because the law told her the money was there to be spent. 'If he wants me like, then of course Ah want him too.'

'Did he come last night?' Gladys asked tentatively.

'Well, no. 'Im came dis morning. Overtime, you know. Many people done dey die for dat hospital.'

They were both quiet after this. They were not babies. They knew that so far as James was concerned, there was not going to be any trouble. Many, many more people did not need to die to keep him away, he could always invent some other excuses. Was it not a coincidence that Mrs Allen knew exactly in which market and at which stall to find Sonia? After all, they were uppish blacks who did not need to make that long journey from Kentish Town to Finsbury Park. They could afford to buy the meat they needed from any butcher's shop. Their likes did not need the Indians.

Sonia looked up from the tea she was drinking and her eyes met Gladys's. And they both smiled. Sometimes, some truths are better not said.

'When will we go and see Gwendolen, Sonia?'

'Ah tole you, when me see that gal, me kill 'er, you know.'

Gladys dropped the subject, but she made sure she took Gwendolen's address.

As for James, he solved his own problem. He stopped visiting the Brilliantons because the work in the hospital became too heavy. Sonia did not bother to tell him about his wife. He probably knew already.

Winston's case was settled out of court. And after all had been deducted, Sonia was left with a little over £1,000. The solicitor would not let her touch the children's money, not even to pay part of her debts. The kids would decide what they would do with their money when they came of age, not before. Sonia should make do with her Widowed Mother's allowance.

Sonia knew she would go back to her church soon, but not immediately. The curses she had rained on Brother Simon and Sister Esmee and the rest of them were still too fresh. She would wait until they had forgiven her. But she would go back. It was clear they had something against Winston but not against her and her children. She would go back one day soon.

She changed her name to Jane and took up a cleaning job

late in the evenings. There she worked with so many Nigerian women, cleaning libraries around Camden Town. Many of them had so many names, they could hardly remember which one they were using at which library. And some of them still collected the dole. Sonia used to think that all this was wrong when she and Winston lived together. Now she was beginning to see why these women were doing what they were doing. It was very exhausting, but they said that stolen water is sweet. That kept them all going.

Despite her pleading with the big furniture shops in Tottenham Court Road and promising that she would pay, they still came to collect their stuff. It looked as if her going to tell them what had happened hastened their decision to repossess their goods. But the manager with the drooping moustache and with furrows on his forehead pretended to understand.

They took the desk and the canopied bed, the plush leather suite and the dolly dressing-table. The latter hurt her most, because she had called in all her neighbours to see it, the day it arrived. And now the removal men were making so much racket taking it away that Sonia thought everybody on the estate was aware of what was happening. Somehow she knew people were not laughing at her. She could not imagine the same situation in Granville. She would have been forced by shame to leave town. Here people were friendly in a lukewarm manner, but they were not sufficiently interested in her affairs to make her worry about them. She was none the less ready to blast anybody who asked her any silly questions. But nobody did.

However, a week or so later, the whole world seemed to have collapsed on top of her. The thought came suddenly to her that the court must have paid Gwendolen her share of the money, because the lawyers had said she would need it now for her child. And here was she, Sonia, Winston's wife, not knowing how she was going to manage. What would the world say if they knew that she felt like killing her own daughter? Would they say she was mad? Would they be able to understand her? She could bear it if they had not given all that money to Gwendolen. After all, it was she who had married Winston, not Gwendolen, not Ronald, not Marcus. She did not worry so much about all that money being kept for the younger ones. But Gwendolen! God must have sent that daughter to destroy her!

How could your daughter be your downfall? Gwendolen had been brought here to help her mother with the children and to improve herself, and what did she do? She allowed that white boy to mess her up. Since then the wrath of God had descended on her family. Sonia took the kitchen knife and hid it in her shopping bag. She had two shopping bags. The one for the big shopping was mounted on a trolley. That one Mrs Allen had smashed up the other day. Then she had one she had bought from her local Woolworths in Camden Town, specially for mid-week shopping. She put the knife at the bottom of the bag and covered it with a lot of old paper bags. She looked as if she was going to do her evening cleaning, but as far as she was concerned, she was going to have it out with Gwendolen. Something had happened when she went to Jamaica, something terrible must have happened to warrant God's anger.

Finding the flat was not so difficult because the social worker had described it to her several times. She had told her which station and which turning to take after Seven Sisters Road. Sonia walked very fast, her suspense and anger lending lightness to her walk. She did not mind the quiet streets, she did not care that she was walking alone on a late winter evening in Tottenham.

She found the number of the house in a very neat street lined with identical houses. The houses were of red brick, the area beautiful and even more private than their grey and white council estate in St Pancras Way.

She rang the bell and Emmanuel opened it.

'Wharr, wharr are you doing here, this time of night? Whey June-June?' Sonia pushed Emmanuel out of the way and walked purposefully into this nice flat.

The flat was lovely and yet so different – so much so that she felt like asking Emmanuel whose flat it was and who lived there. Baby sounds coming from a white basket placed in the front room with plastic birds and aeroplanes hanging from its canopy stopped her thoughts. Sonia went towards the cot and was transfixed. She opened her mouth and closed it several times as if she was drowning. Winston's dark-rimmed eyes seemed to jump from the child's face to mock her. She saw Winston's round face shrink to the size of the child's, and the child's face balloon to the size of Winston's; Winston, the baby, the baby, Winston, in rotation. Sonia held on tightly to the edge of the basket to stop her feet from buckling under her. Her eyes wandered to the square nails, the very shape of the nails by which she identified Winston's body. Those nails had now shrunk on to the tips of the baby's fingers. And Winston's square-shaped hands seen in miniature were now waving a rattle.

Mercifully, there was another ring at the door. Sonia breathed in deeply when she heard Gladys's voice.

'Oh, so you came at last,' cried the African woman.

'Yeah, me come,' replied the woman from the Caribbean, in a voice so deep that it was strange and distant even to herself.

'Mrs Odowis, me blind you know. Me so blind. To think me think Winston 'tupid.'

'No, Sonia, you're not blind. You refused to see what you did not wish to see. Who could blame you for that? We do it all the time.'

'You tink me know all the time?'

'That's right.'

'Oh, Mummy, I knew you'd come one day. I knew you would.'

236

Sonia turned from the cot to see Gwendolen standing there, a grown woman in a white running suit, carrying a tray full of tea-things. She placed the tray on a plain pine table with no runner or antimacassar and ran to her mother. 'Isn't Iyamide wonderful? She's so good.'

Sonia started grunting like Winston. She did not know what to say. She found a seat and sat down. She stared at the cot. 'Is dat her name? Iya . . . mi . . . de?'

Gwendolen nodded. 'See, you can pronounce it very easily. It is a Yoruba name.'

'That no Christian name. You give the baby uncivilized African voodoo name?'

Gwendolen looked at Gladys Odowis, and they both tried to suppress the laughter that was bubbling inside them.

Sonia turned her anger to Emmanuel. 'Wharr you doing here, eh? You gave her the idea of this heathen name. This chile not yours, you know.'

Everybody just started to laugh, dispelling the tension.

'Oh, Mum.' Gwendolen moved closer to Sonia on the chair. 'Iyamide means "My mother is here". It is symbolic. It does not mean you're no longer my mother, it means everything I ever wanted, warmth, security, comfort, is all here in a female form. That is going to be her Christian name. But it is a name with a meaning, and see, you can pronounce it.'

'I know people who still can't say "Gwendolen" and say it's "Granada",' Gladys put in with a hint of impatience, wondering when these Caribbeans would stop calling Africans uncivilized as if they were civilized themselves! Whatever that word meant.

Gladys got up. 'Well, Gwendolen, I come to see how you are coping, and you are doing very well. We'll be going now. Come on, Sonia.'

Sonia got up stiffly, still clutching her bag. Then she turned to Emmanuel. 'You come with us? Ah tell you this child not yours.'

'I know that, Mrs Brillianton, and it does not matter. Gwen is my friend, you see. I baby-sit for her so she can go to her singing lessons. She sings at a gospel choir now, you know. And isn't Iyamide adorable?'

'Come on, Sonia, this is not our world.' Gladys was now gently pulling her friend.

'You'll come again, won't you, Mum?' Gwendolen asked. And Sonia nodded mutely.

Outside, Sonia cried, 'Lawd ha' mussy, Ah been so blind. Everything change so fast in this kontry, you know.'

'Come on, grandmother. They are the future now. We can't hold them back with our fears and prejudices.'

'Me no know nutting no more,' said Sonia suppressing a sob.

'Don't worry, Gwen is a big girl now. She can take care of herself. She'll find her own identity.'

The two women walked into the street and the biting wind. Sonia looked this way and that in the darkening night. She saw a huge dustbin in front of a badly lit house and walked towards it. She lifted the lid gently so as not to alert the occupants of the house; then she took out the kitchen knife she was carrying. She plunged it fiercely several times into the rubbish bin, with all her might and with as much anger and frustration as if she was stabbing a snake that had just bitten her. At the same time she was muttering to herself. Then, when she seemed exhaustedly satisfied, she heaved a sigh as if at a job well done, and used her bare hands to bury the knife in the bin. At length, she placed the bin lid back reverently. It was like a ritual. She walked back to her friend, who stood on the pavement watching spellbound, not knowing what to say or do.

Sonia started walking briskly back to the tube station, with Gladys following silently, very much shaken. It became clear to her that Sonia was not going of her own free will to offer any explanation, for her face was bent down as if she was counting the concrete pavement slabs.

Gladys peeped into her face and asked, 'What were you burying, Sonia?'

Sonia stood rigid. She stood at attention right there in the middle of the pavement, almost like a puppet whose strings had suddenly been pulled tight. Her face stared into the dark night. She looked as if she was talking to the few stars that dared to twinkle.

'Winston Brillianton!'

There was nothing more to be said.

Sonia's voice had the finality of a closed door.